BECOMING GHANIYAH

BY

PAUL BLADES

I0690211

Dark Visions Publications

darkvisionspub@gmail.com

Previously published:

Watch for publication of the other books in the Maddy Saga:

Other books by Paul Blades:

Klitzman's Isle
Klitzman's Empire
Klitzman's Paradise
Klitzman's Pawn Part One
Klitzman's Pawn Part Two
Slaver's Dozen- A Tale of Klitzman's Isle
The Taking of Cheryl Part One
The Taking of Cheryl Part Two: Slaver's Bait
Comfort Girl No. 4
Sacrifice to the Emerald God
The Blue Cantina: Anna's Surrender
The Warlord's Concubine, Books 1, 2, 3 and 4
Dreams and Desires, Books 1 and 2

CHAPTER ONE

Leslie Harrington watched from the balcony of her third story bedroom as the early morning sun broke over the far distant horizon. The whitewashed buildings of the small, Tunisian town glowed light pink and orange as they caught the first rays of the emerging orb that would later punish them with its stifling, merciless heat. At 6 a.m., though, the air was still redolent with the cold of the neighboring desert night. Leslie took a deep breath, reveling in her good fortune.

The 22 year old, shapely, Bryn Mawr graduate had jumped at the opportunity to become the private secretary of Mr. Hassan Ben Moussa. She had been out of school for about six months and heard about the job from a professor at her college. She had been hired based on her resume, her recommendations and a telephone interview. She had to send a picture too. She had made sure she sent a good one and had paid a friend who was a professional photographer to take some really good shots, ones that showed her serious, competent side, but also a little cheese-cake. It never hurt, you know?

Mr. Moussa was the wealthy owner of an international trading company based in the small town of Dar Al Jamah located a few miles from the Mediterranean coast and about 85 miles southeast of Tunis. Leslie had studied both French and business back at Bryn Mawr and the job was a golden oppor-tunity to gain experience in both while, at the same time, satisfying her desire to see more of the world than presented by the rolling Pennsylvania countryside. Mr. Moussa needed a secretary who could decipher both English and French as he dealt with American and European companies, trading the numerous commodities that flowed from the Middle East and Africa to the developed world and then back again as finished products.

She had only been at her job for a little over two weeks. So far, she had seen little of the town itself, having been driven here directly from the airport in Tunis by Mr. Moussa's chauffer. It was tantalizing to have seen from the back seat windows of the long, stretch Mercedes the desert countryside, the looming Atlas Mountains far off in the distance and the exotically bedecked natives. She had even seen some camels driven by white robed men along the sparsely traveled roadway.

Dressed in her sheer, flowing, blue tinted, lace trimmed nightgown, Leslie relished the slight breeze that wafted its way over the rooftops below, lifting loose strands of her shoulder length chestnut colored hair. It was early March and the harbingers of the desert spring were in the air. She knew that she should not be showing herself at the window dressed as she was. Mr. Moussa's aide, Faraq, had given her a stern lecture about the differences between local sensibilities about women's bodies and that of the West. She was not in the more cosmopolitan capital of this Muslim country where some deviation from strict dress codes was tolerated. Leslie had seen some burkha clad women when they had driven through the town's narrow streets on the evening of her arrival. The young girl had shivered as she thought of the constrictions the young women had to live under.

Now, looking over the panorama from the balcony off of her luxurious bedroom, Leslie peered cautiously about to make sure that no one could see her. Seeing no one, she stretched her long, thin, graceful arms up over her head and let the early morning sun flow over her. Her motion stretched the bodice of her filmy nightgown tautly, pressing it hard against her firm, heavy, young breasts. The nightgown was long and rose to the tops of her ankles as she spread her feet widely. A close observer would have been just able to make out the dark red, almost purplish areola that adorned her sweet orbs, the light brown, trimmed bush that covered her sex and the soft, pinkish flesh of her graceful, smooth thighs.

Today was an off day for Leslie. Mr. Moussa was away in Paris for business. He had taken Faraq with him. Leslie did not like the tall, thin, surreptitious looking man. His face, unlike Mr. Moussa's, carried more than a hint of cruelty and disdain. Leslie had the distinct impression he did not approve that his employer and master had hired an infidel from the West to do his work when a good local Muslim girl would have suited him just fine. But translating documents into English from French or vice versa required a delicate sensibility to the nuances of language and idiom and Leslie was sure that she was the right choice to do the work. She was confident in her abilities.

She was also sure that Mr. Moussa was happy with her services. He was a pleasant, older man, in his sixties, she believed. He had strong, noble features and wore expertly trimmed, sliver hair with a finely sculpted Van Dyke beard and mustache. His interactions with her were always suitably formal and decorous. Leslie had been worried for a while, when she was pondering whether to accept the job in the faraway land, that her employer was just seeking a pretty young thing to serve as his mistress, not that she would have necessarily rejected that out of hand. She just hadn't seen how good looking Mr. Moussa was. She had had a few flings and knew that love and sex didn't necessarily need to go together. But Mr. Moussa turned out to be nothing like that.

The only unpleasantness, other than the sour attitude of Faraq, was Mrs. Moussa. Her first name was Halima, but she was instructed specifically never to call her that. Mrs. Moussa was a beautiful woman in her early forties. She had long, full black hair that she kept in a bun, was svelte and dressed always to the nines. Leslie knew a little bit about fashion and she recognized Mrs. Moussa's outfits as being the latest from Paris and New York. She wondered why the woman spent so much effort in looking pretty when, every time that she went out, she covered herself in a deep blue abaya.

Well, Mrs. Moussa was imperious and none to happy about her husband's selection of a secretary. Her interactions with Leslie had been hypercorrect, bordering on rudeness. Leslie ate dinner every night with the family and Mrs. Moussa never spoke to her. When Mr. Moussa tried to engage her in conversation, Mrs. Moussa always interrupted with this or that. Worse, she only spoke Arabic to Mr. Moussa at the table, although she was very conversant in French and English, making it impossible for Leslie to know what they were talking about.

The other occupants of the house, aside from servants, were the Moussa's son and daughter. Hajib was a little over twenty three years old, a little older than Leslie. He spent much of his time in Paris partying with his friends, but Mr. Moussa had called him home because of a few escapades he had been involved in. So he was basically home cooling his heels until his father gave him permission to return. The daughter, Jana, was twenty five. She had been married at one time, but her husband had been killed in a terrorist bomb blast at a nightclub in Tunis a year ago and she had come back home in her widowhood. So neither of the Moussa children was particularly happy to be living under the Moussa roof. It made for a somewhat tense atmosphere at dinner time.

Jana was proper but curt in her limited dealings with Leslie. Hajib was something else. It was clear to Leslie that the boy lusted after her. He took every opportunity to talk to her, offer her tea, chocolates, a walk in the garden. He was polite, but his politeness did not disguise his leers as he stared at her breasts. When Leslie walked up the stairs to go to her room on the third floor, Hajib often stood at the bottom step, his eyes glued to her legs. Leslie was sure that he couldn't see more than a glimpse of thigh, she wore knee length skirts, but it was disconcerting nonetheless.

As she peered over the roof tops, Leslie heard the sound of a wailing call to prayer. There was a mosque a few blocks away from the large, elegant Moussa residence and Leslie had begun to get used to hearing the undulating tones three times a day played over the mosque's loudspeakers. She decided that it was time to step back from her balcony, for modesty's sake, and get dressed.

She stripped herself of the fine, translucent garment and went to her dresser to decide what to wear. Today, she had resolved she would go into the town. She had been warned against it by Faraq and Mr. Moussa, but she was dying to discover more about the mysterious urban center. After all, she didn't take this job so that she could sit in an air conditioned house all day.

She removed a pair of pink, lacy panties from the drawer and put them on. She bought them in Paris on her stopover on the way to Tunisia. They were bikini cut and made of silk. They felt luxurious next to her skin. She had decided that she would wear as daring underwear as she could, seeing that she had to dress hyper modestly on the outside. The panties had come with a small, matching bra. It barely covered her nipples and lifted her breasts seductively.

"That will give Hajib something to stare at," she thought. After she put it on, she stepped over to the full length mirror that covered the door to her closet and admired herself. She had been always a little chunky in high school and in the first years of college. She had thinned out admirably after she turned 19. It was a combination of diet, exercise and having naturally shed the baby fat that had adorned her hips. Since she had arrived in Tunisia, she had been unable to exercise except for the push and sit ups she did in her room every night. She was worried that she would begin to put back on the pounds that she had lost. A good long walk around the city was just what she needed.

As she admired her curvaceous form in the mirror, she could not help speculate what Hajib would do if he saw her like this. He would probably attack her, she thought. Now, if Mr. Moussa ever gave her any hint that he wanted to see her in her undies, that was something else. He featured greatly in her nightly fantasies as she stroked herself to her daily orgasm. He was everything that she admired in a man. He was strong, aloof, dignified. He seemed to ooze charm. Not the false charm of his randy son, but a sophisticated, make your pussy wet charm. Mrs. Moussa was right to be nervous at her presence.

She pushed her breasts together and up, accentuating her already pleasing cleavage. She could just make out her dark areolas behind the lacy screen of her bra. "Would you like a taste, Mr. Moussa?" she said to the mirror. "Go right ahead." She laughed.

In her closet was her longest skirt. She had bought it in contemplation of walking the Arabic streets. It was light cotton, blue. It had no adornments other than the sparkly, gold belt she liked to wear with it. She also selected a modest, white blouse. It had half sleeves with a little lacey fringe on the ends. She looked in the mirror to make sure that her bra did not show through. If you looked closely, you could see just a faint tinge of pink. That was okay. She had seen Mrs. Moussa wearing things much worse.

The last adornment was a pair of sensible shoes. During the day, while she worked for Mr. Moussa, she usually wore high heels. Today she would wear her flats, a pair of shiny, black slip ons. She would have rather worn her Nikes but didn't think them appropriate. Only an American would wear sneakers with such conservative but elegant attire, she thought. And she didn't want anyone to think she was American. She liked to think of herself as French, sophisticated, continental.

Once dressed, she grabbed the kerchief she had bought at the airport in Tunis, bright red with blue and white fluer de lis imprinted on it. She knew she would be arrested for certain if she walked about without a hair covering. That was the last thing that she wanted to have happen. It would be so embarrassing.

Leslie ran down the stairs to breakfast. She wanted to get her walking done before noon to avoid the extreme heat of the later hours. She figured she would walk one hour out and then another back. That would bring her back around 9 o'clock. Nobody would even know she had gone.

After wolfing down the thick, tart coffee and an apple croissant given her by the ancient head cook, Leslie headed for the back door. She wanted to slip out without anyone noticing. When she opened the rear door, she saw that no one was there. She closed it quietly behind her, strolled quickly out to the street and she was on her way.

It felt wonderfully liberating to be out of the house. She was finally going to have an adventure.

Her kerchief tied tightly around her neck, her head covered modestly, Leslie strolled the narrow streets. They were mostly deserted. The buildings were almost uniformly of whitewashed stone, at most two stories high. The streets were cobblestone. Here and there a shop owner was opening up. She passed a couple of cafés with seated men clad in white shirts and slacks drinking coffee. They gave her intense looks as she passed. It was nothing she couldn't handle. She knew that even her demure skirt and blouse couldn't hide her luxuriant curves. She didn't blame them for staring.

When she came to the street with the mosque on it, she hurried past. She dreaded being confronted by some mullah outraged by her Western garb.

The town was hilly and the walking was a little tiring. She could feel herself sweating steadily despite the early morning hour. She crossed what she assumed was the city center. A few more people had hit the streets. Most of the women, and there were only a few, were robed head to toe. She saw one girl dressed like she was, but she hurried off and was picked up by a taxi.

On her way back, Leslie was tired. She thought to herself that she had been a little overambitious in deciding to walk for two hours in this heat. She was thirsty and was looking forward to getting back to the Moussa compound. Out of the blue, a shiny, black Mercedes came to a screeching halt right in front of her. Two men jumped out. They were dressed in beige colored caftans and had maroon colored, round hats on their heads covering their wild, black hair. They both carried long, heavy sticks and had badges pinned to their breasts. They immediately started screaming at her in Arabic, waving their ominous sticks around.

A pit opened up in Leslie's belly. Maybe this hadn't been such a good idea. She was only about five or six blocks away from the Moussa house. If only she had walked a little quicker.

Her skirt had a little pocket on the side and Leslie's hand reached for it. She suddenly realized that although she had meant to bring her passport, she had forgotten it. An icy feeling went through her.

The men continued to shout at her. She tried to speak to them in French to tell them that she was sorry and would go right home. One of the men swung his stick hard at her legs, catching her on the back of her shins. She screeched in pain and fell to her knees on the hard, white sidewalk. Tears came to her eyes. The other man grabbed her by the back of her hair and started to drag her to the car. People had come onto the street and were watching. Leslie called out in French for help, but no one took any steps to interfere.

She struggled, resisting the force that was impelling her to the car. She knew that once she was inside she was lost. The man who had struck her struck her again, this time across her back. She moaned in pain. Realizing that further resistance was useless, she allowed herself to be dragged to the back door and thrown in. It slammed closed behind her. The men got in the front and the car sped away.

Leslie sobbed heavily as the car caromed through the narrow streets. She had never been so scared in her life. The doors had no interior handles. They were taking her in the opposite direction from the Moussa mansion. She realized that she didn't even know the phone number there.

Her ride took about twenty minutes. At one point she tried to speak to the men in the front seat, but the passenger turned and gave her a vicious poke with his stick right in the ribs. Leslie gasped and fell back onto the rear seat. She was quiet after that.

The car pulled through a gate into a large courtyard. They came to a halt in front of an ominous looking, white stone building. The men hopped from the front seat and the door on the driver's side opened. Leslie was too scared to get out. The driver reached in and took hold of her hair again and dragged her from the car. She fell to the ground outside. It was covered with sharp, white, crushed stones. Leslie screamed in pain. The man just kept dragging her until they reached a large, steel door. Leslie was doing everything to get back on her feet, but the man was moving too fast. He banged on the door with his stick and it opened. He dragged her in.

Once inside, the man paused so that Leslie could regain her feet. He held on to the hair at the back of her head and, when she was steady, started dragging her again down the hall. Leslie was screeching in pain and terror. They went down a long hallway and then down some narrow, cement stairs. They waited while a heavy wooden door was unlocked from the other side and then she was pulled past it. She went through another door, down another set of stairs and then was brought into a large, well lit room. There were desks set around it with caftan attired men, cookie cutter versions of the men who had seized her, sitting at or standing next to them. She was brought over to a long high desk with a high, caged window. A man was sitting behind it writing on something. It took a moment for him to look up.

The man who was holding Leslie spat some words in Arabic at him. He leaned over the desk to take a look at Leslie's attire. Her powder blue skirt was dirty and torn from being dragged through the parking lot. She had lost one of her shoes. Her ribs, back and legs ached where she had been struck. She was bent over and had to look up to see the man. She realized that she was at some kind of booking station and that the moment to speak up had arrived. Once she was actually booked, she would be mired in the local criminal system and who knew what could happen after that. She hoped desperately to be able to talk her way out of this mess.

The man behind the desk asked Leslie's captor a question and he responded curtly. He raised Leslie's head so that the man behind the desk could see her face. He asked Leslie a question in Arabic. "My name is Leslie Harrington," she started to say in French. The men looked at each other quizzically.

The man behind the desk repeated his question.

"Please! Please!" Leslie blurted out in English. "I'm an American. I work for…"

The man who was holding her slapped her viciously across the face. She screeched in pain.

"Pleeeeeeease!" she shouted again. The man holding her gave her another blow and yelled back at her.

Weeping disconsolately, Leslie decided that she best keep quiet. The men had a further conversation and some decision was reached.

Leslie was dragged over to the door that led to the area behind the caged window. It was opened on the inside and she was hauled past some desks to another door. This was made of steel and a man standing next to it opened it with a large, steel key. When the door swung open, Leslie saw that she was in a cell block. There was a long hallway with a shiny concrete floor. Larger heavy, wooden doors lined it. Each door had a huge lock on it and a small trap door on the top so that someone on the outside could peer into the cell. Leslie was dragged down to the fourth or fifth door on the right. The man who had been standing by the outside door fumbled with some keys and opened it. Leslie was pushed inside.

She fell to the floor of the ten by ten foot cell. There was a grungy, old, narrow pallet along the right wall and a disgusting looking bucket in the corner. The two men who had arrested her followed her in. The door closed behind them. Leslie's stomach went sour as she anticipated what was to come next. What happened was not calculated to reassure her.

One of the men jabbed her with his stick and yelled at her, using his free hand to indicate to her that she wanted her to stand up. Frightened beyond all belief, Leslie complied immediately. He jabbed her with the stick again and gave her a command. She didn't understand it and he jabbed her harder. She fell back, clutching her stomach in pain. Tears were streaming down her face. The man stepped forward and took hold of her skirt, pulling on it and repeated his command. Leslie understood at once that he wanted her to take it off.

"Please, don't do this," she moaned. "Please!" The man raised the stick over his head as if to strike her a mighty blow and Leslie at once gave up her objections to stripping. Her hands were sweaty; she had a hard time undoing her belt and loosening the buttons on the back. When they were free, she hesitated for moment and then quickly stepped out of her skirt. She proffered it to the man, who took it and handed it to his companion. He then repeated his command and pulled at the tail of Leslie's blouse. She obeyed at once, unbuttoning the front and then pulling it off of her shoulders and arms. Shaking, she handed it to the man who passed it on.

Things happened fast after that. The man grabbed her arm and made her turn around. Her arms were drawn behind her back and she felt cold steel being applied to them. She was handcuffed. The man turned her around again and produced a long chain. There was a hook in the ceiling above her and he clipped one end to it. The other end he ran under her handcuffs and then brought it back up. He kept pulling it until Leslie was standing on her toes. He then clipped it to one of its links.

When he stepped away, Leslie realized that she could not lower herself to her feet without putting a strain on her confined arms. It was a position that would become tortuous very quickly.

"Please don't do this," she uttered meekly. All she earned was another viscous slap across her face. The force of the blow made her totter on her toes and her arms pull up behind her. She moaned from the pain.

The men seemed satisfied with what they had done. For the first time since she was arrested, they seemed to relax. They took the time to examine her near naked body. The man who had been driving reached out and took hold of her left breast, squeezing it and saying something humorous to his companion. The other man laughed and made some kind of suggestion. The driver laughed back and he took the cups of Leslie's lacey, pink bra and pulled them up over her breasts, exposing them. There was a moan of appreciation from both men. They took turns cupping and squeezing them.

Leslie recoiled at the offensive contact of the hot, rough hands. She tried to back away, but the chain holding her wrists aloft wouldn't let her. She was only able to back off a few inches and one of the men, taking hold of her nipples, dragged her back. He gave them a mighty pinch until Leslie called out in pain. The men laughed.

At that, they seemed satisfied. One of the men produced a black hood and it was pulled over Leslie's head and drawn tight at her neck. The other leaned over and removed her remaining shoe. The men walked away and she heard the door open and slam shut behind them. Then the lock turned with a heavy sounding, 'clank!'

The unhappy American girl realized that she was in deep shit. No one knew where she was and she had no way of relating to the men who held her captive who she was. They didn't really seem to care. That was the worst part. The slamming of the door when it shut had seemed so final. It took her moment to realize that she was sobbing uncontrollably. Her sobs were muffled by the hood which covered her head. It was pitch black inside. Her shoulders ached from the chain pulling her wrists toward the ceiling behind her and her toes were already becoming cramped.

She could feel her loose breasts swaying as she tried to keep her balance.

She heard the trap door on the upper portion of the door open and then men's voices. There was laughter. She realized that the men were staring at her naked breasts. It shamed her to be seen by unknown men this way. By any men. She thought of her long, shapely legs bared for the men's view and the slight bulge that her pubic hair made on her loins under her panties.

Chagrinned, she tiptoed until her back was to the door, depriving the men of their show. She knew that they were looking at her firm, plump ass, but that was better than having her breasts exposed to them. She heard one of the men make an unhappy comment. The trap door closed and a moment later, the door opened up again. Men, she believed there were two of them, came into the cell. They were laughing. They grabbed her ankles and pushed them together. She felt a pair of handcuffs being applied, locking them to each other. She was turned around to face the door again and she felt something tugging on the cuffs as if they were being affixed to something on the floor.

When the men stepped back, Leslie realized that she had been anchored in place. She could no longer turn her body to hide her breasts. She whined in unhappiness. The men played with her soft mounds for a little while, squeezing and caressing them. One of them placed his mouth on a nipple and suckled it until she felt an unwanted pull in her loins. The other man said something in Arabic and they made as if to leave. Then one of the men, as if he had forgotten something, returned. She felt his hands on her hips take hold of her panties and pull them down past her knees to her ankles. Both men laughed again. Then they left.

CHAPTER TWO

Leslie stood that way for it seemed like hours. Every once in a while the trap window to her cell would open and she could hear the snickering of the men. Each time a wave of humiliation passed through her, bringing on a new cascade of tears.

Nothing in her life had prepared her for such treatment. Hers was a middle class upbringing where all significant problems occurred to other people. She had never been in trouble and never even known anyone who had. Life was supposed to be a progression from one safe, comfortable environment into another. Standing virtually naked, her arms tortuously held up behind her back, her feet cramped and swelling, being the object of the lewd leers of unknown, foreign men was not the way things were supposed to be.

The men had not gagged her, and her moans and cries were able to overcome the black hood that encapsulated her head. She pleaded for mercy, for forgiveness, for an end to her torment, but there was no one to hear her and no one to reply except the faint echo of her supplications on the cold, stone walls.

Leslie wondered what Mrs. Moussa would do when she was found to be missing. Since Mr. Moussa was out of town, she was the only one who could help her. Leslie remembered her disdainful looks, her haughtiness, and realized that if she found out that Leslie had been arrested by the morals police, she would probably do nothing. When Mr. Moussa returned, she would tell him where she was and how wrong he had been to employ an American, an outsider. She would undoubtedly lose her job and have to return to America in disgrace. She would eventually be released from the prison, she knew that. What could they really do to her except expel her from the country? She was an American citizen after all.

But then she thought about some of the stories she had heard about women being beaten for dressing immodestly. A shiver went through her body when she thought of that. It would be horrible to be struck by a cane. She prayed that that would not happen to her. She would do almost anything to avoid it.

It was about three hours later that the door to her cell finally opened. The pain in her shoulders had become a dull ache. The pain in her distended feet was becoming excruciating. The door shut again right away and Leslie sensed the presence of another person in her cell. A male person. She heard him walk around her as if on an inspection. She whined in fear and in supplication. Then she felt a large, rough hand on her naked ass. It caressed it gently as if appreciating its delicate curve, its soft firmness. The hand was hot. It traversed both of her rear globes and flitted between her thighs. She had pressed her thighs together as closely as she could, but she knew that her compressed vagina, due to her posture, would be visible to the man. She felt a finger trace a line along her love lips. It followed up over her perineum, up between her soft rear cheeks and halted at the little brown star. She felt the finger begin to probe her there. She mewed in protest and tried to move away, but her confinements left her little room for maneuver. The finger penetrated her rear opening, just dipping slightly past her pursed, brown tinted ring, and she gave out a little squeal. "Please don't," she managed to plead from beneath her hood.

The finger left her back passage abruptly to her relief. But a second later, the hand descended forcefully on the tender skin of her rear. It made a loud, 'smack!' and an immediate, harsh fire erupted there.

"Ooooooooowwwww!" Leslie shouted.

A second later, the hand descended again. "Smack!"

"Ooooooowwwwww!" Leslie shouted even louder. "Please don't hit me! Please!" she begged. The hand came down again, harder still.

"Smack!" and then repeated itself five times quickly in a row. Leslie began to howl. "Oh stop! Stop! Please stop!" she yelled. "Ooooooooooowwww! Oooooooooowwwwwwww!"

There was a pause. Her cries of pain still reverberated in her ears. Her ass seemed to be glowing with heat from her assault. Then the hand touched her again. A finger traced a line from the middle of her lower back, down, down, down, until it had regained her smaller portal. A moment later, it had penetrated her once more.

Leslie moaned and cried as the finger explored her anus. There was nothing she could think of that could be more humiliating. The finger moved back and forth, penetrating her small ring deeply and then running back until its tip was just inside and then in deep again. It was like the finger was fucking her there. It felt offensive and wrong. She tried to clamp her rear cheeks shut, but the man's other hand held them open. There was nothing she could do about it. She knew better now than to utter a protest. She didn't want to be spanked again. Whatever the man was going to do, he was going to do and she was powerless to prevent it.

The finger finally pulled out and she thought that her ordeal was at an end, but she was wrong. Within a second, she felt two fingers now probing her sphincter. The presence of the single finger had been humiliating, but now two stretched the tender tissue just a little bit more than was comfortable. She moaned as the fingers began a slow, steady rhythm back and forth. Her rear channel felt strangely filled and the abrasion of the fingers across the tender ring of skin at the entrance was producing an unfamiliar tingling in her loins. She mewed and cried again. She wanted it to stop. Needed it to stop. Begged God to make it stop. But the fingers continued their remorseless journey back and forth, in and out. It was a weird sensation, to be utterly sightless, the hood extinguished all light, and yet have her body subject to some strange, unknown man's casual use. It was like her body and her mind were in two separate places.

It was when the third finger joined the two that had been exploring her small, rear opening that Leslie began really to worry. That brought the man's actions way beyond the teasing stage. He was definitely preparing her for something. The addition of the third finger stretched her anal ring, creating little, tiny cracks in the membrane, cracks that stung and hurt.

"Ohhhhhhhhh!" she moaned. She yearned to call out for pity, to protest her treatment, but she could still feel the heat where her rear cheeks had been struck so harshly a little while ago.

The force of the fingers going back and forth caused her body to shift backwards and forwards in her bindings. Her bound arms were pulled more tightly upwards behind her as she moved forwards, making her moan with pain. Her breasts swung back and forth, free beneath her chest. "Ooooooooooooooh!" she moaned.

And then the fingers left her. She could feel her anal ring gaping. She heard the sound of a zipper lowering. A hand took hold of her hip as if to hold her steady.

"Oh, nooooooooooooo!" she screamed. "Please don't do that! Please! It'll hurt! I know it will! Please! Please!"

Despite her now vociferous protests, she felt something hard and soft at the same time probe at her rear entrance. It was thick and round. It pressed against the stretched but still small opening. Its progress halted for a moment, having encountered resistance, but then pressed slowly, inexorably forwards, expanding her anal ring and filling her like she had never been filled before. She screamed in pain as it gained entry. And then, remorselessly, it sank itself fully within her.

Leslie cried and moaned as the man fucked her rear passage. He was in no hurry. He had hold of both of her hips now and pushed and pulled her in time with his slow, steady thrusts. "Oh! Oh! Ohhhhhhhhh!" she cried as the cock crossed and recrossed her tender anal ring. She could feel the man's immenseness in her bowel each time he thrust himself home. She cried and shook and moaned. Her mind refused to believe what was happening to her even though her body told her unmistakably that it was. Was she really a helpless prisoner in an Arab jail being butt fucked? Could this really be happening to her?

An arm snaked its way around her waist, pulling her rear more tightly against the huge belly of the man who was fucking her. She could hear him now, grunting and groaning his satisfaction. His other arm went past her hip and grabbed one of her dangling, flopping breasts, squeezing it tightly. His fingers pulled and pinched fiercely at her teat until she howled with pain. He was pounding away frantically now, his belly slapping against her rear cheeks, his fat cock pistoning within her. He began to groan, "Ugh! Ugh! Ugh! Ugh!" each sound timed to match a fierce inward thrust of his cock. She felt his body tense and he emitted a loud, almost mournful groan. His cock began to throb within her and she felt the hot splash of his come. She moaned and cried out in frantic disgust.

When his cock's explosions were at an end, he kept leaning against her, his prick firmly lodged in her ass. His body was hot against her back. She could feel his chest rising and falling rapidly from his exertions. He massaged her breasts and laid his fat, sloppy lips on the back of her neck, murmuring some word in Arabic over and over.

Finally, he released her. His softened cock slid free. He gave her an appreciative slap on her ass and laughed. She heard his zipper being pulled up. He stepped over to the door, opened it and left. It closed again with a loud, heavy thud.

Leslie sobbed and sobbed. This was the worse experience of her young life by far. It was worse than anything she had ever reasonably expected to suffer. She had been raped, in the ass, by a man she could never identify other than by his groans. How many more men would come in and fuck her like that? How long would they keep her prisoner? How long would she have to be so cruelly confined?

And yet, to her shame, there was something exhilarating about being fucked in the ass and being unable to prevent it. It had not been a wholly disgusting procedure. The scraping of the cock along the ring of her rear entrance had sparked heat in her loins. The man's firm hands, his casual use of her had seemed oddly right. But what was she thinking? She had always considered ass fucking to be disgusting and dirty. She had never let any of her boyfriends, and there had been more than one, go near there with their hands, never mind their cocks. It was demeaning and unsanitary, and worst of all, it had been against her will, without her consent. She had been used worse than the lowest whore. And on top of everything else, it still burned back there where her anus had been stretched.

It was not long after that the door opened again. Two men entered. She felt the chain that held her wrists high being lowered. She moaned with relief. The other man unlocked her ankles. Her hands were freed. The bag was pulled off of her head.

Before her stood a tall, dark haired man. He was dressed in what looked like a military uniform. His khaki blouse had red epaulettes and there were gold bars on his collar. He looked maybe forty or so, a very young forty. His face was clean shaven and he carried himself with an air of authority. The other man was one of the jailers, dressed in Khaki as well, but obviously an underling. It was the tall man, the officer, who spoke to her.

"Dress yourself, you pig!" he spat at her. "What do you think parading yourself naked like that?"

"But, I…..." Leslie started to protest.

"Silence!" the man screamed. "Prisoners are to remain silent!" he yelled.

Leslie began to cry. It was so unfair. It hadn't been her idea to strip like that. Afraid of further reprimand, Leslie quickly pulled down her bra to cover her breasts. She leaned over and pulled up her panties. The underling had her skirt and blouse and she quickly donned them.

The officer watched her disdainfully the whole time. When she was done, he spoke to her again, his voice rude and cold.

"And I understand that you enticed one of my guards into fucking you! Is this true?"

"No, I didn't, I, I, I couldn't help it," she whined meekly.

The man lashed out, his hand slapping her face harshly. Leslie screamed and fell backwards. "Liar!" he roared. "You are a whore! A slut! Do you think you can come to our country and poison us with your foul Western ways!"

Leslie was too scared to respond. She rubbed her face where he had struck her and cried. It was too unreal. She was being blamed for the men stripping and fucking her? She had nothing to say about it! What was happening here?

"Your attempt at bribing my guards with your body will be added to your charges. Tell me, where are you staying? Where are your papers? What is your name?"

"I'm personal assistant to Mr. Hassan Ben Moussa," she whined. "My name is Leslie Harrington. I left my papers at his house. I was only going for a walk…"

The hand lashed out at her again. She screeched as he struck her cheek. She backed up and bent over, holding her hand to her face, tears of fear and pain flowing from her eyes.

"Did I ask you what you were doing?" the man screamed. "I know what you were doing! You were parading your lustful body for all the men to see! You're disgusting! And you work for Hassan Ben Moussa? I don't believe it! He would never hire a lascivious slut like you! We will see! If you are lying, I will add that to your charges! Now follow me!"

The underling snapped to attention and opened the cell door. The officer walked briskly out. Leslie was afraid to follow him, not knowing where they were going. The underling took hold of her arm just above the elbow, squeezing it hard, and marched her along after him. They went back along the row of cells and exited into another corridor. They walked along its length. When they came to another large, locked steel door, the officer rapped on it loudly with his fist. The door opened and a tall, heavyset woman dressed in a blue ayala appeared. Her face was covered by a veil. The officer spoke to her in Arabic. She nodded and replied to him in kind. The officer took Leslie by the arm and forced her through the doorway. It slammed shut.

Leslie was on the verge of hysteria. She couldn't believe how much trouble she was in. Being underdressed was one thing, not that she thought she had been, but she knew that bribery was a serious charge wherever you went. She could go to prison! She was in prison! They could keep her here a long, long time! She started to cry all over again.

The ayala clad woman lowered her veil. She had a stern, homely face. She looked to be in her late forties or early fifties. She had dark eyes and a dark brown complexion. Her eyebrows grew across her forehead, connecting with each other. Her nose was long and hooked. Her lips were thick. She said something to Leslie in Arabic.

They were standing in what seemed to Leslie to be some kind of an anteroom. There was a steel door just like the one she had just come through on the other side. There was a small, ancient looking, battered, wooden desk by the wall and next to it a thick, wooden chair. The walls were stone block and covered with a faded and peeling whitewash. The floor was stone too, slate. Its coolness reminded Leslie that they had not returned her shoes to her.

She had no idea what the Arabic woman had said or what she wanted her to do. She stood there dumbly, her eyes watering with tears, her lips trembling. She had her hands clasped together before her and she writhed them together frantically. The woman stood about half a foot taller than her and was broad shouldered. She had an 18 inch long, thick club in her left hand. Her face wrinkled up in an impatient grimace and she repeated the Arabic words to her.

"I don't under...." was all Leslie got out.

The hand with the club in it moved like lightning. It struck Leslie on her right arm between her shoulder and her elbow. It made a dull thud when it landed.

"Ooooooowwwwwwwww!" Leslie yelled. She stepped back and bent over, clutching her left hand to her arm. There was a painful, dull throbbing in her arm where she had been struck. "Ohhhhhhhhhh, god!" she exclaimed. "Ohhhhhhhhhh, please don't hit me! Pleeeeeease!" she cried desperately.

The woman raised the club again. Leslie backed away from her until her back was against the wall. The woman screamed the Arabic command for a third time.

There was only one thing Leslie could think of. She began immediately to strip off her clothes. The Arab woman lowered the club and smiled.

Leslie sobbed while she once again discarded her clothes. When she had her blouse and skirt off, she paused and looked at the woman to see if that was enough. The club came flying again, striking her on the right thigh.

"Ohhhhhhhhhhhhhhh!" Leslie moaned again. She fell to the floor. The woman raised the club and gave her order for the fourth time. Sobbing heavily, Leslie rose to her knees. Frantic to avoid another blow from the club, she put her hands behind her back and unclasped her bra. She lowered it off of her arms and tossed it onto the floor. She reached into the gusset of her lacey, pink silk panties and pulled them to her knees. Keeping her eyes glued to the Arab woman, she sat back and brought her legs in front of her. She slid her panties down her shins and over her feet. They joined her matching bra on the floor.

The Arab woman screamed another command. This time, she waved her hands upwards and Leslie understood that she was being ordered to stand. She scrambled to her feet. The woman's free hand made a turning motion and Leslie obediently turned and faced the wall. She felt the club jammed against her back, pushing her closer. Defensively, she put her hands up against it. Issuing what sounded like a curse, the woman took hold of her hands, one by one, and spread them further apart. She tapped the club on the inside of her thighs, forcing them wider and wider until they were stretched to their limit and then on the fronts, until Leslie edged her feet back.

Leslie was leaning over, her legs spread wide with her hands against the wall. If she pulled her hands from the wall, she would fall on her face. Her feet were arched and she was standing on her toes. They began to cramp almost immediately. She turned to look behind her to see what the Arabic woman was going to do next. The club flashed out, this time catching her on the ribs on her right side.

"Auuuuuuuugh!" Leslie moaned. The force of the blow forced her off of her toes. The pain flowed through her, giving her a sickening feeling. The woman screamed the curse word again and Leslie, crying and moaning resumed her position immediately. The woman stepped forward and, grabbing her by the hair in the back of her head, pressed her face towards the wall, holding it firmly so that her gaze was fixed on a spot on the wall before her. She uttered a sharp, acerbic sounding word for emphasis. Leslie got the picture. She was to look straight ahead and nowhere else.

The woman seemed temporarily satisfied. Leslie heard her step away and heard the sound of the club being placed down on the desk. A drawer opened and she heard the sound of elastic snapping. Then there was the sound of a jar opening. The lid and then, a moment later, the jar, were placed on the desk. The woman stepped back to her.

Her hand reached between Leslie's naked thighs and Leslie felt a gooey substance being applied to her pussy. Rough, thick fingers insinuated themselves onto her love lips and then into the gash between them. Leslie gritted her teeth and whined as she felt the fingers prying their way into her canal. Despite the lubricant, it hurt as her pussy's walls were forcibly widened. The fingers delved around inside her as if they were searching for something. Her stomach went queasy and she began to break out into a sweat. Besides being ass fucked, it was the most humiliating thing that had ever been done to her.

The fingers slid all the way in. Finding no barrier, the woman laughed and said something caustic sounding in Arabic. Leslie knew that the woman was commenting on her lack of virginity, something quite common for a 22 year old woman back in the States. Here, she knew, it was a sign of what would be considered extreme licentiousness for an unmarried woman.

Satisfied that she was hiding no contraband in her vagina, the fingers withdrew. They immediately began to probe at the delicate, irritated ring of flesh between her rear cheeks. Leslie issued a groan of unhappiness as she felt the fingers slide right in. She knew that she was hiding nothing there, but also knew that the spume of the man who had raped her had been slowly leaking out of her rear ever since he had withdrawn his softened prick from it. The woman discovered it right away.

She gave out a shriek of disgust and gave Leslie a fierce slap on her buttocks. She slapped her two, three, four, five times. Leslie wailed and cried as she hit her. She yearned to pull her hands from the wall to defend herself, but knew that the only result would be another blow from the woman's club. Leslie screamed and cried in pain. When the slaps ceased, the woman roughly thrust her fingers back into Leslie's rear hole and twisted them brutally around and around. Leslie's knees went weak. "Auuuuuuuuuuuwwwwww! Auuuuuuuuuuuuwwwwwwww!" she screamed. "Please stop! Please!" she yelled.

The woman pulled her fingers abruptly from Leslie's ass and then struck her three more times on her buttocks, issuing a harsh command, which Leslie understood as an order to keep quiet. She closed her mouth, sniffling and sobbing. The fingers thrust themselves back inside her, circled around the area nearest her anus and then withdrew.

Leslie was sickened with shame and humiliation. Her face was awash with tears. Her toes and feet ached and her shoulders had begun to hurt. She issued a little prayer of thanks that her ordeal was done, but she was wrong. The Arab woman stepped up next to her. One hand grabbed her cheeks firmly, squeezing her mouth opened and the slime covered, gloved hand was thrust into her mouth.

Leslie groaned with misery as the fouled fingers explored her oral cavity. They passed over her teeth, between her gums and her lips and then all the way to the back of her mouth to the edge of her throat. Her mind reeled with the thought of the filth laden fingers in her mouth. It seemed to take forever, but only lasted a few seconds. It was an experience she knew that she would never forget as long as she lived. When the fingers withdrew, it was all she could do to prevent herself from vomiting. Her sobs of misery echoed off of the stone walls.

Her examination complete, the woman withdrew to the desk again. Leslie heard the sound of the jar being capped and put back in the drawer. She heard the snap of the glove being removed. She heard a faint sound as it was tossed into the garbage.

There was silence behind her. She got the feeling that the woman was scouring her naked body with her eyes. She had never felt so vulnerable in her life. She just wanted her ordeal to end. She knew that there was a prison cell waiting for her and she yearned for its relative safety.

She heard the woman stepping up closer to her. Her rough hand slid up and over her right buttock. The sensation made Leslie's body run cold. The hand slid over her other rear cheek as if appreciating its softness and roundness.

The woman said something. While her voice up to now had been stern and demanding, this time it was soft and warm sounding, like you might talk to a favorite pet. The woman brought her body closer to Leslie. The rough fabric of her ayala rubbed against Leslie's hip. The hand kept running over her rear mounds again and again, caressing them while the warm, singsong voice continued. Leslie was keeping her eyes pinned to the wall in front of her. She could feel the sweat running off her underarms. Her skin was prickly. She tried not to know what was happening, to pretend that it couldn't be happening. But when the woman's hands slid between her thighs and trickled across her outer labia, she could pretend no more.

The woman had a soft, tender touch, which was surprising given her previous coarseness. The fingers gently caressed Leslie's sex while the warm, insinuating voice continued. The woman's body was closer to her now, right up against her. Her face was only a few inches from Leslie's ear. She was whispering, a whisper of encouragement, of enticement. Leslie could feel her hot breath. She was holding her air in tightly. It was as if any movement she made would serve as further encouragement to her assailant. When the woman's finger began a soft, circular motion on her bud of pleasure, Leslie felt a tingle flow through her body and her breath hissed out of her like a long, prolonged, lover's sigh.

This seemed to amuse the woman. Her singsong voice became lighter and rose higher. The finger, clearly expert at its task, slid off of her now stiffened clit and slipped along the crevasse below it, gently pushing her love lips aside, delving inside, covering itself with her incipient moisture. When the slickened finger returned to Leslie's pleasure button and resumed its tantalizing motion, Leslie moaned.

It was, seemingly, the signal the woman was looking for. As her finger continued its torment of her clit, her other hand slid over her hip, then across her belly. The hand was hot and seemed to melt something inside her. When it seized one of her breasts, gently cupping it and then giving it a loving, soft squeeze, Leslie moaned again.

Propped up against the wall, naked and defenseless, her toes digging into the stone floor, Leslie's mind screamed at her helplessness. All of being wanted to move away from the woman, to close her distended thighs, to pull her full, throbbing breast away from the hand that had captured it, to move her body away from the ominous presence of her assailant, but she was locked in place, bound in position, no less than is she had been placed in implacable, steel chains.

The woman began to slide two thick fingers in and out of Leslie's distended, moisture laden crevasse. The hand on her breast tightened its grip, its fingers closing in on her rigid nipple, pinching and teasing it. The voice went on and on. Its tenor had become passionate, loving. The hand switched breasts, caressing and squeezing the mate while the fingers probed deep within her churning tunnel, in and out, in and out, faster and faster.

Leslie's moans became steady and louder. Her hips began an involuntary movement, encouraging the assault on her sex. The fingers slipped up over her clit again, pressing down on it firmly, massaging it. Leslie's lust grew higher and higher. She felt her orgasm building. She gritted her teeth and closed her eyes, trying to fight it off, but the hand between her thighs was incessant, insistent. All of her weight was on her hands, pinned to the wall, her breasts were tight and hot and the woman continued her assault on them, squeezing them tighter and tighter, giving her nipples sharp, harsh tugs. Leslie tilted her neck back, groaning as her climax marched closer and closer to completion.

And then it struck. Leslie gave out a long, wailing moan. Her hips shuddered, her thighs trembled, her body shook. The woman's voice was excited, egging her on. It felt to Leslie like it was coming from inside her, her own, personal demon drawing out her baser lusts. "Ohhhhhhhhhhhhh! Ohhhhhhhhhhhhhhhh!" Leslie moaned. "Ohhhhhhhhhhhhhhhhhh!"

When her orgasm had crested, the fingers in her coosh slowed their motions, but did not stop. The aftershocks of her climax caused her pussy to clench and her body to shake. Tears of shame filled her eyes. She had lowered her head back into position, but kept her eyes clenched closed, too humiliated to absorb the reality they would perceive.

The woman did not withdraw her hand until she was satisfied that Leslie's tremors had finished. She gave each of her plump breasts one last squeeze and then, leaning forward slipped her tongue in her ear, causing a wave of revulsion to flow through the young girl. After a few moments, the woman withdrew, said something and then laughed.

A feeling of complete powerlessness flowed through the unhappy Bryn Mawr graduate. In the last few hours, there had been a complete paradigm shift in her life. She had gone from a. happy, independent, self assured, confident young woman to a miserable, forlorn, humiliated prisoner. She wondered dismally what other unpleasant and distasteful things would happen to her. She had been swept up into a world that she had hardly known existed. These people had no respect for her rights. And what was worse, they were perfectly satisfied that she could devise no remedy for their abuse of her. No court would ever hold them to account. They would suffer no consequence for the things that they did. It was their world she was in now and it had a whole new set of rules.

Leslie vowed to obey whatever commands she received to the letter. She would do nothing to incur the wrath of the people who had control of her. The problem was, though, that she did not understand the rules. When the fierce woman in the anteroom with her had given her orders, she had not understood them and suffered immediate, painful violence when she did not obey. What was she going to do? How could she avoid more punishment? Her arm, her thigh and her ribs ached awfully where she had been struck. She was sure there would be deep purple bruises there before long. She had to face the facts. She was in the midst of a terrible nightmare from which there would be no deliverance until either these people were finished having their way with her or Mr. Moussa came to her rescue.

The woman stepped up behind Leslie and took hold of her hair at the back of her head. She pulled on it harshly, forcing Leslie to lean back and withdraw her hands from the wall. The young girl sighed as the strain on her thighs and toes was finally relieved. The woman took hold of her arms from behind and brought them behind her back, crossing them at the wrists. She said something imperative which Leslie interpreted as meaning that she should keep her arms that way until further notice. The woman took hold of her hair again, grabbing it so tightly that Leslie whined from the pain. She forced her head down until she was almost bent over double and then brought her to the steel door on the other side of the small room.

She knocked on it three times. A panel opened in it and a pair of female eyes looked out. The woman said something to the eyes and the panel shut. Leslie heard the sound of a heavy steel bolt being opened on the other side of the door. The woman holding Leslie's hair opened one on her side. The door swung open.

There was a brief conversation between the two women while Leslie was kept bent over, her hands glued behind her back. The second woman was dressed in a thin, dark green, shirtwaist dress that went down below her knees. It had half sleeves and the woman's arms were thick and strong like she had worked in the fields for most of her life. There was an identity card with her picture on it pinned to her uniform, over her right breast. She too was heavyset. Her dirty brown hair was done up in a bun on the back of her head. Leslie was just able to stare up at her from her position. She looked even uglier and meaner than the woman who had been tormenting her. Leslie trembled when she thought of what she might be in for.

When the conversation was over, the first woman handed Leslie off to the second. She took a firm grasp of Leslie's hair and pulled her away from the door while she closed it. She threw the bolt home just as it closed from the other side. It made a loud 'clang!' that echoed down the long hallway. When the echo ended, there was absolute silence.

The new guard brought Leslie to the wall next to the door and gave her the same order that the first woman did, the one that Leslie thought was a curse. She knew what to do now and as the woman released her hair, she plopped up next to the wall and placed her hands on it. She scooted her feet back until she was leaning forward and then spread them. She was a bright girl who didn't need to be told things twice.

The new guard picked up the handset to a wall mounted telephone and punched in a number. A moment later, she barked something or other into it. She waited for a response and then gave out a sound of affirmation. She hung up the phone.

The woman took a seat next to a large wooden desk by the door. She had apparently been reading a magazine. She went back to her task.

Leslie stood there for a long, long time. Her toes and the arches of her feet had started hurting almost right away. Her calves began to ache soon afterwards. Her eyes were pinned to the wall in front of her. It was made of cement blocks that had been coated with a thin screen of plaster and then painted a pale yellow. The grey of the underlying blocks showed through in several places. There were cracks running up and down them here and there. Leslie counted them a number of times. There were seven blocks going up and down. Within her vision, there were five blocks across. That was all she could see, all she did see for almost an hour. She counted the cracks. She counted them again.

Time passed slowly, time to fret about her future, to relive the torment the first guard had put her through, time to regret ever coming to this cruel land. The pain in her feet was becoming excruciating. It was hard to suppress the whine that kept wanting to come out, a whine of pain and misery. The sun outside was turning the inside of the prison into an oven and sweat was pouring off of her body. She was thirsty and tired and very, very scared.

She felt so vulnerable, naked and alone amidst this cold stone and steel. She heard no voices, although there certainly had to be other people in here. She had caught a glimpse of a long line of cells on one side of the hallway, the cold steel bars going all the way up to the twelve foot high ceiling. There had to be women in some of them. Were they condemned to perpetual silence?

Only once did she hear any sound other than the turning of the pages of the guard's magazine. Far away, there was the sound of heavy steel clanging against heavy steel. Then she heard a loud voice yell something. The voice was harsh and angry. It was a woman's voice. There was a pause, and she heard the unmistakable sound of a woman's scream followed by a heart rendering series of desperate pleas. The angry voice rang out again. There was another scream and then sobbing. This was followed by the loud, harsh sound of steel on steel again, as if the door to a cell had been slammed closed. The sobbing continued for a while, getting fainter and fainter. A door slammed and then it went away.

The sounds terrorized Leslie. It was clear that she was in a cruel, hard place. She tried not to imagine what the angry woman had done to the other to make her scream so loudly and frantically. It made her blood run cold. She tried not to envision where the angry woman had taken her and what she was going to do to her there. She just trembled and tried not to cry.

When almost an hour had passed, Leslie heard the sound of heavy steps sounding on the shiny, tiled floor of the hallway. They were coming closer and closer. The footsteps stopped right behind her. She heard a new voice, a woman's voice, somewhat lighter and less harsh than the first two guards. Guard number two answered her back. Then the new guard issued an order that Leslie hoped was meant for her. She turned her head slowly. The new guard was thinner than the other two. She was a little younger and her face seemed less cruel. She was dressed in the same thin green dress as the second guard. She issued the order again and Leslie moved herself off of the wall, still not sure if she was doing the right thing. She suppressed a sigh of relief as the pressure eased off of her feet and toes.

The new guard didn't react to what she had done so far. Leslie's heart was thumping and her eyes flitted between the two women so she could prepare herself for a blow if one was coming. It was so strange and humiliating to be stark naked in front of the two conservatively dressed women. She remembered the first guard's instructions to her and she quickly placed her hands behind her back. The new guard gave her a careful lookover. It seemed to Leslie that her gaze lingered on her plump breasts and the hairy bush between her legs. The guard then nodded at her, her expression deadpan, and she gave a jerk of the head as if telling Leslie to follow her.

They strode quickly down the hallway. Leslie was able to glance in several of the cells and she saw women lying on cots in some of them, but the rest were empty. They were wearing plain, light brown dresses. When they reached the end of the hall, it turned right. They passed another long line of cells and reached a steel door. The guard had a circle of keys on a ring attached to her belt. She took it in hand, isolated a key, and then opened the door. They walked through it.

This looked like part of the administrative wing. It had white plasterboard walls and a low ceiling. There were several brown wooden doors along the hallway. They stopped at one that was a half door with the top open. The bottom half had a shelf on it.

A thin, elderly woman dressed in a light brown shirtwaist dress was sitting on a chair in a small stockroom. She had wispy, gray hair. Her face was heavily wrinkled. She was short, about 5'5" and slightly bent over. Her eyes were dull.

The guard gave her an order. She smiled obsequiously and got up from her chair. She went back in the stockroom and returned with a thin, worn, brown blanket, some sheets, a small, dingy towel and a dirty old pillow. She put them on the shelf. She took a look at Leslie, letting her eyes wander over her body and then went away again. She came back with a folded up, brown, shirtwaist dress and a pair of dark brown, cloth slippers. She placed them on the pile. She walked away again and returned with a clear plastic bag that had a toothbrush, a small tube of toothpaste, a small bar of soap, a long, black, plastic comb and one tampon in it. With an air of finality, she placed them on the pile, smiling. Leslie noticed that she was missing a couple of teeth up front.

The guard gave Leslie an order which she assumed meant that she should pick up the pile of stuff. She did as she was told and followed the woman back down the hall. She opened the door they had come through and led Leslie off to the right, the opposite direction in which they had come. They went down another long line of cells. They stopped at one of them. The guard took another key and unlocked the cell door. She motioned with her head for Leslie to go in and she did. Without comment, she clanged the door shut, relocked it and walked away.

There were two cots in the room, about three feet separating them. The one on the right was made up with the same type of blanket Leslie had been given. It was pulled tight in a military style and the pillow was placed neatly at the head of the bed. The top sheet was folded over the top of the blanket, showing about four inches.

There was a toilet between the beds. The bowl and seat were made of steel. Next to it was a small sink. It too was made of steel. There were two small tin cups on it. There was only one spigot. Cold, Leslie assumed.

The cot on the left was unused. On it sat a thin, lumpy mattress. There were several large, dark stains on it that looked like blood. All of a sudden where she was and what had happened to her came down and punched Leslie right in the gut. She collapsed on the bed and started to cry. She had, at first, been thankful for getting the dress, but now she realized that the other things they gave her, the blanket and sheets, the pillow, the toothbrush, all bespoke the permanency of her status. They were going to keep her overnight, maybe indefinitely!

Mr. Moussa was out of town. Even when he returned, there was no reason to believe that he would lift a finger to help her. She had disgraced him. She had only been working for him for a couple of weeks. She had been warned not to go out. He had no real obligation to her. He could probably get another secretary by picking up the phone. She was in a whole world of shit and there might not be any way out of it for a long, long time.

When her sobs subsided, she tried to gather herself together. She picked up the dress from the pile of bedding and put it on. In was made from thin, coarse cotton and it scratched her skin as she drew it over her body. But at least it was something. It was too small though. The buttons on the front just barely closed. Her breasts pushed out the thin fabric tightly. Across her hips, the fabric strained. The hem was just above her knees, a tad longer than a miniskirt. She wondered if she was going to get any underwear.

She tried on the slippers. They were too small and her toes jammed up inside them. She wondered if the old lady had given her things that were too small for her on purpose as some form of nasty joke or whether she was just senile. She wondered how long the woman had been in here and what she might have done. And how about the other inmates? Were they innocent victims of a tyrannical religious establishment like her or were they real criminals, thieves, drug dealers, murderers? Someone owned the bed across from hers. What would she be like? Would she be a hardened criminal or some girl like her, just a victim of circumstance? She had heard some pretty bad things that went on in women's prisons, although she really didn't believe half of them. But if even half of them were true, it would be terrible. The way the first guard had treated her was not comforting. Her ears still burned from humiliation at that thought of what the woman did to her.

And when she thought of that, she thought too of the man who had raped her just a few hours ago. Were there any male guards? Would she be raped again?

After a while, Leslie grew tired of all of her frantic speculation. She got up from the bed and put the sheets and blanket on it. She tried to make it as taut and as military looking as the other one. When that was done, she lay down on it and waited for something to happen.

The cell block was absolutely silent. The cells were separated by concrete block walls and so she couldn't see into the cells to the right or left of her. In front of her was just a blank wall. There were long, narrow windows at the top covered with iron bars that let in a little light. In the middle of the corridor outside her cell were long, fluorescent lights. Inside her cell was a single bulb behind a steel cage. It was not on.

She had to wait a long time. All kinds of things ran through her head. She tried to stop worrying. Somehow things would work out, she knew that. She really hadn't done anything that bad. All that talk of bribery and such was just ridiculous. She had been raped, for Christ's sake!

After a while, she had to pee. It was strange to sit on the toilet and see the open corridor in front of her through the bars. It felt like she was on stage. There was a small roll of coarse, brown toilet paper. She used it sparingly. She was thirsty after a while and she opened the faucet in the sink. A heavily clouded liquid poured out of it. She wasn't that thirsty yet, she thought.

But she was hungry. She didn't know what time it was. She had been picked up around 9 o'clock. It had to be after 3 by now. And where were all the other inmates?

Her answer came about an hour later. She heard a steel door opening and closing down the corridor. A minute later a single file line of women came walking down. They were all dressed like she was. She could see that they were all natives, with black or dark brown hair and tawny skin. They paraded by her cell. There were young ones and old ones, and ones in between. All the women had deadened, blank looks on their faces. They were utterly silent. Their uniform dresses were raggedy and sweat stained. A couple of guards came walking down next to the column, dressed in their green dresses, swaggering, their clubs held idly in their hands.

The inmates all looked at her as they passed. Some were indifferent, some looked curious. Others leered at her hostilely. After about thirty or so of them passed, a whistle blew and they came to a halt. One woman had stopped just opposite the door to her cell. She was scrawny, about 5'6" tall, with dirty, black hair that came down to her shoulders in a ragged cut. The dirty brown dress she was wearing, unlike Leslie's, came down below her knees. She looked to be in her late thirties, but her age was hard to tell because she looked so rough. She gave Leslie a malevolent look.

The sound of cell doors being opened and closed rang out. It came closer and closer. The one of the guards came and unlocked the door to her cell. The mean looking woman came in. The door was shut and locked.

Giving Leslie a dirty look, the woman went right to the toilet. Leslie tried not to look at her while she pissed. When she was done, she got up without wiping, went over to the sink and poured some water into one of the tin cups. She drank it down, poured another and drank that too. When she had finished her third cup, she put it down and stepped over to her bed. She sat down on it and looked at Leslie. She said something low in Arabic. It was slightly louder than a whisper and Leslie had a hard time understanding it.

"I'm sorry, I don't speak…." Leslie started to say.

"Shhhhhhhhhh!" the woman hissed violently. She looked furtively out of the cell. Seeing no one, she turned back to Leslie.

"British?" she asked in a whisper.

"American," Leslie whispered back.

The woman laughed. "You in big trouble," she said, smirking. "Drugs?"

"N,no," Leslie answered. "I was walking down the street. I was wearing a skirt. They arrested me."

The woman laughed again. "You in big trouble. Prostitute."

"No, no, I'm not a prostitute!" Leslie returned forcibly.

"Shhhhhhhhh!" the woman hissed again. "No loud!" she whispered emphatically.

Leslie nodded.

"They say you prostitute, you prostitute," the woman said definitively. "You have big trouble."

Tears welled up in Leslie's eyes. "I'm not a prostitute," she murmured sadly.

The woman laughed. It was like sandpaper scraping along wood. Then her eyes lit up. "You get towel? Soap?" she asked.

"Y,yes," Leslie answered.

"Me see," the woman demanded.

The towel was folded up on Leslie's bed and the plastic bag with her toiletries was on top of it. She picked them up to show the woman.

The woman moved quickly. She got up and snatched the towel and bag of toiletries from Leslie's hand.

"Hey!" Leslie said. "They're mi…."

The woman's hand shot out like lightening and slapped Leslie viciously across the face.

"Owwwwwwwwww!" Leslie shouted. Her voice echoed down the corridor. Within a second, one of the guards was at their cell. She banged on the bars with her club and shouted something in Arabic.

"But she stole my towel!" Leslie exclaimed.

The guard, her eyes flashing fire, banged even harder on the bars and shouted again. Leslie took a look at the heavy club, remembering her prior encounter with one and remained silent. Her eyes were filled with tears. The guard looked at the other woman in the cell with her and smirked. Then she walked away.

The other woman had sat back down on her bed. She was smiling. "No make noise. Get beaten," she said.

She reached under her bed and drew out a long wooden box. It had no lid. She reached inside it and pulled out a grimy towel that looked like it hadn't been washed in a year. She threw it at Leslie. "Yours," she said. She took out a shopworn toothbrush and threw that at Leslie too. "Yours," she repeated. Lastly, she drew out a dirty black comb with several teeth missing. She threw it at Leslie. "Yours," she said.

Leslie despondently gathered the things that the woman had thrown at her. She knew that there was nothing she could do. There was no way she was going to get into a fight with her. The woman looked as mean as a junk yard dog. She was obviously an old hand at prison life. Leslie knew that she wouldn't stand a chance.

The woman shoved the wooden box back down under her bed and then lay down on top of it. She folded her arms behind her head and closed her eyes.

A half hour later, there was another whistle. Leslie's cell mate got up and stood by the door. Leslie got up and stood behind her. She wasn't sure she was supposed to, but she was hoping it was the dinner call and she didn't want to miss that.

A guard came down the line of cells opening them. Leslie's cell mate just stood there waiting. After a few minutes, another whistle blew and she stepped out. Leslie stepped out behind her. They turned to the right. There was a whole line of women standing outside of their cells in front of them, their arms behind their backs. The whistle blew a third time and they began to walk.

Leslie followed the column of women as they walked down the corridor. They went through an open steel door and down another corridor. At the end of the corridor was another steel door. When Leslie walked through it, she saw that she was in a cafeteria. She said a prayer of thanks.

The line became all jammed up, women pushing anxiously from behind. They turned right when they entered and proceeded along the whitewashed, cement block wall. There were at least fifty women ahead of her. At the head of the line, she could see women picking up trays and moving along what looked like a chow line. Green garbed guards were patrolling between four long lines of old, wooden tables.

All of a sudden, someone pushed into the line behind Leslie. She turned and looked. It was one of the other inmates. She was at least 6' tall and broad shouldered. She had matted, black hair, cut short to below her ears. She looked maybe forty five or so. Her face had deep creases, and her nose looked like it had been broken several times. Her arms were thick and she had large breasts that pushed out against the blouse of her dress. She smiled at Leslie.

Leslie turned away to look up ahead towards the chow line. The woman leaned over and whispered something in her ear. Leslie ignored it. The woman leaned over and whispered in her ear again. It sounded creepy. She tried to pay it no attention.

Then she felt a hand on her ass. A chill went through her. She reached down and tried to brush it away. The woman quickly jammed two stiff fingers in the side of her head. "Ow!" Leslie exclaimed. Then she looked around quickly to make sure that none of the guards heard her. No one was looking at her.

The line was moving slowly. She felt the hand on her ass again. This time it rubbed up and down, causing her skirt to move. Leslie went to bat it away, but the two fingers jabbed into her head again, this time harder.

"Ow!" Leslie exclaimed again. She turned to look at the woman. She was smiling lasciviously at her. A chill went down her spine.

As soon as she turned her head to look forward again, the hand came back. Leslie, angered at the woman's rudeness, swatted it away, harder this time. This time, the woman gave her a punch on the side of the head.

"Ohhhhhh!" Leslie called out. She staggered to her left, moving out of the line. One of the guards saw her. She moved to her immediately. She was small, about 5'4" tall, but she was compact and looked muscled. She seemed to be in her late twenties. Without saying a word, when the guard reached her, she took her club and jammed it fiercely into Leslie's ribs.

"Oooooomph!" Leslie spat out. She doubled over. The guard pushed he club under her chin and forced her head up. The she jammed it against her chest, forcing her back in line, shouting out some invective.

Leslie tightened her lips, trying not to cry. The tall woman was still behind her. This time, when she placed her hand on her ass, Leslie did nothing.

She suppressed a whine as she felt the hot hand move up and down her rear cheek. The woman was using her right hand, closest to the wall, so that it couldn't be seen by the guard. She could feel the hem of her skirt going higher and higher. When the hem was high enough, the hand reached under it and made contact with her naked flesh.

The hand was rough, but the touch was gentle. A sourness erupted in Leslie's stomach. She held her hands together in front of her tightly. At the same time, the heat and gentle friction from the hand was making her loins tingle. It moved up and down her thigh, it brushed over her rear cheek and then went back again. Slowly, the touch became firmer, more confident. Leslie couldn't believe that she was being sexually assaulted in the middle of a vast crowd of people and that there was nothing she could do about it. She tried to deny the heat that was rising within her.

She looked ahead. They were coming closer and closer to the chow line. Once she was there, she knew that the woman would have to stop.

It took about another five minutes for her to reach the line of steam tables where the food was handed out. The big woman's hand continued its assault on her tender flesh all that time. A thick finger traced its way up from the base of her perineum, along the crack of her ass until it reached the dainty portal itself. It flitted at it, teasing it, and then ran its way all the way back down again. Leslie kept her thighs mashed together as much as she could. She took tiny steps each time the line moved. The last thing she wanted was the woman's filthy finger on her sex.

Although she felt revulsion at the woman's touch, there was something about the situation that was raising her lust. There was something about the utter feeling of helplessness she felt while the woman took her liberties with her. The hand was hot and, while rough, the woman had a deft touch, letting the tips of her fingers drift across her flesh, up and down her thigh, all over her rear cheeks. There was something exciting about having her passion raised against her will. Her nipples had stiffened and her breath had grown short. It was as if the hand was, since she had no power to resist it, giving her the chance to enjoy her baser, darker instincts without guilt. It was somehow, deeply compelling. Leslie shuddered with revulsion.

When they reached the head of the line, Leslie grabbed a dirty and scratched, dark brown plastic tray divided into three compartments and a large steel spoon. It was the only eating utensil there. A guard was standing there watching carefully so that no inmate would take more than one. A spoon might not seem like much of a weapon, but if you spent a hundred or more hours rubbing its edge against a wall or the steel frame of your bed, it would become razor sharp.

The inmates behind the steam table seemed healthier and more robust than their mates. Kitchen duty is one of the most coveted jobs in a prison. You get first dibs on everything and eat as much as you want. There were four servers dressed in the standard drab, light brown dresses. They stood over large tubs of yellow, green and brown mush. The fourth was handing out what looked like a tiny little cube of thick bread. A fifth inmate stood at the end handing out tin cups filled with a greenish, yellow liquid. A green garbed guard patrolled behind them.

When Leslie passed down the line, one of the servers looked up at her. She smiled and gave a nudge to the woman on her right. That woman looked up and nudged the woman on her right. They were all tough looking women with dark, dirty hair and dark, sullen eyes. Leslie became self conscious of the tight pull of her dress over her breasts. She looked down at her tray. The servers plopped large spoonfuls of the mush onto it. One of them tossed it down forcefully so that it sprayed up on Leslie's dress. Leslie gave a short hop back in surprise and then looked up at the woman. She gave Leslie a wink and made a kissy face. Leslie looked quickly back down and moved on.

When they left the chow line, the inmates filed towards the tables, filling them up as they went under the direction of one of the guards. Leslie had no choice but to follow her cellmate, who was still ahead of her, down one of the aisles and then sit next to her at a table. The tables were so close together that there was no room to move between them once she sat down. To her dismay, the big woman who was behind her sat down at her right.

There was so little room on the bench that the women sat with their hips pressed together. A wave of revulsion passed through Leslie as she felt the heat of the big woman's body. As Leslie was beginning to tentatively dip her spoon into the unidentifiable slop, she felt the woman's thigh press up against hers. She decided to try and ignore it. She put a small sample of the yellow glop in her mouth. It tasted salty and pasty. She had no idea what it was. She looked around and all the other women were scooping it up hastily. A dismal chill went through her as she realized that if she spent more than a few days here, she would undoubtedly sooner or later become just as enthusiastic at the chance to consume it.

She was just getting a small spoonful of the brown mush to her lips, it looked like there might be some kind of beans in it, when she felt a hand on her right thigh. She froze as it drifted down its length all the way down to her knee and back again. On its way back, it dragged the hem of her garment with it, exposing her skin.

Leslie didn't know what to do. She withdrew the spoon from her mouth and pushed her elbow and hip into the big woman next to her to try and communicate her rejection of the advance. The hand left her thigh for a moment and then came down harshly, formed into a large fist. It struck her right on the muscle of her upper thigh. The pain went up her thigh and into her belly. She groaned and leaned forward. Leslie gave the woman a plaintive, begging look, but she just smiled. Leslie looked around for a guard to help, but there was no way a guard could see what was going on.

When the hand returned, Leslie knew that there was nothing she could do about it. She scrunched her shoulders together in dismay and tried to concentrate on her food.

The hand kept gliding back and forth over her smooth skin. Leslie cast a furtive glance at her assailant. While her left hand was stroking Leslie's thigh, her right hand was dutifully and regularly spooning loads of the glop into her mouth.

Leslie tried a few more small spoonfuls of the food. It was getting harder and harder to ignore the hot hand on her thigh. When the fingers tried to insinuate themselves between her legs, Leslie pushed them tightly together. Stroking her thigh was one thing, but there was no way, she was going to let the woman touch her down there.

She was mistaken. The hand rose again and once more came down forcefully on her thigh. Leslie groaned with the pain. Then the woman grabbed a thin slice of the flesh on her thigh between her thumb and forefinger and gave it a harsh twist. Leslie dropped her spoon and her hand went down to her thigh to try and free her stinging flesh, but the woman kept twisting harder and harder. Tears were coming to Leslie's eyes. The women across from her were looking up from their meals and smirking at her. Finally, in desperation, Leslie let her thighs open. The fingers released her flesh and slid between them.

Not satisfied with Leslie's surrender, the hand pulled her right thigh harshly until it was more widely separated from the other. Then, slowly, it flitted over the inside of her thigh, up over her belly and down to her furry treasure.

A thick finger began to delicately worm its way into the gap between her outer labia. All of the contact to her naked thigh had unwillingly caused Leslie's puss to moisten. The finger was able to glide easily into her already heated crevasse.

Slowly and steadily, the finger started to excite her. She had given up on trying to eat. She sat there, hunched over, humiliated and shamed at her powerlessness. The other women were snickering and smirking. One of them, seeing that she wasn't eating it, snatched her tiny piece of coarse bread from her tray. Another one grabbed her tin of juice and replaced it with her empty one. Her cell mate, to her left, picked up her tray, sliding her empty one in its place, and started to wolf down her food.

Tears were flowing down Leslie's face. Her puss was becoming mushier and mushier and the woman was able to slide two of her thick fingers into it. They slid in and out, abrading her stiffened clit with each motion. All of her being wanted to clasp her thighs back together, to interrupt the assault on her sex, to drive back the rapidly rising need. She closed her eyes tightly, trying to shut out the image of the other women watching her, trying to take herself anywhere but here. But the relentless fingers kept sawing and sawing, running seemingly deeper and deeper within her. When the fingers withdrew and began to concentrate on her pleasure nubbin, Leslie gasped. They were moving rapidly now, bedeviling her throbbing, slick clit. Leslie clenched her hands into fists. She felt her toes curl. Her breathing became deep and labored. And then it hit.

The first waves of her climax tore through her like a railroad train. Her thighs shuddered. She kept her lips tightly pressed together in an attempt to suppress her moans of pleasure. She had abandoned resistance to her assault. She rocked her hips back and forth. Her heart beat wildly in her chest. Her blood was pumping hot.

As her pussy's tremors eased, the fingers lazily slipped back and forth between her engorged love lips, delivering delicious aftershocks. Finally, they abandoned her, wiping themselves on her still trilling thigh. The hand gave her a loving pat and then withdrew.

It took Leslie a few moments to return to full consciousness of what was around her. When she opened her eyes, she saw that the other women at the table were eying her lasciviously. She turned to look at her assailant to her right. The woman was beaming with satisfaction, smelling Leslie's odor on her hand.

CHAPTER THREE

A whistle blew. The tables started to empty. When it got to their table, Leslie picked up her tray and stood. She was still ravenously hungry, but at least her ordeal was over. They marched out towards the door in reverse order than when they came in. They passed a station where the inmates dropped off their trays and their spoons. Suddenly, Leslie realized that her spoon was missing. She couldn't imagine where it had gone. When she got to the station, she put her tray down, tossing her tin cup into a plastic bin. When the guard saw that she had no spoon to return, she immediately came alive.

She poked Leslie in the chest with her baton harshly and began to scream at her. Leslie didn't know what to do. It was hard for her to believe that the guard was making so much fuss over a spoon. The guard reached in, took a hold of the front of Leslie's dress, and dragged her out of the line. Another guard came over. The one who had assaulted her gave the other an animated explanation. The second guard became livid and grabbed Leslie's hair at the back of her head. Leslie whined and screamed as she was pulled across the cafeteria.

When they reached the middle, the guard released her and started yelling an order at her. Leslie, near hysteria, didn't know what the guard wanted her to do. The guard jabbed her fiercely in the gut with her baton, knocking the air out of her. She fell to the floor. The guard struck her on the shoulder and hip savagely. Leslie moaned and cried. Fingers pried into her hair again and she was yanked to her feet. The guard started screaming again and pulling at Leslie's clothes. Still desperately trying to catch her breath, she began a panicked unbuttoning of the front of her dress. When she got it down to her waist, she pulled it over her head and dropped it to the floor.

Tears were flowing down her face. Her hip and shoulder were throbbing. The guard spat an order at her, raising her hands and Leslie raised hers in imitation. The guard moved her arms out wide at shoulder level and Leslie desperately followed suit. The guard banged her baton between Leslie's thighs and she dutifully spread them wide.

The guard walked around her. She felt up the crack between her rear cheeks. She pressed her finger into the dainty hole and rummaged around. The she came around the front to examine her pussy. Leslie quailed at what she knew she would find. When the guard's fingers detected her still slippery cunt, she screeched and slapped Leslie across the face.

The blow stung harshly and knocked Leslie off balance. She brought her arms in instinctively. The guard jammed her baton into her ribs and yelled out another order. Leslie quickly resumed her position, arms out, thighs spread and broke out into sobs.

The cafeteria was still emptying out of sullen, brown clad inmates. A couple of them sneered and snickered as they passed by. Another guard came over. She had a brief talk with the other guard and then laughed. She stepped up to Leslie and rubbed her hand over her vulva, her finger intruding inside and she laughed again. She then poked two fingers into Leslie's crevasse, felt around for the missing spoon and then withdrew.

They left her standing there. Before she left, the second guard laid her baton under Leslie's chin and then raised it. Leslie was forced to raise her chin and then, when the baton kept going, raise herself to her toes. The guard said something that Leslie interpreted as, "Stay as you are," and then walked away.

Leslie stood like that for the longest time. The women who had been working in the kitchen came out to clean up. One became busy wiping down tables while two of them began to clean the trays, brushing dirty, pungent rags over them. Another started to sweep while the fifth brought out a bucket and mop and started cleaning the floor.

The pain in Leslie's toes quickly became intolerable. Her arms became heavier and heavier and it became more and more difficult to hold them up. The inmates on kitchen detail kept looking at her and smirking. One of them, the one who had made a kissy face at her, as she was washing the floor around where Leslie was standing stark naked, gave her ass a little pinch as she passed by. Leslie whined with dismay. It was clear to her that she was considered as fair game for all the other inmates. She was young and attractive and, relatively innocent. Her skin was a pearly white and she had an alluring, hour glass figure. In her distress she wondered how long she could survive. When she thought of going back to her cruel cellmate, she felt queasy and desperate.

When the inmates were done cleaning the cafeteria, they retreated back into the kitchen. Leslie was left alone with three of the guards. She had lowered her feet due to the intense pain on her toes and one of the guards put her baton under her chin and raised it until she was restored to her former position. Leslie whined. Her lips were trembling. She was alone with three guards. There were no witnesses. They could do anything they wanted to her. She was naked and vulnerable and alone without a friend. The pain from her distended toes and her outstretched arms was disabling. She could see that the guards were contemplating something. A great empty space opened in her belly.

Just then, another guard walked in. Leslie noted right away that she had some stripes on her sleeve. She carried herself with an air of authority. The other guards came to order, stiffening at her presence.

The new guard asked a question. One of the guards gave an explanation. The new one nodded. She stepped closer to Leslie.

"So, what did you do with the spoon?" she asked in English, her voice brisk and clipped. It carried only a slight accent. She looked a little older than the other guards. She was about 5'10" tall. While she seemed strong, her body was trim and somewhat graceful. Her hair was short, cut primly just below her ears, and had a slight wave to it. Her face was not unattractive. Her eyes communicated a sharp intelligence and a certain coldness.

"N,nothing," Leslie said miserably, trying not to cry.

"Say, 'Nothing, sayyidati.' It is more polite."

"N,nothing, sayyidati," Leslie replied.

"Who did you give it to?"

"Nobody, sayyadati," Leslie eked out. "Somebody took it while I wasn't looking."

"You are awfully careless with the State's property, aren't you?" the woman asked. There was a hint of amusement in her voice.

"Y,yes, sayyadati," Leslie croaked. "I'm sorry! I didn't know!"

"My guards here think you should be taught a lesson. Do you need to be taught a lesson?"

Leslie started to cry. "N,no, sayyadati," she pleaded. "It won't happen again! I promise! I didn't know," she repeated.

"Since this is your first day, I'm going to let you off the hook, as you say. The next time I won't be so forgiving. Do you understand?"

"Y,yes, sayyadati! Thank you! I promise it won't happen again!" Leslie said emphatically, her voice whiney and shrill.

"My name is Sergeant Malikah. It means 'queen'. Captain Khalil is the commander of this prison, but I am its ruler. Do you understand?"

"Y,yes, sayyadati," Leslie replied. Her toes hurt so bad she didn't know if she could keep up on them for much longer. Her arms felt like lead and her shoulders ached terribly. She was afraid that if she lost position, the sergeant might not be so forgiving. Tears were streaming down her face.

The sergeant ran her eyes up and down Leslie's delectable body, appraising it. She had a baton in her hand and she brought it up between Leslie's legs, brushing it along her exposed love lips. She had a pensive look on her face, like she was under a spell. Her eyes were following the slowly sawing baton. And then she broke it off.

"You can get dressed now," she spat out. "Corporal Hanin will take you back to your cell. I'll see you tomorrow."

With that, the sergeant barked a command to the other guards and then turned and left.

Leslie looked carefully at the other guards before she lowered herself from her toes. She went down slowly, ready to jump back up at the slightest indication that she was committing a sin. One of them, a disappointed look on her face, bent over and picked up her dress from the floor and threw it at her. Leslie caught it and hurriedly, gratefully, put it back on. The guard nodded her head toward the doorway. Leslie crossed her arms behind her back and followed.

When they got back to her cell, her cellmate was lying on her bunk. She was reading a copy of the Koran. She gave Leslie an amused look as she entered. Leslie went straight to her own bunk and lay down.

She realized what a close run thing it had been. If Sergeant Malikah hadn't come in, she was sure the other guards would have given her a beating. She had been overjoyed to hear the sound of English. There was finally someone she could talk to, that she could understand. She didn't feel much like talking to her cellmate, whatever her name was. She had stolen her towel, her toothbrush and her dinner.

She was desperately hungry. She knew she wouldn't have the chance to eat anything until breakfast, whenever that was. Her stomach growled and she put her hand on it, rubbing it as if somehow that would make the hunger pangs go away. Her body ached where she had been struck.

Sergeant Malikah, the Queen, had said she would see her tomorrow. Was that a good or a bad thing? The woman seemed civil and civilized. But there was something about her that made Leslie fear her. She had noticed the way that she had looked at her pussy and rubbed it with her baton. Why did she want to see her? Would she make her submit to more foul acts? It seemed like everyone here was sex crazed. She closed her eyes and issued a desperate prayer. "Oh, please, God, let Mr. Moussa come here tomorrow! Please get me out of here! Please!" She turned her face to the wall.

About an hour later, a whistle sounded. One of the guards came walking by, letting her baton clatter over the bars to their cell. Leslie's cell mate put her book away in the box under her bed. Leslie called out to the guard.

"Please! Please! Can I talk to you," she asked plaintively. The guard stopped. She stared at Leslie. She repeated her question in French. The guard gave her no response. "I need to know, will I get to see a lawyer? Can I make a phone call?"

The guard slammed her baton on the bars to the cell and shouted something at Leslie that she took to mean, "Be quiet!"

Something snapped in her. All of her mean treatment, all of the insults to her body and her psyche rushed into her brain. "Please!" she begged. "I need to get out of here! I'm sorry! I didn't mean to do anything wrong! Won't somebody listen to me? Please!"

The guard's face turned red. She slammed her baton on the bar again, ordering Leslie angrily to quiet herself. But the dam had been broken. Leslie couldn't have stopped if her life depended on it.

"Please take me out of here! I can't stand it! I'm sorry! I'm sorry!" She had broken out into miserable sobs. She knew that her pleading was useless, but she had to do something or she would go insane.

The guard just stood there glaring at Leslie. She said something that sounded ominous and then she walked away.

"Oh, you have big trouble now," Leslie's cellmate said.

Leslie looked at her. What did she mean? What were they going to do to her?

Her answer came a moment later. The original guard came back with two of her sisters. She was holding some kind of leather thing in her hand. She smiled at Leslie, tapping her baton on her thigh as one of the other guards unlocked the cell. The cell door swung open. They were on her in a second.

Two of the guards jumped on her, grabbing her arms and pinning her to the bed. The third guard took hold of her cheeks and started squeezing them.

"What are you doing! Let me go! Let me go! You're hurting me!" Leslie shouted. She saw that the leather object had a long, thick prong on it. The guard was trying to jam it into her mouth. "Mmmmmmmmmm! Mmmmmmmmmmm!" Leslie moaned, her lips sealed tight. She was shaking her head wildly, trying to prevent the prong from going between her lips.

The other two guards placed their knees on her arms and took hold of her head. One held it still while the other pushed on her jaw. Leslie felt her teeth coming apart.

"Mmmmmmmmmmm! Mmmmmmmmmmmm!" she moaned again. She was twisting and contorting her body to try and get loose. But the women were too strong and determined. They had obviously done this before. The end of the prong started to probe between her teeth. The guard who was holding it was pressing down harder and harder. Her jaw started to creep down. "Naaaaaaaaaaaaaa!" Leslie called out. And then the thing went in.

The prong was attached to a thick, leather shield. It banged up against her lips. The prong filled her mouth and went almost all the way to her throat. "Mmmmmmmmmmmmm! Mmmmmmmmmmmmmmmm!" Leslie screamed. A triangle type strap went over her nose and then was pulled back over her head. The shield encompassed her whole jaw. The guards took straps leading from it and, pressing Leslie's head forward, buckled them behind it. They pulled it very tight, jamming her jaw closed, pressing her teeth into the rude intruder. Two of the guards grabbed her arms and brought her wrists together. The original guard had a long, leather thong and she tied Leslie's wrists off quickly. Then they brought her arms back and tied them off to the head of the bed.

Their work done, the three guards got up and stood there, appreciating their work. "I'm sorry! I'm sorry! I'm sorry!" Leslie tried to scream. "Please don't do this! Don't leave me like this!" But her voice emerged only as grossly distorted sounds. "Pllllllleeeeeeeeeeeease!" she shouted again desperately.

The guards laughed. One of them leaned over. "You learn be quiet," she said merrily. She reached out and tweaked Leslie's breast hard.

"Owwwwwwww!" Leslie screamed. But the sound that emerged was low and soft. The guards laughed again. They left, slamming the cell door shut behind them.

Leslie desperately pulled and yanked at her bound hands. They were tied together tightly by experts and would not loosen. She shook her head violently. She bit down hard on the leather mass inside her mouth. She screamed again. It was no use. There was nothing she could do. She broke down and cried.

After a while, her sobs subsided. She heard the striking of a match and then smelled the unmistakable smell of tobacco. She looked over. Her cellmate was smoking a hand rolled cigarette. She was smiling mockingly at her. "I bet you learn good now," she said.

A moment later, the lights in the corridor dimmed. The cell became darkened. Every third one of the fluorescent lights was still on, casting an eerie light into their cell. She could see it gleaming in her cell mate's dead eyes. She turned her face to the wall.

She lay there for a long time commiserating with herself. It had been the hardest day of her life. It was the worst thing that had ever happened to her. She thought of her home in Philadelphia, her mother and father, her sister. She wanted desperately to go home. She would never travel anywhere again. She just wanted a quiet life where no one would bother her. She would never do anything bold or daring again. She had learned her lesson.

Finally, she fell asleep. She had dark, disturbing dreams. Her body twisted and turned. In one of the dreams, something had gotten hold of her leg and was pulling it. She tried to pull back, but whatever it was was too strong. She tried to move her leg, but it was held fast. When she felt something on her other leg, she awoke. Her cell mate was on her bed! She was naked! She had hold of her left leg and was tying it with something to the rail under her mattress. She had pushed her leg back so that it was almost up by her hip.

Leslie began to struggle. She tried to kick the woman away. She yelled into her gag. But she was too late. The woman had some kind of cloth. She had tied it around Leslie's ankle and was pulling the knot closed tightly which bound her to the bed frame. Leslie's legs were spread wide. Her short skirt had ridden up to her lap. She tried desperately to yank her legs free, but they had been tied too tightly. The woman was kneeling between her legs. Leslie couldn't see her face in the darkness, but she got the distinct impression that the woman was leering at her. A hollow formed in her belly. "Please!" she whined. The sound of her supplication barely emerged from her mouth.

"Now we have some fun," the woman whispered. She began to unbutton Leslie's dress. Leslie tried to shake and squirm, but she was powerless to prevent it. When the buttons were undone, the woman spread the bodice open wide, letting her large, plump breasts fall out.

"Mmmmmmmmm!" the woman moaned appreciatively. "Nice titties!" she whispered. She placed her hands on them, caressing them weighing them. "Niiiiiiiice!" she repeated. She leaned over and subsumed the nipple on Leslie's left breast into her mouth. She suckled on it slowly and gently. Her left hand was on Leslie's other breast, squeezing and caressing it. The hot mouth brought a tingle to Leslie's loins. "Noooooooo!" she screamed, making only a low gurgling sound. She bucked her hips and arched her back trying the throw the woman off. She abandoned Leslie's breast and took hold of her nose, squeezing it shut. Leslie immediately became desperate for air. "Mmmmmm-mmmmmm! Mmmmmmmmmmmm!" she moaned.

The woman whispered in her ear. "You better be still, prostitute, or I suffocate you. You wake up tomorrow dead. Eh? You want?"

"Mmmmmmmmmmmm!" Leslie moaned, shaking her head desperately.

"Then you lie quiet, little whore. You lie back. Enjoy it."

The woman released Leslie's nostrils. She stroked her head a couple of times, staring into her eyes. "So pretty," she said, her voice low and tremulous.

The impassioned woman bent down and took hold of the hem of Leslie's dress. She pulled it up her belly until it was under her breasts. It wouldn't go any further until the back of the dress was pulled up too. When she went to pull the back of the dress up, Leslie kept sitting on it firmly in an attempt to frustrate her. The woman merely took hold of Leslie's nipples, twisting them hard, making Leslie whine with pain. This time, when the woman went to pull up the back of her skirt, Leslie sadly relented, lifting her buttocks so that it would come free.

The woman pushed her dress up all the way to her neck. Leslie was completely nude from the neck down. She felt frightened. Her breasts were bare and vulnerable as was her belly and her sex. The woman stroked Leslie's leather covered face several times and whispered, "We start all over now, eh?"

She leaned over and began to kiss Leslie around her face, her neck. Leslie could feel her breasts pressing up against her own, her bare hips against her naked thighs. She moaned and squirmed as the heat of the woman's body started a glow in her own. She whined and her bound hands strained to free themselves. She could feel the woman's hot tongue as it scoured her flesh. It ran under her chin and then down her neck. It floated over her chest and between the gap of her breasts. Then the mouth seized a nipple, the tongue washing it. Her other breast was captured by her rough hand. It gently massaged it, cupping it, squeezing it.

Leslie's loins had started a slow burn. When the mouth shifted teats, she emitted an involuntary moan.

"Mmmmmmmmmmmmm," the woman hummed. "Such pretty titties. You like, eh? You like? I like. So tasty," she said under her breath.

She resumed her oral massage of Leslie's teat, her right hand taking hold of her other breast. Leslie could feel the hot tongue running over her stiff point. When the woman sucked on it, harder and harder, she could feel a pull in her loins, as if there were a direct connection between the two.

When the tongue abandoned her breast and began a slow, leisurely descent over her belly, Leslie knew what the woman was going to do. The thought of a woman supping at her crevasse repelled her. The feel of the soft feminine body between her thighs was repulsive to her. And yet her lusts were rising, her breathing was getting deeper, her heart was beating faster. She pushed up with her hips, strained to pull her thighs together, issued a moan of protest, tried to arch her back in an attempt to throw her assailant off. None of these things affected in the slightest way the relentless progress of the tongue and lips to her loins.

The woman ran her hands over the tender insides of Leslie's thighs, sending a message of unwanted pleasure to her brain. They ran over her belly, slid over her taut, hot breasts, gave her nipples sharp little pinches. Then they slid down again,, crossed over her belly, went up and down her thighs once more and then settled in the crux of her legs, to each side of her throbbing outer labia and the tongue and the lips of her insistent, unwanted lover took hold of their prize.

Leslie hissed as the tongue flitted over her stiff nubbin. It circled it, pressed down on it, washed it and then ran the length of her widening divide. The hot hands pressed on and massaged her love lips while the tongue entered her depths. She could feel its tip deep inside.

"Mmmmmmmmmmm! Mmmmmmmmmmmmm!" the woman moaned. She raised her head. "What lovely pussy," she whispered. "So soft and hot. We going to have such fun together my little whore. I own you now. You belong to me. I'm going to make you scream with pleasure! You see! You see!"

When the mouth descended down to her burning quim once more, the tongue began to play a lust driving symphony. When the woman took hold of her trilling clit with her teeth, biting down on it just hard enough to send Leslie a tiny message of pain, she moaned. When the lips began a gentle suckle that became gradually harder and harder, Leslie could not help but grind her hips against it.

But it was when the woman slipped her thumb inside her exposed, helpless, tender rear ring and began a slow, luxurious abrasion of the delicate tissues there, that Leslie became overwhelmed with passion.

The combination of the active, expert tongue and lips, and the gentle but remorseless sawing of her digit inside her anal passage drove Leslie into delirium. Her need for completion kept growing and growing. A hand seized a breast, squeezing it harshly, the tongue flitted incessantly over her clit. The thumb began a swift, rhythmic traverse over her dainty ring. Leslie tried desperately to hold back. She tightened her muscles, closed her eyes, strained at her bonds, but nothing would stop the inexorable march of her lusts towards explosion.

When it came, it was as if a jolt of electricity had gone through her. Her body convulsed as her leaky, buzzing channel clamped down on itself again and again. She moaned deeply, her thighs quivered, her toes curled. Her pussy's deep, soul wrenching throbs went on and on so fiercely that she felt like her whole body was going to be sucked down into her fevered passage.

The woman was not satisfied with one climax. She went on, ignoring Leslie's muffled pleas for cessation. Within a minute, her organ surged again. Leslie's eyes rolled back, her thighs jerked, her back arched, her pussy burned.

As her second climax began to abate, the woman slowed her ministrations. She gently rubbed her hands up and down Leslie's defenseless thighs, cooing and moaning.

"Mmmmmmmmmmmmm!" she moaned. "You like, eh?" she whispered. "Yessssss, you like! Jamilah know how to suck pussy, eh? You learn too. I show you. You mine now. Jamilah show you good time every night. You show Jamilah too. You see."

It was the first time Leslie had heard her cellmate's name. She cringed at the prospect of a nightly assault and being made to serve the pussy of the older, callous woman. It was like she had been dropped into a surreal version of hell where her bodily pleasures were her assigned torment. She whined in dismay.

Jamilah had risen to her knees. Her hand was gently stroking Leslie's still throbbing mons. "Mmmmmmmmmm, such a pretty pussy," she whispered, her voice low and quivering. "But now it Jamilah turn, eh?" she said.

She leaned forward between Leslie's forcibly distended thighs. She matched their bellies together. And then she gave Leslie's quim a long, impassioned stroke of her own. "Mmm-mmmmmmmm," she moaned. "That nice."

Lowering her torso onto hers, Jamilah began a series of languorous strokes of Leslie's sex. She moaned and quivered. She placed her lips on Leslie's neck, sucking at it, kissing it. Her breasts pushed against Leslie's. Every few strokes, she would press her pussy down hard against Leslie's, grinding their clits together. Leslie could feel her heat building again. Her mind clouded over. Her thighs pressed against Jamilah's hips. Her pelvis began a rhythmic motion, encouraging the scouring of her puss. She bit down hard against the infernal presence in her mouth and moaned.

It did not take Jamilah long to come. Her body quaked and her motions accelerated. She grunted and moaned. Her excitement was contagious and Leslie's well worn purse renewed its throbs and convulsions. The two women groaned and moaned as their passions overwhelmed them.

The callous woman was not satisfied with one orgasm. She continued her motions, grinding her pussy harder and harder against Leslie's. The pleasure was so intense that Leslie began to cry.

"Oh, yes! Oh, yes!" her cellmate called out. "Oh, yes, my pretty little whore! Make Jamilah come! Make Jamilah come! Ahhhhhh! Ahhhhhhhhh! Ahhhhhhhhhhhhh!"

Slowly, Jamilah's hips wound down their assault. Her body went limp and she collapsed upon Leslie's. Her chest was rising and falling intently as she began to recover from her paroxysms of pleasure.

Finally, she withdrew. She patted Leslie on her belly and sat up. "You good whore," she said happily. She got up from the bed and rummaged around in her box under her bed. Leslie watched in the slight light as she rolled herself another cigarette. She dipped her head under her blanket and lit it, causing a brief explosion of light underneath. Then she came out and returned to Leslie's bed.

While she smoked, she gave Leslie's mushy crevasse gentle, loving strokes. "I been here five year," she said. "Four more to go. You the best I had. Pretty, little whore. We have many night together. You love Jamilah. You see."

Leslie moaned at the prospect. She prayed that what the woman said was not going to come to pass. She didn't know how she could live like this. She would go insane. It wasn't right! It wasn't fair! She began to cry again.

The other woman noticed her sobs. "No cry, little whore," she said, wiping at her eyes. "It be okay. You see. Jamilah take good care of you. You Jamilah pretty little whore now."

Leslie moaned at the prospect.

Jamilah finished her cigarette. She had smoked it down to a tiny, little nub. She crushed it against the bedpost and then tossed it into the toilet. Her hand had continued its caresses to Leslie's puss and her thumb had entered her canal. She began to rub it over Leslie's sensitized clit. Leslie's pussy had begun to get warm again; she sighed.

"We go one more time, okay?" Jamilah said. Then she lowered her head and put her lips to Leslie's quim.

CHAPTER FOUR

Jamilah eventually let Leslie go back to sleep after two more explosive climaxes. She untied her ankles and retreated to her bed, but not without giving each of Leslie's teats a warm suckle. Leslie was so exhausted by their encounter that she passed into somulance almost at once.

She awoke to the sound of one of the guard's whistles. Another one came down the line of cells and dragged her baton along the bars making a noisome clatter. Leslie suffered some confusion at first, trying to figure out where she was and why she couldn't move her hands. When she figured it out, a pall passed over her.

Jamilah jumped out of her bed and took a long pee. Then she washed her face at the sink and dried it off using Leslie's fresh towel. She brushed her teeth with the new toothbrush. She pulled on her dirty, light brown dress and then sat on the bed smiling at Leslie. There was a spark in her that was not there yesterday as if claiming Leslie as her property had presented wonderful, new horizons for her.

Another whistle blew and Jamilah got up and stood by the door. Leslie struggled at her bonds. She was desperate that she would not be given a chance to eat breakfast. Her stomach ached with hunger. Jamilah just smiled at her.

The guard came by and unlocked the cell. Jamilah dutifully stepped outside, turned right and waited. The guard came inside and gave Leslie a studied look. Her skirt was still up around her neck. Her breasts were dangling out. The guard gave Jamilah a sidewise look and then smiled, having put two and two together. She leaned over and unfastened Leslie's gag from behind her head and then undid her wrists. When Leslie got up to get in line behind Jamilah, she gave Leslie a little pinch on her ass.

All the way to the cafeteria, Leslie agonized as to whether the big woman who had assaulted her yesterday would make another appearance. Just before they entered it, Jamilah surreptitiously stepped out of the line for a second and let Leslie pass. Then she got in line behind her.

A few seconds later, the big woman appeared and made to cut into the line behind Leslie. Jamilah made a hissing sound and uttered something that sounded like a curse as she shoved the woman away. The woman cursed back and got in line behind Jamilah.

A wave of relief passed through Leslie. She would be able to eat her meal in peace. There was some benefit, she saw, from her assault last night. Jamilah must be one tough cookie, she thought, if she was able to oppose the big woman so fearlessly. Maybe having her as a cellmate had some advantages. Wasn't it better to be subject to one woman's abuse without having to worry about the others?

When they went through the chow line she picked up a large, brown, wooden bowl and carried it in. She took a spoon and held in firmly in her hand. One of the women behind the counter spotted her right away and nudged the woman on her right. She, in turn, nudged he woman to her right. It was the woman who had made a kissy face at her yesterday. She made another kissy face today and gave Leslie an extra large portion of mush. It was brownish and looked like some kind of oatmeal. The woman at the end of the line handed her what looked like a mug of black coffee. She too gave Leslie a pleasant smile.

The line continued further and filed in between the tables. Leslie took a seat on the same bench she was on yesterday. The same women were sitting on the opposite side and a couple of them smirked when they saw her. There was a slight commotion to Leslie's right. Jamilah and the big woman were jostling for position. The big woman put her bowl of mush down on the table and reached into the pocket of her uniform. She brought out two tightly rolled cigarettes. Jamilah set her bowl down, took the cigarettes and let the big woman pass. She smiled as she sat down next to Leslie.

It was just like the day before. Her big, hot hand started in on Leslie's thigh right away. Leslie closed her legs, but the woman gave her skin a pinch and she reluctantly opened them again. She realized that Jamilah had sold her use to the big woman for two cigarettes. She knew now what Jamilah had meant when she said that she owned her. She was her whore to be rented out at her pleasure and for her profit. A wave of misery passed through her even as the big woman's fingers began a tantalizing drumming on her puss.

This time, Leslie made sure she ate. It was hard to concentrate on the meal as the big woman's fingers expertly raised her lusts. She had to stop when the tell tale surge in her loins told her that her climax was imminent. She grabbed her bowl with her free hand so no one would take it away. She bowed her head as the waves of pleasure went through her. When they passed, she tearfully resumed her meal.

Leslie hadn't peed yet that morning. She had been too anxious not to miss her meal so she had skipped it. Her need came on her intently as the line of women worked its way back to the cells. As soon as the cell opened, she dashed for the toilet. She uttered a sigh of relief as the water passed from her making a loud splash in the bowl. When she was done, she went to take a piece of toilet paper from the slender roll, but Jamilah snatched it away. "Paper for shit," she said caustically.

Grimacing, Leslie got up and went to her bed.

They lay on their beds for about a half hour before the whistle blew again. Leslie glared at Jamilah the whole time, cursing her in her heart. The older woman just smiled and took out her Koran.

When the whistle blew, Jamilah stood and waited by the cell door. Leslie got up behind her. The guard came and opened it. When Leslie started to step out, the guard barred her way. "No work," she said curtly and slammed the door shut.

Leslie went back to her bed. Forlornly, she watched the line of women pass by. She didn't want to spend the whole day alone and locked in her cell. Even Jamilah, as evil as she was, was better than no company at all. When the last inmate passed out of sight, Leslie lay down, turned her head to the wall and crunched up into a little ball.

She was distraught beyond all belief. Who could ever have imagined her life plunging so low, to such a desperate state? Her comeliness, her beauteous aspect, which had once been her pride, was now her curse. Everyone she came into contact with seemed to lust after her. She no longer belonged to herself, but to those who had power over her. They had forced her to spread her legs, to surrender her most private places. She thought of that sweet divide between her thighs. It had become the most important part of her.

And yet, her pussy began to tingle when she thought of her helplessness last night when Jamilah had assaulted her. She had never had such body wrenching orgasms before, ever. She would never have surrendered willingly to the coarse, callous older woman, or to any woman for that matter. But something inside her yearned for it to happen again.

Her hand drifted down between her thighs and she discovered that she was wet. She glided a finger along her crevasse, gathering her moisture and spread it over her love button, making it slimy and slick. She rubbed it tenderly, luxuriating in the delicious messages it was sending her.

Then, when she realized what she was doing, when she realized the despicable nature of her thoughts, she quickly drew her finger back.

"I'm not like that!" she asserted to herself tearfully. "I'm not perverted. I don't want it to happen again! It's just horrible!"

She spent the morning tossing and turning on her bed. She looked into the box underneath it and brought out her personal copy of the Koran. It was, naturally, in Arabic and she couldn't read a single word. After flipping through it a couple of times, she put it back in the box and lay down again.

After a few hours, an old inmate came by pushing a cart. She was accompanied by a guard. She stopped at Leslie's cell and passed a wooden bowl of mush under the bars. It came with a wooden spoon. Leslie scooped it up and ate it quickly. It was salty and pasty and had little kernels of something in it. When the old woman returned, Leslie passed the bowl and the spoon back out to her.

That was her excitement for the morning.

A little while later, she decided to make use of her relative privacy to move her bowels. Although she was full, she had a hard time getting her wastes to pass. When she was done, she took a small piece of toilet paper and wiped herself. She didn't know how long the tiny roll would have to last. She washed her hands with the coarse soap, dried them on her dingy towel and went back to her bunk.

Some time in the middle of the afternoon, one of the guards came by her cell. Leslie was floating in between sleep and consciousness. The guard banged on the bars twice with her baton and barked something out to get Leslie's attention. When Leslie stood up, she opened the cell door and motioned for her to come.

Leslie followed the guard with foreboding, her hands behind her back. Sergeant Malikah had said that she would see her today and she was sure that that was where she was going. They entered what appeared to be the administrative wing of the prison and walked down the hall. They passed the door where Leslie had gotten her supplies yesterday. Leslie thought for a moment about asking the guard to let her stop and get a better fitting dress, but she gave up the idea when she realized that she would just be inviting a blow from the guard's baton. Her body was already black and blue in several places and her wounds were sore. She didn't want to add to them today if she could help it.

They stopped at a door and the guard knocked. There was a sign on the door with Arabic lettering that looked official. A voice shouted out from behind it and the guard opened it. She stood back and invited Leslie to pass her. When Leslie entered he room, she closed the door.

Leslie was standing in front of a large, heavy wooden desk. It had a two level tray of papers on it. There was a tall, ornately decorated cup holding some pens and pencils, a stapler, a tape dispenser, a black telephone with numerous buttons. One of the batons that the guards carried was lying next to the phone. Besides the large, green desk pad, that was all there was. The walls of the room were bare except for what looked like a diploma or certificate on one wall covered with shiny glass with a black frame around it, and on the other side of the room, a picture of the country's ancient dictator sitting behind a desk and smiling. In one corner of the room was the national flag hanging limply on a pole. In the other was a coat tree. A bright blue ayala was hanging on it as well as what looked like a multi strapped whip. The tips of the strands were tinged red.

Behind the desk was Sergeant Malikah. She was dressed in the green uniform of the guards. She had a thin file opened and she was reading it. Leslie stood there anxiously, her hands behind her. After a few moments, the sergeant looked up.

"Good afternoon, Miss Harrington," the woman said. Her voice was pleasant but had a steel edge to it.

"Good afternoon, sayyadati," Leslie said uncertainly. It was the first words she had spoken all day.

"I've been reading your file. Assault on an officer, immodest dress, prostitution, bribery, failure to carry documents, blasphemy. These are all serious charges, Miss Harrington."

Leslie trembled as she heard the list of charges. Assault on an officer and blasphemy were new to her. And there was the bribery charge. She started to shake and tears came to her eyes.

"I,I didn't do anything, sayyadati," Leslie blurted out. "I was out for a walk. They assaulted me. And I was raped," she said. Her voice had a distinct element of panic to it.

The sergeant raised an eyebrow. "Should I add slander against the state to these charges?"

"N,no, sayyadati," Leslie whined. "Please don't. Please!"

"The report says that you were naked in your cell and enticed a guard to have anal intercourse with you. I'm surprised that you weren't charged with crimes against nature and adultery. The guard, I understand, was married."

Leslie started to cry. "It's not true, sayyadati," she moaned. "It's not true. And I didn't blaspheme!"

"Three people at the scene have sworn that you called out, 'A curse on your Allah!' when you were arrested. Are you saying that they are lying?"

"Y,yes, sayyadati," Leslie moaned. "It's not true!"

"Well, there will have to be a trial. You are fortunate that blasphemy is not a capital offense in Tunisia, not like some other backward countries. But it does carry very stiff sentence. Twenty years."

"Twenty years!" Leslie cried out. "Oh my god! It can't be true! I didn't do it! I didn't!" Her knees went weak and she became dizzy.

"And 100 lashes," the sergeant added.

"Ohhhhh, no!" Leslie screamed. She fell to her knees. It was a nightmare! A horrid, horrid nightmare! It couldn't be true! How would she ever stand it! It was like a death sentence! She would never go home!

"Get up!" Malikah shouted. She stood from her chair and slammed the baton down on it. "Get up on your feet or I'll give you a beating you'll never forget!"

Leslie jumped back to her feet. Her face was awash with tears. She put her hands behind her back. Her lips were trembling. Her chest was heaving. She felt like she was going to throw up. She stared at the angry guard, her eyes pleading.

The sergeant calmed herself. She sat back down in her chair.

"Of course," she continued, "that is the maximum sentence. A lot will depend on your behavior while you are our guest. I'm willing to help you. And, let me say, that can mean a lot."

"Ohhhhhhh, pleeeeeeease! Pllllleeeeeease, sayyadati ! Pllllll-lleeeeease help me! Pllllllllleeeeease!" Leslie begged.

Sergeant Malikah sat back in her chair. She still had the baton in her hand. She was patting her palm with it slowly. She was staring at Leslie intently. She licked her lips. Her eyes seemed to be devouring her hungrily.

She slowly rose from her chair and walked around the desk. She walked around behind the prisoner and then back again. Leslie was sniffling. The administrative wing was air conditioned, but she had started sweating heavily, even though her body had run cold. She felt the eyes of the 'Queen' running over her body. She jumped slightly, although she was not surprised, when she felt the woman's hand on her rear cheek. It caressed it and then took hold of the fabric of her skirt and slowly began to edge it up.

"You are a beautiful, young woman, Miss Harrington. Or should I call you Leslie?" Malikah said. Her voice was husky. When she had brought the fabric of Leslie's skirt up to her waist, exposing her rear mounds, her hand slid along Leslie's exposed flesh, ran under the curve of her cheeks and up the divide between them.

Leslie's stomach was churning. She didn't know what to do. It seemed unreal that she was facing all of those charges. She thought of Jamilah who had only spent 5 years as a prisoner here. Was that what she would be like in 5 years? Would she have to spend years and years as somebody's, maybe everybody's, fuck toy? If she gave in to the Queen, would she keep her word? Would she help her? Or once she had her in her power, would she make sure that she stayed here forever? How was she to know?

The Queen drew her hand back from Leslie's ass and stepped in front of her. "No," she said. "I think I'll call you Ghaniyah. It means 'the beautiful one.' For you are very beautiful. It's no wonder that you were able to inflame the lusts of a happily married man. I will give you lessons every day. Right here in my office. When you have learned to be holy, I will help you convert. It will help you before the judges to show your repentance. Do you want to repent, Ghaniyah? Will you suffer the lessons I will give you?"

Leslie knew that she had no choice. If the Queen could help her, she could hurt her too. She would do anything to shorten her stay in this hell. Even if she was lying, and would be no help to her at all, she could make her life very, very difficult. She knew that the whip hanging on the coat tree as not just there for show. She was at the mercy of the guards and the other prisoners. She needed all the help she could get.

"Y,yes, sayyadati," Leslie murmured. "I'll do whatever you say."

"Take off your dress," the cruel sergeant ordered.

Leslie shuddered at the order. It was not unexpected. Her stomach turned sour at the thought of the woman putting her hands on her, her lips and tongue on her, drawing out her deepest, darkest desires.

Her hands shaking, Leslie began to unbutton her bodice. She felt the evil presence of the woman standing behind her. The woman would perform despicable acts upon her, make her perform despicable acts. And she had no power to refuse her.

Something about that thought sent a thrill through her loins. It made her feel shamed at her own licentiousness.

When the buttons were undone, Leslie took hold of the hem of her short skirt and brought it up. As it passed over her head, she reveled in the temporary darkness. If only that darkness would last, she thought. "If only I could pass into nothingness, vanish like I never existed."

When she had drawn the dress over her head, she was about to drop it in the floor when she felt the hands of the Queen taking it from her. She walked past her and placed it on the clothes tree, next to her ayala and the whip. She turned back to look at her. Leslie could see the flame of lust in her eyes.

"Put your hands behind your head," she commanded. "And spread your legs."

Tearfully, Leslie complied. The act of raising her hands caused her breasts to lift and present themselves. She could feel her nipples stiffening. She closed her eyes to try and blot out what was happening to her.

"Open your eyes!" the woman ordered her curtly.

Leslie opened them. Even her right to darkness had been taken from her. She must be a witness to her own demise.

The sergeant placed her baton back down on the desk. She strolled leisurely over the where Leslie was standing. She stepped behind her, came close to her back, and reached around her front, seizing both of her pale, plump breasts. Her hands were hot and sweaty. She closed her hands around Leslie's treasures, squeezing them, forming them into cones. She took hold of her nipples, pinching them, tugging them until her breasts came free of her body, pulled out to their greatest extension. When she released them, they fell, like two heavy weights, vibrating from the motion. Her hands closed around her waist, went lower, lower, lower, until they reached the crux of her thighs. Her fingers flowed along the engorging lips that guarded her divide causing a ripple of lust to flow through the young, defenseless girl.

The woman's breasts were hot up against her back. Her face was leaning over her shoulder and Leslie could feel her hot breath in her ear, on her throat. She felt the woman's chest rising and falling deeply as if her own lusts were beginning to overwhelm her.

The, she broke off. Rubbing Leslie's naked buttocks as she passed, she returned to her desk. She picked up the phone and punched one of the buttons. There was a pause. Her eyes became alert.

She made a short, curt statement in Arabic and then placed the phone back in its cradle and sat back down in her chair.

The room was deathly silent as they waited. Her words ran back and forth through Leslie's head. Who was she talking to? Who was she waiting for? The Queen's steady, cold eyes, which continued to appraise her charms, gave her no clue.

There was another door to the Queen's office, across from and opposite from the one through which Leslie had entered. Her heart jumped when she heard a hand turn the knob. The door opened and someone entered.

It was the officer who had released her from her cell after her assault in the men's part of the prison. He was dressed in the same sharp, crisp uniform. He was youngish, maybe 40. His face was clean shaven and his aspect alert and bright. He was tall, almost 6 feet. His uniform had red epaulettes and there were gold bars on his collar.

Sergeant Malikah stood when he entered. She smiled. She turned to Leslie. "Ghaniyah," she said, "I take it you have already met Captain Khalil."

Leslie began to tremble. Her mouth ran dry and her body began to shake. When he had released her from her chains in the men's prison, he had castigated her, accused her of enticing his man into fucking her. It was he who had brought all of these terrible charges against her, she just knew it. Now she understood what was happening. He had brought them so that she would become his slave, so that she would be at his mercy for years and years and years. He had probably sent the man in to fuck her!

She started to sob. Tears were rolling down her face. The captain smiled as he perused her naked body. He said something to Malikah in Arabic. Leslie heard the name Ghaniyah repeated. Malikah answered him and he laughed.

"I see you have been given a new name, Ghaniyah," he said merrily. "It is most appropriate. We often get pretty girls here in our prison, but not, in recent memory, one as beautiful as you." He had one of the ever present batons in his hand and he laid it on the desk. He strolled over to where Leslie stood, unbuttoning his tunic as he went.

Leslie quailed as he stepped slowly around her. She could feel lines of sweat running down her sides. Her mouth was dry and her knees were weak. When he passed behind her, he casually ran his hand over her rear. His hand was large, larger than the female hands that had been using her, and stronger too. He walked around in front of her. His tunic was open now, revealing a strong, hairless chest. He stood before her and placed his hands under her breasts, lifting them, running his thumbs over her taut nipples. "Very pretty," he said.

He stepped back and removed his tunic. Malikah, the Queen, had been standing nearby, watching her as one would watch a well trained animal. She was smiling with satisfaction.

"Today is your first lesson, Ghaniyah," she said. "I want you to get down on your knees and spread your legs."

With a low pitched whine, Leslie descended to the highly polished, wooden floor. When her knees touched down, she spread them obediently.

"Now, bend over and place your forehead on the floor," Malikah ordered.

Leslie obeyed quickly. Her hands were still behind her head and her elbows were flared out. She heard the heavy boots of Captain Khalil stepping behind her. He crouched down and slid his hand up and down her inner thighs, appreciating the silky smoothness. He captured her mons and stroked it, letting his finger slip between her watering divide.

"Very good, Ghaniyah," he said. "You've passed the first test. You're nice and wet."

The man's words opened a wound inside her. She was shamed at her lasciviousness, shamed that her body would evidence desire amidst her humiliation. When she felt the man's finger tarry on her button of pleasure, she gritted her teeth lest her moan betray her passion.

The man rose. She heard Malikah's feet step towards the corner of the room, pause, and then return. Leslie desperately wanted to know what the woman was doing, but she dared not raise her head to see. She found out soon enough.

She felt something trail along her back. It had several strands and was stiff at the ends. She recognized it immediately as the whip she had seen hanging on the clothes tree. It ran up her back and then over her defenseless, pale white, plump rear mounds.

"I'm only going to give you a few strokes today, Ghaniyah, just so you know what it is like," she said. "Should we have any problems, I will string you up and whip you until your back is raw."

"Noooooooooooo! Pleeeeease sayyadati! Please don't whip me! I'll do whatever you want! Pleeeeeeease!"

"And you were doing so well, Ghaniyah," Malikah said in mock sympathy. "The first rule is that you remain absolutely silent. I'll have to put something extra in it to teach you a lesson: do not speak unless spoken to. Burn that into your brain with each blow."

With that, Malikah let the whip fly. It landed across Leslie's proffered rear cheeks. "Aaaahhhhhhhhhhhhhhhoooooowwwwww!" Leslie screamed. "Ohhhhhhhhhhhhhhhh!"

"Since it's your first lesson, whore," Malikah said, "you can scream all you want. In the future, you'll have to do better."

Her rear cheeks felt like they were afire. The Queen's harsh words and dire threats pierced her to the heart. She gripped the hair at the back of her head tightly and clenched her teeth. The second blow came quickly after. It scoured her rear like the claws of a tiger.

"Ahhhhhhhhhhhhhooooooooooowwwwww!" Leslie screamed. "Ohhhhhhhh! Pleeeeease stop! Pleeeeeeeeeeeease!"

"It seems that our pretty American whore cannot keep her mouth shut, Sergeant Malikah. I'm sure we have a remedy for that," the Captain said. Leslie knew that his words were meant for her ears since they were spoken in English. She knew she should be quiet, but she couldn't help herself.

"Ohhhhhhhhhhhhh, by all that is sacred, pleeeeeeeeeease stop! Pleeeeeeeeeease!" she screamed.

The captain said something to Malikah, amusement in his voice. She laughed.

"The captain is right, Ghaniyah. Pleading to God is quite inappropriate for a blasphemer. You're not helping yourself one bit. I'll have to make a note of that in your file for the court."

"Ohhhhhhhhhhhhhhhh!" Leslie moaned. She was sobbing intently. She hardly noticed it when the Queen went back to her desk and then returned. A hand fastened itself in her hair and she was pulled up. Her hands were yanked behind her and she felt a pair of handcuffs snapped on to them. She turned to look and beg that she not be bound when a thick prong of leather came towards her mouth. She tried to blurt something out in protest, but the thick wad of leather went right in. The captain fastened its straps behind her head and pulled them tight while Malikah idly swung the tassels of the whip back and forth. Leslie's head was forced back down to the floor.

The Queen stepped up quickly and gave her another vicious stroke. This time, Leslie's screams of agony were blocked by the fullness in her mouth and all that emerged was a muted, high pitched squeal.

Two more cruel blows were directed at her lava hot rear cheeks. Leslie screamed helplessly at each one. Her supplications for mercy emerged as garbled, muffled sounds.

They waited silently while Leslie's sobs of misery quieted down. When she had recovered a semblance of rationality, Malikah spoke to her again. "I was only going to give you five strokes, Ghaniyah," she said. "But I have to give you another for talking out of turn. I'll save your punishment for your blasphemous outburst for your next visit."

At this news, Leslie released a heart rendering moan. Malikah let the whip fly one, final time. Leslie screamed and sobbed as if all the sorrows of the world had been poured into her.

She knelt there for a while, her muted sobs winding down. She heard her assailants moving about the room. There was the sound of liquid being poured into glasses and being downed. Malikah laughed and there was the sound of a kiss. Then they turned their attention back to their prisoner.

Malikah prodded Leslie with the tip of her boot. "Get up, whore. Kneel up straight," she said.

Anxious not to provoke any further abuse, Leslie dolefully raised her torso. Captain Khalil had stripped to the waist. He was in the process of lowering his fly. He reached in and drew out his sleek, stiffened prick. Leslie's belly turned over when she saw it. She felt the buckles on her gag being released. The thick wad of leather was withdrawn from her mouth.

"Now it is time for your second lesson of the day, whore," Malikah said. "There is only one good use for the mouth of a filthy slut like you. Open it up and admit the captain's prick. All American girls know how to suck pricks," she opined. "We've had a few of you through here over the years, so don't try and tell me different. I want you to give Captain Khalil your best effort or it's back to the whip!"

Leslie grimaced. It was true that she had experience in this department, but only a couple of times. She really didn't like it. The thought of taking a man's spume into her belly was repulsive. And the thought of holding it in her mouth while he came so she could spit it out was even worse.

She knew she had no choice. Sadly, she opened her mouth and awaited the insertion of Captain Khalil's prick.

It was long and thick. Holding it steady in his hand, he advanced on her. He placed his other hand on her head, taking hold of her hair, and slid it in.

Leslie moaned as she experienced the presence of his salty tool in her mouth. Reluctantly, she closed her lips upon it and started to suckle it. Khalil gave out a little groan as her moist heat transferred itself to his rigid rod. He began to pump slowly at her orifice, forcing her head back and forth to meet his movements. Leslie's hands writhed in dismay behind her back as the despised presence worked its way over her tongue and lips.

Khalil was not satisfied with her efforts. "Suck harder!" he ordered her. "Use your tongue!"

Fearful of Sergeant Malikah's whip, Leslie redoubled her efforts. She suckled and slurped, washed the pistoning meat with her tongue. All the while, she felt the cruel eyes of the Queen on her, assessing her efforts, taking amusement from her degradation. She tried not to think about it, but she knew that this was only the first of many times that she would be performing this service for the captain. Tears flowed down her cheeks. Wave after wave of despair flowed through her.

When the captain's efforts became more determined, when she heard him groan and felt his hand tighten in her hair, she knew that the ultimate moment was coming. She started an involuntary whine. Her eyes had closed the moment that the conscienceless prick had crossed the threshold of her oral cavity, and she clamped them even tighter as if she could blot out the moment of her ultimate humiliation.

Khalil's groans became more urgent. His thrusts came faster and harder. Leslie lost all ability to suckle the raging member and she concentrated on forming a warm, wet tunnel for its enjoyment. Suddenly, Khalil gave a shout and his cock began to throb and pulse in her mouth. His spume jetted out, filling her. Desperately she tried to swallow it all, fearful of the consequences of the alternative. Nonetheless, some of it burst from its confinement and spilled out over her lips. She coughed and choked, her stomach soured. Her body shuddered.

Once his salty flow had begun to abate, Khalil slowed his motions back to a languid series of long, satisfied strokes. His hand loosened its grip on her hair. He let out a long, appreciative moan.

Leslie's lips were trembling when the cock slipped from between her lips. She looked up anxiously at her tormentor for a sign that she had performed her task satisfactorily. He looked back down at her, a smile on his lips. "Good work, Ghaniyah," he said. "Not bad for a first effort. You'll get better, I'm sure."

Leslie heard Malikah laugh. "You'll get plenty of practice," she said. "But now it's my turn. Let's see how you do at sucking my pussy."

Leslie groaned at the news of her new task. Malikah advanced on her. First she wiped the spilled cum off of her lips with her finger and ordered Leslie to lick it off. Then she took hold of her hair and forced her to knee walk to the other side of her desk. When they reached her plush chair, she reached under her green dress and lowered her panties. She pulled them over her boots and then sat down in the chair, spreading her legs widely. She pulled the hem of her dress up to her hips, revealing a bushy triangle of curly, jet black hair. "Come, whore," she said, her voice husky with anticipated pleasure. "Get to work."

Leslie moved morosely towards the sneering, callous woman. When she reached the edge of the chair, tears in her eyes, she leaned forward, her tongue jutting slightly out of her mouth, and applied it to the sparkling wet divide between her outer labia.

The odor of the Queen's arousal was overpowering. Leslie whined as she tentatively slipped her tongue along the length of the woman's gash. Malikah took hold of her hair, brought her head back and shook it violently.

"You better do better than that, whore, or it's the whip for sure!" she said threateningly. Leslie gave an abject nod and Malikah pushed her face forward once again.

Conscious of the eyes of the captain on her back and rear, Leslie performed as commanded. Suppressing her revulsion, she thrust her tongue deep into the slick divide, pressing her lips on its outer guardians. She dragged her tongue upwards, wriggling it all the while and then slipped it over and around the stiff nubbin at its top until she heard the woman sigh.

It took longer to satisfy the cruel sergeant. She kept starting and stopping her, prolonging her enjoyment. She issued curt instructions, "Deeper! Harder! Faster!" She ordered her to subsume her hardened clit into her mouth and suckle it, compelled her to flatten her tongue and lick the length of her divide and then to use her rigid tongue as a cock, thrusting it in and out of her needy hole.

Khalil crouched down behind Leslie and slipped his hand between her thighs. He began to massage and stroke her pussy, tickling her clit, thrusting his fingers in and out of her. His other hand crept around her torso and began to massage and caress her breasts. He urged her on, calling her a whore, a slut, a pig, a filthy dog. He warned her of terrible torments should she let up on her efforts.

Leslie's lusts grew higher and higher. She tried to will away the tantalizing sensations on her sex, but to no avail. She knew she was lost when she moaned into the Queen's cavern. Her assailants laughed and her torment continued. She came twice, issuing body wrenching orgasms to the amusement of her captors.

Finally, Malikah's passions grew too high for her to resist letting Leslie drive her to completion. She groaned and moaned. She pushed Leslie's face hard into her loins. Her thighs closed over her cheeks. Her grip on her hair became so tight that Leslie feared she would rip it out of her head. When she came, her hips bucked, her thighs swung in and out. She grabbed Leslie's head with both of her hands and moved it up and down over her pulsing pussy. She shouted out something loud in Arabic. Her hips thrust upwards and her back arched.

She hummed languidly as her contractions subsided. She brushed her hands tenderly over Leslie's head, stroking her hair like she might a favorite pet. When finally satisfied, with a deep sigh, she pushed Leslie's head away.

"You have found a new talent, Ghaniyah," she said, amusement in her voice. "I think we are going to be great friends." And then she laughed.

Leslie thought she was done. But Captain Khalil's lusts had been resparked by the vision of her gemauching his partner and the handling of her delectable flesh. He pulled her up and bent her face down over the sergeant's desk. He lifted her hips, spread her legs and pierced her slit.

"Ahhhhhhhhhhh! So good! So good!" he repeated over and over as he fucked her. The iron pole energized Leslie's puss once more and he soon had her panting and gasping with pleasure. She gave out powerful, unrestrained moans as the relentless rod traversed her clit. She wanted to cry out for mercy. The pleasure was so intense, her lusts were raised so high, that she thought she might explode. When the captain gave out a great groan and his cock began its dance inside her, her pussy erupted into fierce, body wrenching throbs.

She lay there listlessly as the captain readorned himself with his tunic. Malikah emerged from her chair and slapped her viciously on her ass. "Don't get his cum all over my desk, whore," she spat out. Leslie struggled to her feet. Malikah unlocked her handcuffs and handed her her limp, dirty brown dress. "Put this on!" she ordered.

Exhausted by her ordeal, Leslie pulled the thin garment over her head and drew it down her body. She fumbled as she tried to button it. Malikah brushed her hands aside and completed the job for her. She pointed to a spot in front of her desk and told her, "Stand over there."

Leslie watched as the captain and sergeant gave each other an impassioned kiss. Khalil picked up his baton, gave Leslie an ironic smile and left. Sergeant Malikah sat down at her desk.

She opened a drawer and pulled out a hairbrush which she quickly ran through her jet black hair. When she was done, she tossed it back in the drawer and looked at Leslie. "You will find that I am very generous person, Ghaniyah," she said. "But everything depends on your cooperation. Do you understand?"

Leslie had placed her hands back behind her and was standing with her legs apart. "Y,yes, sayyadati," she murmured morosely. Her backside still burned and she could feel the captain's spunk dripping down her thigh. She still had the taste of the Queen's quim in her mouth. Her eyes were pointed downwards, unable to look in the face of her jailer. There was a moment's silence. Malikah picked up the phone on her desk and punched in a number. She rattled off an order in Arabic into it and then placed it down into its cradle. A moment later a guard came in. "Take inmate Ghaniyah back to her cell," Malikah said in English. And then, to Leslie, "I will see you again tomorrow."

It was late afternoon when Leslie got back to her cell. She could tell by the quality of light being admitted by the long, narrow, barred windows across the corridor from her cell. She knew that Jamilah would soon be back from her work detail. She lay on the bed, on her side, due to the injuries to her bum. She didn't cry. She felt like she had used up all her tears. She kept thinking, "Twenty years! Twenty years! It can't be true! It can't!"

Interspersed with her mourning over the seriousness of her predicament, she castigated herself for her easily drawn out lust while being used by Captain Khalil and Sergeant Malikah. The captain had been right. She had been wet when he examined her. There was something about the powerlessness she felt when under the Queen's orders, something about being subject to the whims of the captain that had sparked her lust. It wasn't that she didn't hate being degraded. She resented it horribly. It was just that something triggered inside her when someone gave her a command that she knew was a prelude to her use.

Leslie was still lying disconsolate on her bed when the other inmates were brought back from their work details. Jamilah came in, repeated her ritual from the day before and then sat down on her bunk. She lit a cigarette.

"So, you see Queen today?" she asked Leslie after a while, her voice low, just over a whisper.

Leslie turned to look at her and nodded.

"She make you dance to her whip?"

Again Leslie nodded.

"Poor little whore," Jamilah said. "But it can be good too. You see."

A little while later, one of the guards came by. She was holding a cardboard box in her arms. She maneuvered it so that she was holding it with one arm and unlocked the cell. She placed it on the floor and kicked it in. When she closed the door, she gave Jamilah an order. Leslie heard her new name, Ghaniyah, mentioned.

"Naäm, sayyadati," Jamilah replied respectfully.

Jamilah immediately pulled the box over to her bunk and began to rummage through it. She pulled out a thick, soft, white roll of toilet paper and smiled. "See," she said to Leslie.

There was a small chocolate bar, some fragrant soap, a hair brush, a small tube of salve, a small, plastic razor, skin lotion and some shaving cream. There was also a small, clear plastic bag with three cigarettes in it. Jamilah beamed. "We rich now," she said. She looked at Leslie. "You good whore."

She put most of the stuff in the box under her bed. "We eat chocolate later," she said. "Guard give me order. I have salve for your stripes. I put on, make you feel better."

As much as she disdained any assistance from her cellmate, Leslie relished having something soothing put on her wounds. She nodded, "Yes," and turned to her stomach. Jamilah came over and flipped up the skirt to her dress. She gave a whistle of astonishment.

"Oooh!" she exclaimed. "Queen get you good."

She opened the tube, placed some salve on her hand and started to delicately apply it to the damage inflicted on Leslie's rear. Leslie cringed when the older woman touched her wounds, but the salve really did make them feel better. Jamilah could not resist the opportunity to give Leslie's ass a gentle caress.

"You name Ghaniyah now," she said. "Pretty name. You very pretty. I like."

Jamilah's attentions were going beyond the medical and Leslie began to feel uncomfortable. Jamilah got off the bed and rummaged in her box again. She brought out the razor and the shaving cream. She came back to Leslie's bunk.

"You turn over," she said.

Leslie turned and looked at her over her shoulder, suspicious of the woman's intentions.

"Order from Queen. Shave pussy," she replied.

"Shave my pussy!" Leslie exclaimed. "No way!"

"Shhhhhhhhh!" Jamilah warned. "If not, we both get whipped. Must do. Turn over and spread legs."

"I will not!" Leslie insisted.

Jamilah slammed the flat of her hand on Leslie's wounded ass. "Oooooooooooh!" Leslie moaned.

"You do what I say," Jamilah hissed threateningly. "Jamilah no get whipped for Ghaniyah. I hurt you bad first."

Realizing she had no choice, Leslie reluctantly turned over. Jamilah flipped up the front of her dress. "Spread legs," she told Leslie. "Raise knees."

When Leslie had complied, she squeezed some shaving lotion out of the tube and applied it to Leslie's pubic region. It frothed up in her wiry hair. Her cellmate jumped up from the bed and went over to the sink where she filled one of the tin cups with tepid water. She returned and insinuated herself between Leslie's upturned thighs.

Slowly, Jamilah swiped away the shaving cream, bringing with it the evidence of Leslie's sexual maturity. Leslie had her eyes closed. She cringed each time the razor slid over the tender flesh surrounding her sex. She fought back her tears. She wondered dismally how many more indignities she would be subject to. She knew that she was utterly under the Queen's thumb. She would be virtually a slave to her, and, through her, to Captain Khalil. Tomorrow, she would suffer her abuse again. And the day after and the day after and the day after.

Jamilah's efforts were making her pussy tingle. As she shaved, she placed her hand here and there, pushing and pulling her skin, pulling taut her love lips, so that she could do a complete job. When she was done, she patted Leslie's denuded quim. "Very pretty," she said, smiling. "You wait here."

She got up, washed out the cup and went back to her box. She pulled out the tube of skin lotion and returned to Leslie's bed. She put some on her hand and began to rub it into the skin surrounding Leslie puss. Despite her hard hands, she had a gentle touch. Leslie felt herself relaxing and getting into the feeling of the soothing lotion being applied. When she felt Jamilah's thumb slip through her love lips and ascend to her clit, he eyes popped open and she went to move her legs together. Jamilah laughed.

"You nice and soft," she said. "And you all wet." She laughed again.

That night, at dinner time, Leslie was able to eat her meal in peace. Apparently having been selected as Malikah's sex slave made her out of bounds for the other inmates, at least for tonight. As long as the sergeant kept Jamilah supplied in cigarettes, maybe she would not be tempted to whore her out, Leslie thought.

As at breakfast, Leslie held on tightly to her spoon and showed it dutifully to the guard as she exited the cafeteria.

Leslie was full of apprehension when she returned to her cell. Soon it would be lights out and she expected another assault from Jamilah during the night. She tried to think of ways she could resist her. But the woman was hard as nails and would certainly hurt her if she did not cooperate.

As promised, Jamilah broke out the chocolate after dinner. Leslie had to admit that it was a little bit of heaven to taste its sweetness. And to give Jamilah her due, she did split it evenly with her.

About a half hour after lights out, Jamilah came over to Leslie's bed. She did not resist when she insisted she remove her dress. What was the use? Jamilah lay down next to her, already naked. She stroked her hair and cooed little Arabic sayings to her. She draped her leg over Leslie's thigh. The heat of her body was raising Leslie's passions. Her voice was so surprisingly soft and gentle, that Leslie began to cry. It was what she needed, comfort and love. While she knew that the hardened convict did not love her, she accepted the illusion.

"It be okay," Jamilah said sympathetically. "You see. Jamilah take good care of you. We be happy together. I give you pleasure every night, kiss you and hold you tight. You Jamilah's little whore now. I make you feel good."

The hard convict's words were comforting. Leslie could not help but snuggle up against her. It was a stark contrast to how the Queen had treated her. When Jamilah put her lips to hers and slipped the end of her tongue between them, Leslie gave out a great sigh, opened her mouth and accepted it.

They made love for about an hour. It was strange for Leslie to feel Jamilah's hand caress her now hairless love lips. It made her feel more naked than naked. Jamilah turned her body and, after drifting her tongue along Leslie's belly, brought her passionate attention to her loins. When Leslie began to moan with pleasure, she threw her leg over Leslie's torso and presented her own sex to Leslie's lips. Without hesitation, Leslie reached her arms around her muscular thighs and buried her mouth in her quim.

CHAPTER FIVE

The next morning, after Jamilah and the others went off to work, a guard took Leslie to the showers. She watched while Leslie cleaned herself with the soap she had been given. Leslie felt ashamed for the guard to see her rudely displayed love lips. She snickered when she saw it after Leslie had undressed.

She had brought some fragrant shampoo and Leslie used it on her greasy hair gratefully. When she was done, there was a clean towel and a clean dress. Leslie brushed her hair out with the brush she had been given. She was bought back to her cell afterwards to await her summons.

The next few days developed into a routine. On only one of those days was Captain Khalil there. After giving her three strokes of the whip for her prior day's blasphemy, this time across her belly and thighs, he had her suck him off and then, when Malikah had taken her pleasure, he fucked her, this time in her rear passage, making her squeal with pain.

On the next day, Khalil was absent. Malikah used a large, black dildo strapped to her waist to fuck her. She sat back on her chair and had Leslie kneel over her lap, her quim pierced by the rigid device. Leslie raised and lowered herself passionately over the thick prong while Malikah kissed her lips and played with her breasts. After she had come twice, Malikah had her kneel on the floor and service her. On the third day, she laid Leslie back on her desk with her legs spread and mouthed her hairless loins while Leslie screamed with pleasure. She then laid Leslie on the floor, covering her face with her coosh, and made her return the favor. She had spared her further abuse from the whip and Leslie tried desperately not to give any reason to complain.

Every afternoon, following her sessions, she received a care package consisting, mostly, of candy and cigarettes. When she came back from work, Jamilah made sure that she shaved and lotioned Leslie's loins so that they would be smooth and pleasant for the Queen's use the next day.

At night, after lights out, she and Jamilah coupled passionately.

Otherwise, Leslie's days were spent in absolute boredom and unhappy lassitude.

On the fourth day, though, after both Captain Khalil and Sergeant Malikah had made use of her, Leslie's journey back to her cell took a detour. The guard took her through a steel door that led to the work areas. Leslie's hopes brightened. If she had to be a prisoner here, at least they could give her something to do. Otherwise she might die of ennui. They walked down a corridor that Leslie took, from the smell of steamed cotton, to be the laundry area. The prison, in order to offset the costs of confining its inmates, took in laundry from the town's hotels and restaurants. They also did their own wash, of course.

They passed a room where several of the prisoners were folding tablecloths, sheets and napkins. None of the busy women looked up as they passed. A little further down the hall, the guard opened a door and waited for Leslie to pass into it. The room was filled with piles of dirty, white laundry. It was dimly lit. At first, Leslie thought that there was no one there. Then, a tall, heavyset figure stepped out of a shadow. It was the inmate who had been assaulting her in the cafeteria. Leslie gasped. She turned around and made an effort to dash from the room, but the guard barred her way and pushed her back. She kept prodding her and pushing her with her baton until she was several feet in.

The inmate came closer to her, smiling. She reached into the pocket of her light brown smock and pulled out a small wad of currency. She handed it to the guard. The guard placed it in the pocket of her uniform, smiled at Leslie and then left the room. Leslie heard the door lock.

A wave of fear passed through her. Where did the woman come up with money? She had heard tales of corruption in prisons, seen the movies. She realized that the inmate was probably the leader of a drug ring, or perhaps just a perpetrator of plain old extortion. The other inmates undoubtedly paid her tribute so that her gang wouldn't harass them or worse. The guards didn't mind since they probably got a piece of it. Friends and family on the outside would send their loved ones money so they could pay for drugs or protection.

The other inmate began to unbutton her dress. Leslie backed away from her and ran to the door. In her desperation, she tried the handle to see if she could get out, but it wouldn't turn. She watched as the inmate pulled her dress over her head. She had large breasts, a broad chest and thick, muscular thighs with a large, hairy bush between them. Her arms were long and looked strong. Ice filled Leslie's belly as she realized what was about to happen to her. Her palms started to sweat. She could feel her body shiver.

When the woman started to come towards her, a look of lust in her eyes, Leslie quickly ran past her and went further into the room. She circled around a large pile of white laundry. She heard the woman calling her name. "Ghaniyah!" her deep voice called out sweetly sickly. "Ghaniyah!" And then she said something meant to sound enticing in Arabic.

Leslie's heart was beating wildly. Her throat was dry. She knew that she would not be able to avoid the woman for long, but she knew that she had to try. When the woman's head peeked out from around the corner of the laundry, Leslie took off again. They repeated their charade several times, the woman calling her name, Leslie retreating further and further into the room. Then, she realized she was cornered. She waited and waited for the woman's head to peep around the corner so she could run the other way. Suddenly, the whole pile of laundry came down on top of her. She fell to the floor. She was still struggling to untangle herself from the winding pile of sheets and tablecloths when the woman pounced.

It was not much of a battle. "No! No! No, please!" Leslie yelled as the woman started to take control of her body. She pushed her aside and was about to get away when the woman grabbed her arm and pulled her back. This time, she covered Leslie's body with her own. Her leg trapped Leslie's. She took hold of her hair and began to pull it. Her other hand took hold of Leslie's wrist and began to twist it cruelly.

"Oh! Oh! Oh!" Leslie cried. "Let go! Let go! Owwwwww-wwwwwwww!"

The woman snaked her arm under Leslie's back and grabbed her other arm. She locked them together under her while shoving her knee hard up into Leslie's crevasse.

"Ohhhhhhhhhh!" Leslie cried as her pussy exploded into pain. The woman's free hand snuck under her skirt and took hold of her delicate love lips and twisted them meanly. Leslie screeched. "Oh, please let go! Please! Please! Owwwwww-wwwwwww!"

The woman slowly loosened her grip. Leslie's body went limp. She knew her struggles were over. Her arms were held fast behind her and her leg was trapped. The woman outweighed her by at least 100 pounds. Tears flooded her eyes.

Pleased with Leslie's surrender, her thick, naked body shoved up against her, the woman began uttering some sweet sounding phrases. She used her free hand to stroke Leslie's breasts and belly over her dress and then down her naked thighs. She leaned over and let her tongue flow inside Leslie's ear and then across her neck and under her chin. Leslie moaned and arched her back, but the woman held her firmly in place. "Please don't do this," Leslie whined weakly. "Please."

The woman paid her no mind. "Me Zarifa. You pretty girl," she said in broken English, her voice scratchy and low. "I like."

When Zarifa began to unbutton her dress, Leslie started to cry. When she had the bodice open, she reached her hand inside and took possession of her breasts, massaging and squeezing them. She kept pulling the fabric until both her breasts were free and then began kissing and suckling at them, all the time issuing a lustful, revolting moan. Leslie tried again to struggle, but Zarifa took hold of one of her nipples and twisted it until Leslie screamed. When Zarifa released it, Leslie's resistance was over.

The larger, stronger woman had her way with her. She took hold of Leslie's cheeks, pressing them to force her mouth open, and thrust her tongue inside. Her breath was stale and sour and it made Leslie's stomach turn. She caressed her breasts while she kissed her, swishing her tongue all through her mouth, pressing her lips down hard. Her hand then slowly descended down

Leslie's belly until she reached her skirt. She pulled it up and caressed the length of her thighs. Leslie had her legs pressed together, the other woman's right thigh between them. When she felt the woman's fingers take hold of a piece of her skin and begin to twist it, she relented, spreading her free leg. She moaned when she felt the hand cover her mons.

Zarifa played with her pussy, stroking it, slipping her finger down its moistening divide, pressing down on her bud of pleasure, plunging inside her. Leslie tried to fight off the feelings of arousal. But the hot tongue in her mouth, the press of the other woman's body against her, the knowledgeable, experienced, incessant fingers on her crevasse, forced her lusts to rise. When the woman thrust two of her thick fingers inside her and began to fuck her with them, she moaned unhappily.

This sparked Zarifa into action. She pushed Leslie's skirt up until it was around her waist and then farther and farther up until it was around her chest. She released her arms and, pulling her up by her hair, forced the dress up over her head and then down her arms. Once the dress was free of her body, she rummaged around until she found some twine that had held the bundles of laundry together. She pressed Leslie face down against the fabric and climbed on top of her legs. She grabbed her wrists and tied them off behind her.

Leslie whined as the woman pulled her up. Apparently she wanted to inspect her prize before she fully consumed it. She held Leslie's face in her hands, licking it and turning it this way and that to get a better look at it. She felt her breasts again and moved her torso so that the dim light shined more directly on them. She pinched and twisted her nipples and then ran her hand over her belly. She turned Leslie over again and caressed her soft rear globes, pushing her finger inside Leslie's delicate anal ring. She stroked her thighs while kissing her rear cheeks, laying her tongue along the valley between them. She grabbed her pussy again, from behind, and stroked and played with it, pushing her fingers deep inside and then pulling and pinching her clit.

Leslie moaned and cried while she was being handled. It was if she were a tiny doll in the bigger woman's hands. The heat of her hands and the sure way that she handled her, made Leslie's blood run hot.

Then, having satisfied her prurient curiosity, Zarifa turned Leslie's body around again and pressed her face against one of her large, fleshy breasts.

Leslie knew what the woman wanted her to do. She opened her mouth and subsumed the long, thick nipple in her mouth and began to suckle it. Zarifa's one hand held her face firmly down against her tit while the other caressed her back. She was moaning low and deep. She shifted Leslie's face to her other massive orb and repeated the procedure. The ease with which the older, stronger woman controlled her, the contact between their naked flesh, she sensation of suckling on her teat, all drove Leslie's lust. She hated herself for it, tried to deny it, but her pussy kept getting warmer and warmer and her heart was beating stronger and stronger.

Keeping a firm hold on Leslie's hair, Zarifa laid back and spread her powerful legs. She forced Leslie's face between them. Leslie took a deep, involuntary breath of the woman's arousal just before her mouth was forced down upon the woman's hairy, messy cunt. Fearful of the woman's retribution, being totally at her mercy, Leslie went to work at once.

Zarifa sighed and moaned as Leslie serviced her. Leslie licked and suckled energetically, knowing that she would not be permitted to remove her face from the musky, mushy organ until she had satisfied the cruel woman. The hand held her head tightly, pushing it down, moving it up and down, encouraging Leslie to suckle at this place or that. When she pushed her head down hard, smothering her face and nose with her flesh, Leslie took this as a signal to probe deeply into the gushing canal. She wriggled her tongue, washed the inner walls, tickled the delicate roof. When her breath became short she began to struggle. She tried desperately to raise her head. Her hands writhed in their bonds. She called out frantically into the deep cavern which yawned before her. Zarifa apparently got the message. She lifted Leslie's head for a moment, allowing her to catch her breath and then pressed it back down.

The woman's need was approaching swiftly. Her mighty thighs began to tremble. Her back arched. Her grip on Leslie's hair became tighter. She began moving Leslie's head up and down rapidly, pausing every few strokes to press it down hard on her clit. Then she grabbed Leslie's head with both hands. She pressed it down hard. Her hips thrust her pussy up, pressing the bone of her pelvis hard against Leslie's forehead. She roared her pleasure. She groaned and shouted something out in Arabic again and again.

Suddenly, as if having become electrified, she raised Leslie's head and pushed her to her back atop the spongy fabric. She reversed herself, throwing her leg over Leslie's torso and then lay down atop her. She spread her legs, pushing her pussy once more against Leslie's face and then leaned down and covered Leslie's mons with her widespread lips.

She attacked Leslie's pussy as if she meant to consume it. She licked and bit and suckled frantically. She pressed her coosh hard against Leslie's face, grinding her hips, thrusting them back and forth. Leslie's lust took off like a rocket. She began to moan and groan too. She spread her graceful thighs as far as they would go and began pumping her hips against the mouth that was tormenting her. Zarifa put her hot, meaty hands on Leslie's inner thighs, pressing them down, raising her hips. Her tongue was snakelike as it twisted and turned inside her, slithered over her engorged, throbbing lips and then pressing down, circling and taunting her rigid love button.

Leslie came first. Her body felt like it was a huge knot that someone was pulling tighter and tighter. Her pussy throbbed and contracted, overriding all other sensations. Enflamed by the rabid tongue and lips that possessed it, it burned brightly as if it were the center of the universe.

Zarifa groaned and her body shuddered as she came too. Her thighs closed around Leslie's head, her arms snaked around her thighs, her hips ground against Leslie's face.

When her assailant's excitation began to wane, she slid off of Leslie's body. They were both straining to catch their breaths. Zarifa let her hand flow across Leslie's belly and breasts, happily.

There was still time left before the guard would return and demand Leslie's release. Zarifa spent it caressing and stroking Leslie's body. She cooed and murmured Arabic phrases. She had Leslie on her lap, her hands still bound behind her, and she kissed her again, a long, impassioned, languorous kiss which Leslie had no energy to resist. She turned Leslie over and spread her across her thigh. Forcing her to spread her legs again, she returned to teasing and tickling her puss, her other hand in possession of her breasts, until Leslie's lust began to return. She slipped two of her long, fat fingers inside her and began to fuck her with them while pulling on and pinching her nipples. Leslie came again almost right away, her moans of pleasure echoing through the room.

Leslie was still cooling down from her forced climax when the door to the room opened. The guard knocked her club against the door and called out something imperative. Zarifa brought Leslie to her feet, scooped up her dress and brought her to the front of the room. Leslie was mortified to have the guard see her naked and bound, her face and chest still flushed from her bout of passion. The guard laughed.

Zarifa gave Leslie another forced kiss before she released her. "Ghaniyah pretty," she said smiling. She left Leslie standing by the guard while she retrieved her own dress. She put it on happily. She gave Leslie's breast a tweak as she passed and exited the door.

The guard did not let Leslie dress, but escorted her back to her cell, bound and naked. When she locked her back into her cell, she threw the dress in after her.

Leslie was lying on her bed, naked and bound when Jamilah returned from her work duty. When she saw her like that, she drew the correct conclusion. "You let Zarifa fuck you!" she said accusingly. "You filthy whore." She gave Leslie several smacks of her hand on her bottom and back. Then she laid back on her bed, opened her Koran and lit a cigarette, one she had earned by pimping Leslie out. It was only when the guard came to call them to dinner that she untied Leslie's bonds and let her dress. At dinner, Zarifa smiled lustfully at Leslie, winking and smirking. She left her alone though. As they were leaving, she dropped a piece of hard candy in her pocket. When they got back to their cell, Jamilah took it away from her and ate it.

That night, Leslie refused to let Jamilah fuck her. She rolled up into a ball and tried to hide herself away. Jamilah jumped on top of her, gave her several hard punches to her body with her fist, reached in and twisted her breasts, pulled her hair savagely and slapped her across the face. Leslie, weeping, gave in. Jamilah made her come three times before she presented her her quim to suckle.

* * * * * * * * * * * * * *

Leslie had given up all hope that Mr. Moussa would come and save her. Frankly, she didn't know if he had the power to, even if he had the inclination. It had been a week since she was arrested. Sergeant Malikah had given her a beating one afternoon for being slow to obey. Captain Khalil had her brought directly to his office one night where he fucked her for two hours. She had been brought again to the laundry room on her sixth day where Zarifa used her again, this time with one of her friends. One day, three of the guards took her to an empty cell where they all took turns having her suck their pussies. It seemed that she was condemned to be the prison's pass around whore, doomed to languish there forever.

Therefore, she was surprised, on the eighth day, that when she was brought to Sergeant Malikah's office, she saw Mr. Moussa and his factotum, Faraq. They were sitting in padded, steel chairs in front of Sergeant Malikah's desk and were both wearing Western style suits. Leslie's heart skipped a beat when she saw them. She broke out into a cold sweat and began to tremble all over. She prayed that they had come to take her away. A vast chasm opened in her belly. She dared not look at them directly, casting only tremulous glances. In conformity with the Queen's number one rule, she said nothing.

Mr. Moussa eyed her with his typical aloofness. Faraq, however, had daggers in his eyes. They lingered on her bare legs. Although she had provided with a clean dress each day before she came to Malikah's office for her daily abuse, they kept giving her the same size as before. The edge of the hem was at least three inches above her knees and her bodice pulled tightly over her breasts.

No one said anything to her. Mr. Moussa was having a pleasant conversation with Sergeant Malikah. They were all sipping cups of tea. Leslie's hopes rose when she noticed darkness flash across the Queen's face like she was being deprived of a favorite toy.

While they talked, Leslie remained utterly silent, her arms crossed behind her back. She felt a little like a small child in the principal's office listening while the adults discussed her latest escapade. Finally, the tone of their conversation and their body language indicated that the discussion had come to its termination. Leslie's stomach fluttered as she wondered what the end result would be. She suppressed a desperate whine. Would she be released or sent back to her cell? For Leslie, it was a life or death question. She was so tense she felt like she was going to throw up. Bile rose in her throat.

It was Malikah who addressed her. "Mr. Moussa is a very influential member of our community," she said calmly and slowly. "He has agreed to go surety for you until your trial. You are to be released into his custody. You are to obey all of his rules to the letter, or he will return you here. Do you understand?"

Tears came to Leslie's eyes. A wave of heavenly relief passed through her. She just prayed that it was not some cruel joke. Her body shuddered and she felt like she was going to faint. "Y,yes, sayyadati," she said, her voice low and tremulous. "Thank you, sayyadati."

"Don't thank me, thank Mr. Moussa. I don't believe a person with offenses as serious as your should be allowed out in the community, but, as I said, Mr. Moussa is a very influential man. He is also a very honorable man and considers it his duty to assist you."

Leslie's lips were trembling. He knees felt weak. She wanted to get out of there as quickly as possible in case Mr. Moussa or the powers that be changed their minds. It was going to be wonderful to be able to be her own person again, to be able to walk around as she wanted, to speak when she wanted. And most of all, to be free from abuse. She would contact the American Embassy in Tripoli as soon as she got out and see what could be done to get her home. It had been a terrible, terrible experience. The things that had happened to her seemed as if they had emerged from her worst nightmare. But soon it would be over.

Malikah spoke again.

"I have told Mr. Moussa that your civilian clothes are on their way here. He will wait outside while you get dressed." Then she said something to Mr. Moussa in Arabic. He nodded, gave Leslie another dispassionate look and got up from his chair. He and Faraq, after appropriate salutations to the Queen, left the room.

When they were gone, Malikah leaned back in her chair, her eyes pinned on Leslie. "As you can imagine, Ghaniyah, we are sorry to see you go," she said imperiously. "We've enjoyed your little visit with us. But don't worry. I will speak to Captain Khalil to see what he can do about moving up your trial. Mr. Moussa's influence only goes so far and our courts have a 95% conviction rate."

She let this sink in for a moment. Leslie shuddered as she received the information.

"Oh, and Mr. Moussa has surrendered your passport, so don't think of going anywhere. You don't want to come back here with new charges, do you?"

"N,no, sayyadati," Leslie stuttered.

There came a knock on the door. Malikah shouted out an Arabic word and the door opened. It was one of the guards. She was carrying a clear plastic bag. In it were Leslie's blue skirt and her white blouse. Her underwear was nowhere to be seen.

Under the watchful eye of her oppressor, Leslie stripped off her light brown dress and then stepped into her skirt. She took her blouse from the guard and put it on. They had not returned her shoes. When she had finished buttoning it, she stood at attention and put her hands behind her back again, awaiting permission to leave.

"Goodbye for now, Ghaniyah," the sergeant said ominously. "I'll be waiting for you." She nodded towards the door to the free world. Leslie hesitated, took a deep breath and then walked to the door.

Mr. Moussa and Faraq were waiting for her in the hallway. Mr. Moussa said nothing. Faraq ordered her to come with them.

They walked down a long hallway, through a locked steel door which was buzzed open for them, down another hallway, past a reception area with a big, wooden desk. There was a pair of glass doors. They walked to them. Faraq pulled one open, and then they were out.

A huge wave of relief flooded Leslie's mind. "I'm out! I'm out!" she exclaimed to herself. She started to cry. The day was sunny and hot. Bright, wonderful colors were everywhere. A woman and a child were walking on the street nearby. There were stores and cars. The air was clean and fresh. It felt so good to be free. A huge weight had been lifted from her. She felt like dancing.

Mr. Moussa's limousine was waiting for them. The driver opened the right rear door for Mr. Moussa. Faraq took hold of Leslie's arm, gripping it tight, and led her to the other side of the car. When he opened the door, Leslie went to get in, but he held her back. There was a pile of steel chains on the seat. Faraq picked it up. Leslie blanched when she saw what they were. He quickly fastened the handcuffs to her wrists in front of her. Then he crouched down and fastened a set to her ankles. These were connected by an 18" long chain. Leslie suppressed a whine. While she was clear of the awful prison, she was still, clearly a prisoner. Sergeant Malikah's words came back to her and she shivered.

It was about a half hour's drive to the Moussa mansion. Faraq rode in the front seat next to the driver. Leslie looked over to Mr. Moussa several times, trying to gauge what his reaction was to all this, but he stoically kept his vision straight ahead as if she were not even in the car. It was not of a nature to reassure her. She knew that things would not go back to the way they were. Too much had gone on. They would certainly make sure that she never left the house again. But she had been forming what she thought was a warm relationship with Mr. Moussa and she didn't want that to go by the boards.

The limo pulled in front of the house. Mr. Moussa's side was closest. Faraq opened his door and he got out of the car and strolled up the six or seven steps and entered. The driver opened Leslie's door. Due to the chains around her ankles, she had to step carefully out of the car. By the time she got out, Faraq was there. He took custody of her and, holding her by the arm, walked her up to the front door. She had to take little baby steps, especially going up the stairs. When they were inside, Faraq locked the deadbolt to the door and withdrew the key from the lock, putting it in his pocket. He began to usher her towards Mr. Moussa's office.

As they were walking toward it, who should come out of a side room, but Mrs. Moussa. She took a look at Leslie and scowled. She released a string of Arabic epithets, concluding with the English word, "Whore!"

The insult wounded Leslie deeply. Maybe it was because it had an element of truth to it. She had bartered herself for her safety. She had received and enjoyed gifts for her services, although the world would consider them paltry. Didn't that make her a whore? She was still repelled by her reaction to having been a sexual thrall. It would take a long time to forget. You never know what you are like deep down under until placed in a position of crisis. She had found out and she didn't like what she saw.

Faraq kept her moving. Mr. Moussa's office was off to the left when you came in the door. There was a secretarial station where she usually sat doing her work, at the beck and call of her employer. She tried to make a mental vision of herself as she once was, innocent and carefree. It was hard to do. That person didn't exist anymore. And while she was free, she understood her freedom to be very tenuous. Sergeant Malikah's promise to be waiting for her knelled in her head like the bell of doom.

Mr. Moussa was not in his office. Faraq led her over to his large, polished, dark brown desk. It was neat as a pin with only a desk pad and a telephone on it. Mr. Moussa was a very orderly man. He had insisted that the letters Leslie sent out under his signature be perfect. He was correct in everything. Leslie was heartbroken that she had disappointed him.

She thought that Faraq was going to lead her to a chair and release her from her chains. She was wrong. He brought her to the side of Mr. Moussa's desk. He crouched down and released one of her ankle cuffs and then clipped it closed around the foot of the desk. She was locked in place. "Stay here slut," Faraq said, and then he left.

A feeling of dread passed over Leslie. She was told that she would have to obey all of Mr. Moussa's rules. Was one of them going to be that she be always chained up? Was she going to be allowed any freedom? When was she going to be able to call her ambassador? Was Mr. Moussa really going to help her or was he just concerned about the disgrace of having one of his employees charged with a crime?

After about a half hour, the door opened and Mr. Moussa walked in. He had doffed his suit jacket but was still wearing his bright white shirt and tie and black pants. He looked at her briefly and then went to sit in his chair. He leaned back as if in deep thought. Leslie's heart trembled as she waited for him to speak. Finally, he did.

"Miss Harrington," he said, his voice low and stern. He spoke English clearly and correctly, with a slight British accent. "I took considerable criticism for hiring an American as my secretary. I was told that American girls were whores, that you would disgrace me. I said, 'Nonsense!' I had read your resume and recommendations and they all supported my belief that you were a decent, modest, professional, young woman."

"Please, Mr. Moussa!" Leslie said. "Please let me explain!"

"Be quiet!" Moussa roared. Leslie took a step back, tautening the chain that held her to his desk.

"I am talking now! There is nothing you can say that will assuage the damage you have done me! I am the laughingstock of Dar Al Jamah! You have involved my family in a terrible scandal! You are a whore and a blasphemer! You assaulted the policemen who arrested you! You seduced a prison guard! And, Sergeant Malikah told me that you engaged in unnatural acts with your cellmate while in the prison!"

"It's not true!" Leslie whined. "I was raped, repeatedly, by Sergeant Malikah and Captain Khalil too. I never blasphemed! I never said anything. They didn't let me. And I didn't assault them. The policemen struck me repeatedly, beat me and dragged me into a car! I'm innocent! You have to believe me!"

Mr. Moussa turned red. "I happen to know Captain Khalil very well. I know his family. It's outrageous that you make such an allegation against him! I ought to take you back to the prison right now! And as to the unnatural acts, I notice that you don't deny them!"

Leslie didn't know what to do. That part was true. Only it wasn't like that. She had no choice. Jamilah raped her and would have hurt her had she not given in to her. How could she make Mr. Moussa understand? She was at first perplexed at how the Queen knew about that but then realized that Jamilah must have informed on her. She was probably purposely put in her cell so that she could report on everything she did.

"She made me do it," Leslie blurted out. "My cellmate made me do it! She was stronger than me, a real convict serving a 9 years sentence. I was afraid. The first night the guards tied me up and she raped me!"

Moussa jumped up from his chair. "I've heard enough of your lies!" he shouted. "You need to be punished like the whore that you are! Lean over my desk!"

Leslie quailed at the order. "Please don't hurt me, Mr. Moussa! I'll be good, I promise! I didn't do anything!"

"Lean over my desk!" Moussa roared. His face was beet red and a mask of rage.

Sobbing, Leslie did what she was told. She leaned over and placed her torso on the desk. She raised her bound hands over her head. Her breasts were pressing against the brightly polished wood. "Please, Mr. Moussa," she started again. "Please......."

Moussa opened a drawer to his desk and he pulled out a thick handkerchief. He stepped towards Leslie and grabbed the hair at the back of her head. He pushed the handkerchief rudely into her mouth. "I've heard enough from you, whore!" he ranted.

Then he stepped behind her. He lifted her skirt. There was a pause and then the palm of his hand came forward quickly and landed on Leslie's tender, naked, rear cheek. It made a loud slapping noise.

"Mmmmmmmmmmmmpf!" Leslie moaned. "..eeeeeeeee-eeease! eeeeeeeeeeeease! ....oooooooon't!" Luckily, the wounds of the other day had subsided. But the hand was brought down so forcefully that it stung like blazes all the same.

Moussa ignored her. He was on a mission of retribution. Unlike the beatings she had received from Sergeant Malikah, which had been instructive, this was vengeful and the tall, broad shouldered man put everything he had into it.

"Slap! Slap! Slap! Slap!" The blows kept going and going. Leslie's rear end was getting hotter and hotter. Each blow hurt more then the one before. She screamed and yelled, the sounds muffled by the fabric in her mouth. She tried to get up, but Mr. Moussa's strong hand pushed her down while the other continued to pummel away.

During her struggle to escape her torture, Leslie's legs spread apart. Suddenly, the hand that had been beating her snuck in between them from behind and took hold of her denuded love lips.

"So, you've shaved you pussy just like a whore," Moussa said menacingly. He gave her labia a fierce squeeze. Leslie moaned and tried to force her legs back together, but the man's fingers had a firm hold on her sex and wouldn't let go.

"Okay! You want to be a whore, I'll treat you like a whore!" Moussa declared.

His hand left her back and she heard the sound of his zipper lowering. "Oh, god, he's going to fuck me!" she screamed inwardly. She tried to get up, but the hand that had hold of her labia squeezed it again harshly. She moaned and desisted her struggle.

The knowledge that he was going to use her against her will sent a wave of lust through her. She had fantasized about Mr. Moussa fucking her, but it had not been like this. In her imagination, it was sweet and tender and sophisticated. Not raw and angry like this. Nonetheless her pussy began to trill and her body got hot. She closed her eyes and whined. She clenched her bound hands into fists. She bit down on the intruder in her mouth. She knew he was going to do it. It wasn't just a threat. And she rued what he would find when he went to penetrate her.

Mr. Moussa pressed his knees inside her thighs, keeping them spread while his left hand held her pinned to the desk. He aimed his stiffened cock at her with his right. She felt his cock probing at her entrance. The tip slid right in. "You're all wet, you whore," he told her. And with that, he plunged himself in the rest of the way.

He pounded away at her unmercifully. His hips crashed against her rear cheeks, making her torso jolt back and forth along the top of his desk. Leslie's rationality went into deep hibernation as her reactive mind took over, relishing the fevered thrusts of her employer. She whined and moaned, she turned her head this way and that. She arched her back. Mr. Moussa's rigid member plowed back and forth incessantly, remorselessly. Part of her desperately wanted it to stop, even if for one moment. The other part was celebrating the river of ecstasy that was flowing through her body. "Ohhhhhhhhhhhhh! Ohhhhhhhhh-hhhhhhhh!" she moaned as her climax drew nearer and nearer. "Please stop! Please stop! Please stop!" she tried to plead even as her pussy relished each determined, powerful stroke.

When her orgasm came, it drove her to delirium. She cried and moaned. Her body shook. Her pussy recorded a rapid series of intense contractions. They had just subsided into levels of tolerance when she heard Mr. Moussa release a loud groan. He fucked her with deep, rhythmic, powerful thrusts. His hands tightened on her hips and his cock began to dance and throb within her. Like the flipping of a switch, her pussy surged and renewed its intense pulses of pleasure. She groaned as she felt him fill her crevasse with his hot load.

When Leslie's mind returned to conscious thought, Mr. Moussa was bent over her, his cock still lodged deep within her. She could hear his deep breaths as he recovered from his bout of passion. Her pussy trilled with pleasure giving aftershocks.

He brought himself erect and his cock slipped from her crevasse. She heard his zipper ascending. He stood there, watching her for a few seconds. He gently caressed her still burning rear cheeks, turned and left the room.

* * * * * * * * * * * * * * *

Leslie was still lying on the table, her skirt flung up around her waist, sobbing bitterly, when the door opened. She just couldn't understand why she reacted with such violent passion each time she was forced to suffer the exploitation of her helpless body. But her unhappy musings were interrupted by the sound of someone entering the room. She hurriedly rose to her feet. Her skirt fell, covering her raw bottom. She turned to see who it was. It was Faraq, Mr. Moussa's major domo.

Ever since she had started to work for Mr. Moussa, three short weeks ago, Leslie had been deathly afraid of Faraq. His face was narrow and hard, his eyes a steely gray. He wore his stark black hair short, perhaps a little more than an inch in length. He was tall and lean but carried himself in a way that advertised his strength. His narrow lips were always taut and colorless. He dressed in black shoes, black, finely pressed pants and an off white, short sleeved polo shirt. There was a fastidiousness about him that bespoke a harsh taskmaster. When he looked at Leslie, it seemed to her that he always scowled, as if he detested the very sight of her.

And now, it seemed, she was in his power.

He said nothing to her as he crossed the room. When he reached her, he crouched down and released the chain that had held her fast to Mr. Moussa's desk and reconnected it to her free ankle. He stood up, took hold of the hair in the back of her head and began to march her towards the door.

Leslie stumbled along as best she could, the chain confining the length of her steps. Faraq kept her at a quick pace as he propelled her down the hall. Leslie was too frightened to say anything or to make any objection as to how he was treating her. Faraq had left in place the handkerchief that Mr. Moussa had stuffed in her mouth, and so there was little she would have been able to say anyway. She had hoped that he was taking her to her room, but they passed the stairs that led to the upper floors. Instead, when they came to the stairs that led to the basement of the building, a place where she had never been, they started to descend them.

Being taken to what seemed to Leslie as the dungeon of the house, propelled Leslie to attempt speech. "P,please, where are you taking me?" she tried to say, but the words came out all muffled and garbled. Faraq ignored her and brought her down, down, down, until they reached the bottom of the stairs.

The stairs emptied out into a long corridor. It was pitch black. Faraq flipped a light switch on the wall and a series of naked light bulbs, some twenty feet apart, lit up. The walls were made of rough stone and the ceilings were slightly arched, giving the corridor the aspect of an ancient passageway. Leslie was still barefoot, and the stone floor was damp and cool. They recommenced their march.

The Moussa mansion was large, consisting of three independent wings. Mr. Moussa's office, and the reception room to the house, was in a central hub. One wing went off to the left and held the kitchen and the family and formal dining rooms. Above that were servant's quarters. The second wing contained Mr. Moussa's extensive library, a salon for entertaining, a gentlemen's room with lounging chairs for smoking cigars and drinking of whiskey or tea depending on the company, and a regulation sized billiards table. There was also what was called the day room, the private preserve of Mrs. Moussa, often referred to as her salon. The family bedrooms were on the second floor.

The third wing went off to the right and contained a small gym, a recreation room where the children when they were younger used to entertain their friends, a game room full of electronic toys and a private theater. Upstairs were the guest rooms. One of these rooms had been Leslie's.

The basement corridor under each one should have gone out in unconnected spokes. Therefore, Leslie was confused when they came to near the end of the corridor to see another corridor going off to the right. She could not see down this corridor because, after it went about twenty feet, it was sealed off by ancient looking bricks in the middle of which was a large, solid steel door. The rust covered door looked as ancient as the bricks. Leslie noticed, however, that a new, shiny, heavy duty lock had been installed on it recently as well as shiny, new steel hinges.

Faraq maneuvered Leslie down the hall and brought her up to the door. It was about seven feet tall and five feet wide. When she saw Faraq remove a key from his pocket and move to unlock the door, a chill went through her.

What Leslie didn't know was that the Moussa mansion had been built upon the former site of a thirteenth century fortress. The still intact chambers of its dungeon had been uncovered when they were excavating for the house. Most of the structures had decayed beyond repair, but this corridor had been preserved. When the rest of the basements were constructed, workmen ran some electric lines down it, some plumbing, had relined the walls with new brick and added a ventilation system. It had been mostly disused for the last twenty five years, but a new use had been found for it.

At the moment that Faraq swung the large door open, Leslie was seized with panic. "Noooooooooooooo!" she screamed through her gag. She began to struggle and tried to twist away from the hand in her hair. Faraq just grabbed it tighter and yanked her along, flicking on the central lights as he passed the switch. Her screams echoed off of the stone walls. She lost her balance and fell. Faraq had to drag her the last thirty or so feet to her destination. There was another door, also made of steel, smaller than the first. It too had a new lock and hinges. Faraq unlocked it. It opened outwards and he swung it open. He dragged the still screaming and struggling Leslie over the transom and into the room.

Faraq pulled Leslie up to her knees. She looked around frantically. The room was large, about 40' by 30'. The ceiling was high, about 12'. A soft, dark red and black rug had been put down on the floor. A mattress had been placed on the floor with its head into the wall shared by the corridor outside. In one corner of the room was a brand new, white port-a-potty. In the other was an unenclosed shower. Under the shower was tiled, a drain in the middle of it, and a three inch high lip all around a three foot square area to prevent water from escaping into the rest of the room. There was a sink, a dark mahogany armoire and a nightstand next to the bed. An antique, darkly stained, oak dresser stood along the far wall together with some wooden chairs. The armoire was locked with a large padlock. There was a small lamp on the nightstand. A small, dim light bulb on the ceiling lit the room.

Along the wall to the right of the doorway was an ominous looking cabinet, also locked and a few feet down from it, hanging down from the ceiling, about four feet out from the wall was a steel chain. At the end of the chain was a pair of closely linked, leather handcuffs.

Leslie shivered with fright. It was clear that this was to be her prison. It also seemed clear that this cell her been especially designed for her. Now she knew why it had taken so long to get her out of prison. They had needed the time to get all this together. That they had been able to do this within a few days said much about Faraq's efficiency.

She wondered how long she would have to stay down here, alone and locked away. There was no way to tell. The presence of the shower and toilet did not comfort her.

Having given Leslie a good, long look at her new home, Faraq yanked her to her feet. He released his grip on her hair and then unlocked her hand cuffs. When he released the chain from around her ankles, Leslie made a mad dash for the door. Faraq was quicker than her, though, and he rose and shot out his hand, taking a hold of her hair and dragged her back. He slapped her twice across the face, vicious, painful slaps that made Leslie screech with pain and then threw her down on the bed. He slammed the door to the room closed, locked it with the key and put the key in his pocket.

While Leslie lay sobbing on the bed, he went to the cabinet and unlocked it. He removed a three foot long leather riding whip. Without announcing his intention, he brought it down firmly across Leslie's rear end. Her body jerked and she screamed again. She hustled away from him, staring at him with fear and wonder. He remained motionless.

In a cold, calm but stern voice, he told her, "Miss Harrington, this is your new room. I don't have to tell you by now that your status here has undergone a significant change. You are a prisoner here as much as you were in the woman's prison, although I might say that your accommodations are a bit more comfortable. If you wish to avoid the whip, you will do as you are told without question and without hesitation. You have proven yourself a whore and you will be treated as one. At the end of every day, you and I shall have a little session where I will administer corrections for your errors. Failure to obey and failure to please will incur the harshest consequences.

Leslie quailed as she took in the cruel factotum's words. She was to be treated as a whore. Did that mean what she thought it meant? Faraq had said she would be judged by how well she pleased. Pleased who and how? Was Mr. Moussa's fucking of her just an introduction to her new role as his fuck toy?

"You have already earned a whipping by your struggle to avoid being brought here and your attempt to escape," Faraq continued. "Do not compound it now by disobedience."

Tears were flowing down Leslie's face. "A whipping! He's going to give me a whipping! Oh my god!" she thought frantically. She began to whine. She pulled at the handkerchief stuffed in her mouth so that she could beg for mercy.

"Get you hands away from that!" Faraq shouted. "Who told you you could take that out?"

Leslie shook her head miserably indicating, no one.

"Get up off the bed and take off those clothes!" Faraq ordered.

Leslie hesitated to obey, but when she saw the fury growing in Faraq's cold eyes, she hurriedly rose to her feet, unbuttoned her blouse and tossed it on the bed. She reached behind her and undid the button to her skirt and then slid it down her hips. Trembling, naked, she crouched down, picked it up and placed it on the bed next to her blouse.

"Come here!" Faraq ordered.

Cringing in fear, Leslie stepped slowly over towards him. She had to go around the foot of the bed to reach him.

Faraq pointed to the toilet. "Use it!" he spat. "I don't want you peeing on the floor when I whip you."

Leslie emitted a miserable moan. She crept slowly to the port-a-potty, pulled up the lid to the seat and sat down on it. And she sat, and she sat, and she sat. Nothing came out. She was too scared.

"Let me tell you, Miss Harrington," Faraq said menacingly, "if you don't pee in the next 30 seconds, I will add to your punishment. And if you pee while I'm whipping you, it will be even worse."

Releasing a sob, Leslie concentrated madly on pushing some water from her bladder. She pushed and pushed and pushed. She felt her blood pressure rise. It felt like her head was going to pop off. Seconds were ticking by at an alarming rate. Having Faraq's cold eyes on her wasn't helping matters. She kept pushing and pushing. And then, when she had just about given up hope, she felt the tell tale tingle that denoted the imminent release of water. It came out in a few drops at first. Then a few more. She pushed again and it released in a steady jet.

She breathed a sigh of relief as she listened to the tinkle beneath her. Her heart was pumping hard and she felt dizzy from the strain. Her relief was short lived. For when she looked up, she saw Faraq watching her coolly, tapping the three foot long whip in his hands on his thigh.

When her water trailed off, Leslie took a few sheets of toilet paper and brushed it along her divide. There was a greasiness there that she had not anticipated, but then realized that it was Mr. Moussa's seed seeping out of her. It was a stark reminder of what it would mean to be the household whore. Who else would she have to fuck? All of them? Surely not all of them!

She tossed the paper in the toilet and pressed the lever that sent the water whooshing into the back tank. Slowly, she got up from the toilet and went to the sink. Slowly, ever slowly, tears of fear running down her face, as if she could delay her appointment with Faraq's whip forever, she took the bar of white soap and washed her hands. Then slowly, as slowly as she could, she dried them with the little towel that was hanging there. When she was done, she put it back, and then turned to face her oppressor.

All of her wanted to fall to her knees and beg him for mercy. Didn't anyone in this foul land have an ounce of mercy for her? She couldn't understand how all this could be happening. How could it be true that within the next minute she would be howling and wailing while this cold, cruel man was belaboring her body with a whip? It all seemed so unreal. And was she really in the bowels of Mr. Moussa's mansion? Was it all some bad dream?

Faraq didn't say anything to her. He merely raised his hand and urged her over. Gritting her teeth, suppressing a sob, a chill running through her whole body, Leslie edged herself closer. When she was standing under the chain that led down from the ceiling she stopped.

Faraq placed the whip under his arm and took hold of her right wrist. She did not resist him when he raised it and enclosed it in one of the leather handcuffs. She did not resist him when he imprisoned the other one, although her knees went weak and her stomach turned sour. The chain led up to the ceiling, through a small wheel, to the wall where it went through another small wheel and fell towards the floor. Faraq grabbed the end of the chain by the wall and gave it a tug, pulling Leslie's hands up over her head. He gave it another tug and she was up on her tip toes. A third tug and her toes were in the air.

Leslie squealed as she felt her weight pull down on her confined wrists. Faraq bent down and she felt a strap going around her ankles. It was tied off and then brought down to a ring in the floor where it was pulled taut and fastened. She was totally immobile and would be unable to dodge or to try and avoid any of his blows. Leslie whimpered and her body shivered. She closed her eyes, not wanting to witness her own torture.

Faraq reached around her head and worked the handkerchief out of her mouth. It was not a very efficient gag anyway and, in moments of extreme distress, a victim could swallow it and choke to death. If he wanted to kill her, he would just do it. He tossed it aside and went back to the cabinet.

Leslie could feel her lips trembling. Faraq had moved behind her and she could not see what he was doing. The answer came when he returned. He carried a wide strap that had attached to it a thick, leather prong. Leslie opened her mouth meekly when he presented it to her knowing that resistance was futile. She mewed while he buckled it behind her head. The strap went under her chin, pulling her mouth closed tightly. It was so tightly sealed that only the most violent screams would emerge, and them as only muted whines. Faraq had no interest, at least today, in hearing her scream.

When Faraq stepped away from her, Leslie knew that her torment was about to begin. "There will be fifteen strokes," he told her coldly. "The first five are for general purposes, to initialize deep in your brain your duty to be obedient in all things. Five will be for struggling outside the door and then trying to run away. Two is for trying to remove your gag without permission. The last three are for taking your time in washing up. I'm sure you will do better next time."

"Fifteen strokes!" Leslie screamed inwardly. "Oh my god! I'll never be able to stand it! It's too cruel! It's too unfair!" Faraq was behind her. His disembodied voice, announcing her cruel sentence, was like a harbinger of doom. She did not see him raise his arm. She did not see him move it forward, but she heard the whip buzz through the air. She was about to scream, "Wait!" when a line of fire erupted across her buttocks. Her body shuddered and jerked. She drew in her breath prefatory to a scream. The second stroke landed immediately after the first. It landed across the back of her thighs. It burned so intently that she momentarily lost her ability to breath. Her eyes rolled back and her chest heaved. The next blow scoured her lower back, just above her hips. Its sting went through her like a viper's bite.

Faraq paused. He waited. Leslie's body was shaking as she tried to recover her breath. It took her a moment. And then she screamed. The sound barely emerged from behind her gag.

She was still screaming when he crossed in front of her. When she saw him, she began shaking her head. Her eyes pleaded for mercy. Tears were streaming down her face. Her eyes widened when she saw his arm raised backwards. The whip came forward so fast that her eyes could not keep up with it. It struck across her breasts before she even knew it. Her body stiffened again, convulsed in her bindings and again, a high pitched, barely audible squeal emerged from her gagged lips. Two more blows followed in quick succession, tearing across her flat, taut belly and the front of her immobile, defenseless thighs.

Faraq waited until she had fully absorbed the blows. When her body stopped twitching and the squeal subsided, he went around back behind her again.

Although he took especial enjoyment in delivering a hellish suffering to this creature who had defiled his master, Faraq went about his task slowly and without passion. He belabored her back and rear again, and again across the back of her thighs. Her screams renewed. He returned to the front. When she was ready, he gave her three more. Again her body shook and contorted, again the barely audible high pitched screams emerged from her mouth. There were three more to go.

Calmly, he stepped back to the cabinet. He placed the whip on its hook and picked out a heavy, four foot long cane. It had no curve to its top, but was designed with a grip on its end so that it could be wielded more easily. There was no sense in waiting for Leslie's sobs to expire. She would be sobbing for a long while yet. But he gave it about thirty seconds. Then, he let the cane fly.

It struck her across her lower back, just above her kidneys, impacting the muscles there. It landed with a loud, 'thump!' Leslie's sobs resolved into a deep, heavy moan. He moved to her front. She looked at him, despair and futility in her eyes. Her nose crinkled and her features, those that could be seen above the wide, leather strap across her mouth, sagged. He reared his hand back and delivered the fourteenth blow. It struck right across the front of her thighs. As she sobbed in misery, he crossed back behind her and gave her a blow across her plump, rear cheeks. He made sure he put his all into it due to the nature of his soft target. It made a loud, 'thump!' as it landed and Leslie's body convulsed and shook for the final time.

Leslie continued to moan and sob while he replaced the cane into the cabinet. He stepped behind her and removed a shiny, gold case from his pants pocket. He opened it and took out a short cigarette with a black tipped filter. They were Turkish, the only brand he ever smoked. He tapped the filter end on his cigarette case twice and then slid the case back into his left pocket. He had a gold plated butane lighter in his right. He removed it, pressed it with his thumb, and a short, brilliant flame erupted. He lit his cigarette and put the lighter back from whence it had come.

The cigarette was short but slow burning. He sat down in one of the chairs, inventorying Leslie's tormented body with his eyes. She was still moaning, although the moans were becoming lower and lower. Her back was to him. There was something eminently satisfying in seeing the American girl's wounds.

He had detested her the first moment he had laid eyes on her. He despised her easygoing ways, the way she assumed that everyone should applaud her voluptuous frame, her innocent mien. And he despised all that she represented, the presumptuous and proud American nation, its wealth and military power, its arrogance and greed. Not that he had sympathies for any of the Islamic madmen with their so called holy war. Their hypocrisy and affected moral superiority sickened him.

He let out another large cloud of bluish grey smoke and looked upon his handiwork with immense satisfaction. Sweat was dripping off of her in sheets. Her forlorn moans were delightful. Every once in a while, her body twitched once or twice and then came back to rest.

After a few minutes, when the cigarette neared its end, Faraq went to the toilet and pinched off its ash. He stripped the remaining paper away so that any residual tobacco would fall into the water. He placed the filter in his pocket for later disposal.

Going back to the cabinet, he began to remove the things he would need for Leslie's next lesson in discipline. These were a series of straps of various lengths and thickness, a leather sheath and a seven inch long cylinder with a bulbous head and a ring on its flat base. When they were assembled on the bed, he returned to his victim.

He lowered the chain holding Leslie aloft until her feet were flat on the ground. She looked at him with doleful eyes as he removed her gag. She fell limply against him when he freed her wrists from their confinements. He held her until she was steady and then told her to turn around.

Her body was covered with angry, red stripes, six on each side. Where she had been struck with the cane was more of a scarlet color. "Stand still," he told her, "or we'll start all over again."

Leslie stood there unsteadily. Her body felt limp and her knees were weak. Her wounds burned and her muscles throbbed where she had been struck by the cane. It took all of her effort to obey. All she wanted to do was collapse to the floor.

Before Faraq had joined Mr. Moussa's service, he had spent five years with the secret police. He was well familiar with all the methods of tormenting the human body. All it took was a call to his former colleagues to obtain the tools for the American girl's subjugation. He already knew how to use them.

He stepped over to the bed and retrieved a leather strap and the black, leather sleeve. Going behind Leslie, he took hold of her arms and pulled them together behind her. He placed them palm to palm. He ran a strap around her wrists, between them and around them again. Then they went under her thumbs, pressing her palms together, then over her thumbs. After tying them off, he ran the ends over her fingers, forcing them together and tied it off again. The strap was tight enough to hold everything together, but not so tight that it would cut off her circulation. It was a difficult art to master, one that, unfortunately, had required much trial and error.

Leslie stood there docilely, letting him do whatever he wanted. It was when he pulled the leather sleeve up over her hands, up past her elbows and almost all the way to her shoulders that she became concerned. Of course, by then it was too late. Faraq quickly pulled up the zipper that closed the sheath tightly around her arms, forcing them so close that her elbows almost touched. Leslie whined at the pain to her shoulders while he laced together the top and tied it off tightly.

Faraq looked upon his work admiringly. Leslie's shoulders were pulled back painfully. Her arms were locked straight and true behind her. There would be more to do, but it was time for a little break.

He took hold of Leslie's shoulders and spun her around. He looked appreciatively into her troubled eyes. Her breasts were jutting out nicely. She was a little over a half a head shorter than him and her breasts were at a convenient level for his hands to reach up and seize them. She whimpered while he caressed and massaged them. He took hold of her stiffened nipples and pulled them upwards, forcing the girl on her toes. He let her whimper there a while and then lowered her slowly. Then he leaned over and one by one, took her teats into his mouth, suckling them, running his tongue over them, giving them bites painful enough to make the girl jump.

She was a beautiful girl with a magnificent body. It had been a long time, two years since he had been with the secret police, that he had had a body as desirable as this at his untrammeled disposal. Her foolish sin had placed her at his mercy. And what was so wonderful about it was that she was not some ignorant Arab girl picked up randomly from the streets as he had done so many times in the past. She was a citizen of the Great Satan, the despoiler of the Arab world. She would pay for her country's sins. He would see to that.

He reached behind her head and unbuckled the gag. Her lips were trembling when he pulled the thick leather prong from her mouth. He tossed it on the bed. He was not done with it. He put his hands on her shoulders and pressed her to her knees. He lowered his fly and removed his already hardened cock. He did not have to tell her what to do. With a high pitched whine, she leaned forward and took it into her mouth.

That was another thing about those Arab girls. They had to be taught to suck cock. Some of them were so shocked that such a filthy thing would be demanded of them that it took several long sessions of the whip to get them to open their mouths. It often took them weeks to get good at it.

The few American and European girls who had passed through their hands were another story entirely. They were only too happy to engulf the cocks of their tormentors if only to interrupt their agonies. And they all seemed to know how to do it well.

Leslie was no exception. She subsumed his cock between her lips and washed it with her tongue. She began to suckle it softly as she moved her head backwards and forwards. She was taking her time, making sure she got it right, anxious to please. As well she should be.

Leslie's gut wrenched when she understood what was being demanded of her. This man had caused her more pain than she would ever have thought her body could tolerate. Her red stripes still burned and her wounds from the cane were throbbing. And she knew, from the binding he had just administered, that he had more torment in mind for her.

Her mind had already formed a separation between all of her prior life and her life to come. One was before her whipping and the other was after. The same person did not exist on both sides of that divide.

Yet she absorbed his cock into her mouth without hesitation. She would give him the best blow job she was capable of. It was not that she thought he deserved it, or was foolish to think that her best efforts would somehow assuage his cruelty. No, it was more basic than that. It was that she feared what he would do if he came to believe that she was holding anything back, being less than enthusiastic, not giving the best that she could give. He had become like a force of nature to her. More than human. A demon who had taken possession of her soul. Her fear of him had become so magnified, that she knew that she had to adore him like a god or face terrible consequences.

Faraq let his hands rest gently on Leslie's bobbing head. He closed his eyes and concentrated on the moist heat, the active tongue, the pursed lips. He let his need slowly build. He was in no rush. And he knew that the girl would remain at her task until she dropped from exhaustion if he so demanded.

When Leslie heard Faraq moan with pleasure, she took this as a signal to accelerate her efforts. He began a low hum as her lips traversed up and down his stiff pole. His hands grasped her head just a little bit firmer. His hips began to rock in time with her motions. When he released a low groan, she reared her head back and suckled the head of his prick, flicking the tip with her tongue, running it around the sleek head. When she pushed it past the fold at the end and ran it across the tip of the tender flesh inside, his body shuddered. Then she knew it was time.

She would think long and hard on it later. There would be plenty of time to do so. The experience of being on her knees to him, of being helplessly bound, globally in his control, and having his hot meat in her mouth, hearing his moans of pleasure, ignited her lusts. She pressed her knees together tightly. She began to issue moans of her own. Her breasts became tight and hot. Her nipples turned as rigid as nails. She started to yearn for the taste of his salty seed, to feel his meat jump and throb within her mouth. Her heart was pounding, her brain was on fire. She couldn't move her head fast enough, make her lips tight enough, make her tongue long enough.

And then he came. He gripped her head tightly. His spume jetted into her mouth. She drank it down hungrily. He moaned, she moaned. He was pistoning his cock back and forth, she was striving to match it.

A feeling of joy filled her as his motions wound down. She suckled on his cock lazily, drawing out every drop of his salty flow, extending as long as she could the aftershocks of his climax.

His motions came to a stop and he slid his softening cock from her mouth. Leslie was out of breath. A feeling of contentment flowed through her. And then she looked up.

Faraq's steely eyes were peering down at her. It was then that what had just happened emerged in her conscious mind. She felt sickened with shame. To have taken pleasure from her abuser, to have had her passion stoked by the man's callous rape of her mouth was the most perverted thing she could think of. There was something wrong with her, she knew it. She began to cry again. It was like some horrible nightmare where some evil spirit had taken control of her. She was going insane. She knew it, she just had to be!

He was amused by her consternation. Her reactions were not that unusual. Stimulated by the pheromones exuded by his loins, the tactile sensation of a hot penis in her mouth, her nudity, her powerlessness, the contagiousness of his passion, all these things often overrode a woman's natural revulsion against being used against her will. We are still essentially animals, after all, and the sexual impulse is quite strong in all of us, not withstanding the shame we might feel when it overflows its civilized bounds.

He replaced his glowing tool and zipped up his pants. She seemed to him to know that the next phase of her torment was to commence as he heard her unhappy whine. He scooped up her gag from the bed and reinstalled it in her mouth, buckling it tightly behind her head. He took a handful of her hair and pulled her to her feet. He pushed her over to the foot of the bed. It was just a mattress and box spring on top of a metal frame. It came up a little more than two and a half feet from the floor. The mattress was covered with a white, cotton sheet. He ordered her to kneel on the bed and to lean over, putting her forehead on the mattress and spreading her legs.

It was important now for everything to go on in the right order. He picked up the cylindrical object and checked its settings. He thought about putting it on low, but then selected medium instead. He crouched down behind her and rubbed his hand over her exposed slit. He chuckled to himself when he found it well lubricated. Applying the nose of the object to the gap between her denuded love lips, he slid the object in.

Leslie felt the object push aside the tender membranes of her canal. It filled her uncomfortably. It was wider than a prick and cool. It had a prong on its end that slid over her pleasure bud. She knew that the object could only have a nefarious purpose. Her body cringed at the threat that it presented. And she was ashamed not only that her crevasse had been ready to accept it, but also that the cruel man had discovered it to be so.

"Get up!" she heard him say. Trembling, she crawled off the bed and rose back to her feet. She felt him clip something to the end of the sleeve that held her hands and arms so cruelly bound. He turned her body so that she was facing him. Her eyes sought for any sign of mercy on his face. She saw none.

Her body trembling with fear, she spread her legs at his command. He crouched down between them. He took hold of the straps that dangled from her confined hands and she could feel him threading them through something on the bottom of the thing he had put inside her. He pulled them forward, ran them up between her breasts and placed them over her shoulders, one on either side of her neck. He turned her around again and threaded the ends through some buckles at the top end of the sheath around her arms. She felt him pulling on them, first one, and then the other. Her hands were pulled downwards and the device was shoved even deeper in her quim. The straps ran tightly over her clit, pressing the prong down hard against it. She could feel the pressure on her shoulders. He went back and forth between the one and then the other, pulling them tighter and tighter, until her back began to arch. She gave out a groan of dismay as she felt him tying off the ends.

"Is he going to leave me like this?" she worried unhappily. She uttered a futile plea from behind her gag, but he merely pushed her back towards the bed. He picked up something from it and turned her to face him. He had two small devices in his hands. He pulled and teased at her left nipple until it was firm and tall and then applied one of the devices to it. It had a hole in its center and her nipple lodged inside. He turned a dial around the hole and it got smaller and smaller until her nipple was caught painfully. It began to sting even as he moved to her other breast.

Leslie's knees went weak and a sickening feeling went through her body as she felt the other device being applied. She whined and shook, making her breast shimmer in his hand. He took hold of her nipple between his thumb and forefinger and gave it a brutal twist. "Stay still!" he spat out at her. Fearful of even worse punishment, she stilled herself while a vision of hours and hours of upcoming torment ran through her head.

When he was done, he pressed down on the devices with the palms of his hands. The devices had sharp teeth on the sides closest to her skin and she could feel the tips prick at her. "Ohhhhhhhhhhh, please don't do this!" she moaned. He paid the murmur emerging from her mouth no attention.

Pulling on the strap that ran between her breasts, he brought her closer to the bed. He pushed her until she was forced to kneel on it. Then he guided her up further to its head. Once her feet were just over the edge of the bed, he pushed her over frontward. He held on to the straps that connected to her confining sleeve, lowering her slowly. When her breasts came into contact with the sheet covered mattress, the points on the terrible devices he had installed pressed in sharply on her areolas. She whined intently and tried to pull off of them by arching her back, but his heavy hand pressed on her neck, forcing her down again.

He worked quickly after that. He reached between her thighs and activated the cylinder lodged in her quim. It began an intense vibration. He strapped her thighs tightly together just above the knees. He went down to her ankles and pushed them together. He tied them parallel to each other, ankle to ankle. Taking her feet, he doubled them back towards her head. He tied them off to the strap around her thighs, pushing them down firmly as far as they would go. Leslie moaned as she felt the immediate strain on her thighs. As a final touch, he ran straps back from the sides of her gag to the sheath around her arms and tied them to a ring in its middle. This lifted her head up and prevented her from moving it from side to side.

Leslie was, for all practical purposes, completely immobile. She was compacted as tightly as a woman could be. She whined and struggled at her bonds and called out through her gag rabid supplications not to be left like this. The prongs were digging deeply into her breasts. Her muscles were strained all over. The gag had been pulled even deeper into her mouth. And the buzzing in her crevasse was starting to drive her mad.

Faraq stood and took in his handiwork. They often left girls like this in the old days. It made them docile and compliant thereafter. They had used dildos then too, of course, but this one had a feature that he hadn't seen before and he was curious on how well it would work. He took out another cigarette and waited.

Leslie knew that he was behind her and watching. As long as she was still in the room there was still a hope that he wouldn't leave her alone in this hellhole, bound into a cruel immobility. She knew that she couldn't stand it for very long. The only things she could move were her toes, her eyes and her hips slightly from side to side. "Why is he doing this?" she asked herself frantically. "I'll do anything he wants! I'll fuck him, I'll suck his cock! I'll be his slave! Please, please, God, don't let him leave me like this! Please!"

The incessant buzzing in her pussy was beginning to drive her lusts. It vibrated against her clit, stoking her desires. She knew that if it kept on, eventually she would come. "Maybe that's what he's waiting for," she thought hopefully. "He's going to stand there and watch me come and come and...."

It was then that it struck her. A fierce jolt of electricity exploded from the device in her quim. She released a long, piteous scream. The jolt lasted about three seconds. Her whole body tensed as if it could burst its bonds. When it stopped she broke out into woeful sobs.

Faraq saw her body jump. It had worked fine. He took a last drag off of his cigarette, blowing the blush grey smoke toward the ceiling and then twisted out the lit end into the toilet. It made a little hiss when it struck the water. He put the butt in his pocket.

Leslie was now way beyond distraught. "...eeeeeease!" she screamed. "...eeeeeeeeeease! ...eeeeeeeeeeesae!" She was screaming at the top of her lungs. She pulled and tugged desperately at her bonds. The only result was to grind the teeth of the device on her nipples deeper into her breasts.

"....on't ...eave ...eee ...ike ...is!" she tried to shout. "I... ...egging ...ou! ...eeeeeeeease! ...eeeeeeeeeease!" she screamed.

Out of the corner of her eye she saw him walk to the door. "This can't be happening! This can't be happening! Oh, god! Oh god!" she thought, a fervid panic forming in her mind. "...eeeeeeeeeease!" she screamed again.

Faraq noted her distress with satisfaction. Her sounds were basically indecipherable, in fact, barely audible, but he knew what she was saying. As a final touch, he went to the sides of the bed, connected straps to rings on the sides of the sheath over her arms and tied them off to rings in side of the bed frame. This would prevent her from rolling to her side to relieve the pain in her breasts.

Stepping back and taking in his handiwork, he could see her muscles straining and rippling. The straps holding her gag in place pulled her head back as far as it would go, forcing it to tilt backwards and directing her vision high up on the cold, stone wall in front of her. Her feet arched and her body shook. Her back had a slight curve to it and her shoulders quivered. He could hear the merciless buzzing of the device in her purse. He had been told that the battery would last at least six hours.

He paused for a moment at the door. He saw her widened, frightened, hysterical eyes peering sideways at him. He gave her a small, ironic smile. Then he flicked out the light and stepped out.

CHAPTER SIX

When the door to Leslie's cell shut, it extinguished all light and sent a slight echo through the room. When she heard the faint sound of the outer door being slammed shut, sealing her prison from all contact with the outside, a wave of profound and soul wrenching sorrow passed through her.

Her eyes strained to pick up any image in the blackness that surrounded her. She tried to remember what the room looked like, tried to recall her position in it. She tried to imagine her remote, isolated, inescapably bound body in relation to the rest of the house. There were people up there, walking around in the daylight, doing their daily tasks. How many of them even knew that she had been locked away in its cold, dark dungeon? Did Mr. Moussa know? Did Mrs. Moussa? How long would Faraq keep her like this? How would she ever stand it?

She stirred her body slightly. The fierce pinpoints on her breasts tore at her skin. She realized that she would have to remain completely still. But she knew that she would not be able to. Sooner or later, the fiendish device in her pussy would shock her again. And then her body would jump and shake and tense beyond her control. It took her a few minutes to realize that she was still crying. She tried to stop it, knowing that it would just drive her mad.

"I can do this! I can do this!" she repeated to herself. "I'll try and think of something, anything to keep my mind off it. I'll try and pretend I'm somewhere else. At home, in my bed, safe and sound."

But the buzzing in her wounded crevasse would not let her. Every time she was about to take her mind somewhere else, it crept insidiously into her consciousness. Her pussy began to tingle. She could feel her passions start to rise again.

She tried to fight it. The last shock she had received came just as her lusts had started to boil. She feared desperately that

that was what had triggered it. She had to fight off the demonic stimulation of her defenseless canal! She just had to! Her mind strained to push the feelings aside.

It did not work. Her lusts continue to grow and grow. The vibrations against her love button sent an agonizing thrill through her. She wriggled her hips. She bit down on the gag in her mouth. She clamped her eyes closed as tightly as she could. She tried to will it to stop. But it just went on and on and on.

Then she could fight it no more. Her body began to trill with pleasure. Her thighs started to quiver. Her feet arched. Her body became taut. She moaned.

She groaned when her pussy began its steady, ecstatic convulsions and her body shook. Her breasts were forced into a reverberating motion that sent jolts of pain into her that mixed with the messages of pleasure. She groaned staccato-like, relishing each violent throb within her.

When her orgasm subsided, her pussy continued to trill as the remorseless buzzing went on. She was relieved that the shock had not been triggered by her rising or completed lusts. But she knew that it was coming. "It has to be coming," she thought frantically. "It has to be co…."

And then it struck again. She screamed and her body jumped. It was a pain like she had never experienced, had never known could exist. Her chest heaved as she sobbed and sobbed. She desperately tried to stop as each deep breath sent another jolt of pain to her through her breasts. She had just started to recover, when the fierce shock deep within her came again, followed by another a few seconds later. She sobbed and sobbed and sobbed for many minutes. When she finally stopped, she realized that her lusts were rising again. She bit down on her gag and moaned.

* * * * * * * * * * * * * *

Upstairs, later, Faraq was finishing his dinner. He had spent some time on the telephone, making arrangements about some of Mr. Moussa's deals. He had discussed certain security arrangements with Mrs. Moussa. He had made one of his inspections of the family cars to make sure that they had not been tampered with. His thoughts turned, from time to time, to the American slut imprisoned in the basement. The image of her body convulsing when the first shock hit her was an enticing one. He almost wished that he could have stayed the entire time. The procedure, however, called for total isolation of the victim and so that wouldn't do. He would watch her another time, when her suffering was less for her edification than for his amusement.

Sitting at the kitchen table, he always took his meals there, sipping the dregs of his thick coffee, he looked at his watch. It had been three hours. That was certainly enough time to show the girl who was boss. He didn't want to drive her insane. She would be worthless then. No, he wanted a totally subservient slut who would jump at his every command without hesitation, would 'accommodate' the other members of the house enthusiastically and without complaint, and would provide a beneficial source of relaxation and amusement for Mr. Moussa.

He had enough pull with the local governmental bureaucrats to delay her trial for many months, maybe years. When she wore out her usefulness, Captain Khalil and his virulently cruel mistress could have her.

Leslie was in the midst of another explosive orgasm when he opened the outer door to her prison and she did not hear it. She was still frantically trying to control her heaving chest when the door to the inner cell opened and the light was flicked on. She cast a piteous, supplicative glance at Faraq as he entered. The sudden influx of light blinded her. He went past her quickly, out of her line of vision. She waited desperately for the feel of his hands untying her and was bitterly disappointed when he did not.

It had been an anguish filled three hours. Her muscles had gone way past soreness and into a deep, dull ache. Her pussy was worn and tired. Her mind was strained to the point of psychosis, fearing that any given second her pussy could explode into excruciating pain.

She heard the man light another cigarette. This signaled to her that her time of liberation had not yet come. She sobbed. She wanted to beg the man with all of her being to release her, to promise to fulfill his most scandalous wishes, to be his slave for all time, anything to win her freedom. She knew, though, that, even if she could talk to him, it would not terminate her torment one second earlier.

Having light all around her changed, somewhat, the quality of her experience. Being in the absolute darkness had been hellish, like she was floating in another dimension where she was the only living soul. Now she could see that she was right where the cruel man had left her and, by his presence, knew that she was not alone in the world.

Her pussy's responses to the interminable buzzing inside it had wound down somewhat over the last three hours. She didn't know how many orgasms she had had, but she felt that her supply had been exhausted. There was something, though, about knowing that the man who had bound her so cruelly, who had stuffed her pussy with the infernal device, was watching, that made her lusts begin to rise once more.

It was something about the shame of being naked and in his power. That and his obvious knowledge of what was going on inside her, and had been going on for the longest, longest time. And the fact that she was his to use at any time and in any way he wanted. She hated herself for it, but nonetheless could not help herself. She didn't want to be the family sex slave, but the thought of it, what they would do to her, make her do, made her blood run hot.

She knew what he was waiting for. He wanted to see her come. That thought itself was enough to stoke her fires. He wanted her to come and she had no choice but doing so. He was making her come, forcing her to come. She would not be liberated until then. As shamed as it made her feel, she had no choice but to let the agonizing vibrations inside her drive her on and on.

Leslie had gone from dreading it to wanting it. She let her mind accept the pleasures the vibrating instrument was bringing her. She thought of the cocks she had had, Jamilah, who she had made love to in the jail, the many times she had rubbed herself to pleasure. Anything to accelerate her passions. Her pussy began to burn with need. Her hips began to rock, her breathing became deep.

And then it struck her, another fierce pulse of pain from the invader in her tender recess. She screamed and her body shook. She sobbed and her mind fled into despair. She overcame it quickly, though. She knew what she had to do. She had to please her master, the man who ruled her. She had to let him see her obedience, her abject compliance with his whishes. He was all powerful; she was nothing. It was a paradigm she would have denied a few short hours ago, but three hours of incessant torture had loosened something in her mind. She was desperate to escape her predicament, and abject surrender seemed the only way out.

Faraq had finished his cigarette and tossed the end in the toilet. He had been amused to witness her reaction to the electrical shock once again. He could watch it all day. Leslie was right. He was waiting for her to come. He wanted to see her confined and helpless body wracked with passion. He closed the lid to the toilet, sat down on a chair and waited.

It did not take Leslie long to build up her lusts again. She had been resisting them all the time she had laid here, but now wanted to feel her pussy explode more than anything she had ever wanted before. She tried to squeeze the humming device with her inner muscles. She rocked her hips. She tried to grind her clit on the bed underneath her. She thought of huge, disembodied cocks, in her mouth, in her pussy, in her rear. She wanted to be filled by a hundred men, a hundred times a day.

"Come on! Come on! Come on!" she shouted in her mind. "Make me come! Make me come! Do it! Do it! Come on, now! Do it! Do it!"

Her pussy's energies were rising. Her blood was boiling. She felt it coming. "For you, master! For you! This is for you!" she thought madly. And then it came.

As far as Faraq could see, there was little difference in her reaction to the explosion of her needs to being shocked with the dildo. Her body seemed to swell and then began rocking and shaking. The only real difference was that she was not screaming. She was emitting a loud, low toned moan. It went on for about 20 seconds and then slowly abated. Her body relaxed and he could hear her sigh.

"She's had enough," Faraq thought to himself. He got up from the toilet and approached the bed. He undid the strap holding her feet to her upper thighs and then slowly let them unfold. When they were resting on the bed, he untied them and then released the strap around her thighs. At the upper part of the sleeve that confined her arms, he undid the straps that went over her shoulders. He released the straps that led to the ends of her gag. Then, after unfastening the straps that led from the sides of the sleeve around her arms to the rings on the floor, he slowly, gently, almost lovingly turned her over.

She was sobbing. He didn't blame her. They all did. What he had done to her was almost unbearable.

He could see from her frantic eyes that she was hoping that he would quickly remove the dildo before it gave her any more shocks. He took his time nonetheless. Before doing anything, he unhooked the nipple clamps from her teats. The nipples were red and would be sore for quite a while. Around them, in a little circle were angry puncture wounds, some of them trailing a little blood. Her eyes kept shifting from his face to the direction of her loins. There was a desperate, pleading aspect to them. When he nodded to her to confirm that he was about to relieve her of the infernal instrument, her eyes glowed with appreciation.

He drew the straps down from her shoulders and then pushed her legs open wide, drawing up her knees. She cooperated easily with him. She shivered with fear as he slid the straps free of the ring on the device. He took hold of the ring, looked her in the eyes and then slowly, slowly, drew it out.

When it emerged from her puss, she broke out into heavy sobs. He pushed her to her belly again and released the straps from the end of the sleeve. He released the strap at the top and zippered the sleeve open. He pulled it off of her arms, tossed it aside and undid the binding around her wrists. For the moment, he left her gag in place.

While the poor girl sobbed her heart out on the bed, he meticulously restored the implements of her torture away in the cabinet. He left it unlocked for now.

Taking a four foot long bamboo cane, he returned to the bed. He tapped her on her rear cheek. She rose from her supine position and looked at him. He pointed the cane at a point on the floor in front of the bed. She scrambled to obey him. She stood before him unsteadily, her body swaying, her eyes pointed down.

"When I command you to stand in front of me," he told her, "you are to place your hands behind your back and spread your legs. Do it now."

His voice was not loud, but it had the hard edge of command in it. Leslie complied immediately.

He tapped the floor with the cane three times. Leslie looked up at him. A look of understanding came across her face and she fell to her knees. She kept her hands behind her back and her thighs apart. She looked up at him to make sure she had performed correctly.

"Very good," he said. Her face seemed to relax, as if she was pleased with herself.

He tapped the floor three more times. Leslie looked up at him, perplexed. He just stared at her, the cane pointing to a spot in front of him. After a few seconds, it was like a light had gone off in her head. She leaned over and placed her head on the floor. "Very good," he repeated.

Her back and rear were full of red stripes. Just above her kidneys it had started to turn black and blue. Her shoulder length chestnut hair was frazzled and was pressed down where the buckle of the gag crossed it. Her wrists were crossed, palms out.

Leaving her there, Faraq walked over to the shower and turned it on. While the water warmed up, he stripped himself. He had a lean, muscular physique. Except for head and his loins, there was virtually no hair on his body. When he was naked, he snapped his fingers sharply. Leslie's head perked up and she turned to look at him. He motioned for her to rise and to come to him. She rose unsteadily, still not over three hours of harsh confinement, and approached him gingerly. He reached behind her head and unbuckled her gag. Then he took hold of her arm and pushed her under the streaming water.

Leslie blanched when the water struck her wounds. It only stung for a moment though. Once she got used to it, it felt marvelous. She obeyed him when he pushed her head under the water and reveled in the sensation of it running all over her. She had been happy to obey his commands, happy that he showed her how to behave in his presence. She was happy to finally have her mouth free.

Faraq took hold of a soft sponge and a tube of body wash and began to bathe her. He patted her gently on her wounded breasts. He ran the sponge over her belly and between her legs. He ran it down her long, naked back and over her rear cheeks. He washed each foot separately. Then he had her kneel down and shampooed her hair.

When he was done, Faraq stepped out of the shower, dried himself off quickly with a towel and then ordered Leslie to stand in front of him. He dried her thoroughly, but gently. He had placed cream rinse in her hair and he took the time to brush it out until it was straight and without knots. He tied it off behind her head.

It was so strange to Leslie to be treated so gently and with such care by the man after he had treated her so cruelly. There was a gentle rhythm to his actions that was comforting. All she knew was that he was in command now and she would do whatever he said. She never wanted to reexperience the torment she had just been through. Never.

He allowed her to use the toilet, something she was very grateful for. Then Faraq snapped his fingers and pointed to the floor. Leslie immediately fell to her knees and put her hands behind her back. She had not seen it when he came in because of the brightness of the light, but he had brought a covered, earthenware bowl with him. He uncovered it now and placed it on the floor before her. It was a spicy mixture of couscous and lamb. Leslie eyed it hungrily. She looked up at him. He nodded to her, and without shame, without hesitation, she leaned over and placed her face in it.

Leslie relished every bite. She gobbled up the meal quickly. She could feel the eyes of her master watching her and felt proud that she was obeying his command. At the same time, she was filled with revulsion at her cravenness. There was not much difference now between her and a slavishly loyal dog. Part of her wondered unhappily if Mr. Moussa's cruel factotum would make her crawl around on all fours and bark for him. And the worse part of it was that she knew she would do it.

She got down to the bottom of the bowl and licked the spicy sauce until it was shiny clean. Regardless of the manner of consumption, her belly felt warm and happy to be filled. It felt wonderful not to be tied up and confined.

She looked up at Faraq. He had a cloth in his hand and he wiped her messy face with it. He put it down and picked up a long, thin green bottle. He put the top to Leslie's lips and she drank long as the refreshingly cool water passed into her. He brought it back every few seconds so that she could take a breath and swallow and then he gave her more. He let her drink until she had emptied the whole thing.

Leslie kept wondering what was next. He was still naked and his long, thick cock was dangling in front of her. It wasn't hard, but it had swelled with the onset of an erection. She knew that it was inevitable that she would have to deal with it before long.

Faraq snapped his fingers and pointed to the bed. Leslie sprung to her feet and got on it. She watched as he went to the cabinet and then returned with a tube of ointment. He squeezed a dollop onto his hand and, crouching down next to the bed, spread some over the wounds around her breasts. The ointment felt soothing.

He snapped his fingers once again and pointed to a spot on the bed a little further up towards the head. Leslie took this as an order to lie down on it. She didn't know whether he wanted her face down or face up. She decided that on her back was probably what he wanted and she lay down on it. Faraq motioned his hands upwards and then out. Leslie lifted her knees and spread her legs.

"Unless I tell you otherwise," Faraq told her, his voice emotionless, "when I order you to lie on a bed, this is the position you will assume."

Leslie nodded her head in understanding.

"If I snap my fingers, like this," he said, "you will turn on your belly, come to your knees, spread your legs and raise your hips. Do it now."

Quickly, Leslie rolled to her stomach. Keeping her forehead on the mattress, she came up on her knees, spread her legs and lifted her hips as high as they would go. She was immediately conscious of the exposure of her twin entrances and understood that this was the whole point.

"When I or anyone else orders you on a bed, either on your back or your knees like this," Faraq continued, "you will immediately, with your right hand, begin to prepare your pussy for penetration. Do it now."

Leslie cringed at the words, 'anyone else'. It was a reminder that he was training her to be the house whore. She slipped her right hand down between her thighs and up over her pudendum. She began to rub the fleshy button at the peak of her crevasse with her long finger. Her pussy began to moisten right away. She slid her finger inside herself, gathering her fluids, and then smeared them over clit. Despite her earlier, prolonged session of stimulation and completions, her lust began to burn. Having her tormentor, her master, peering at her intimacies while she frigged herself, witnessing her lubrication virtually at his command, sent a message of shame right through her.

Faraq let her continue for a full minute. Satisfied at her obedience, he walked over to the cabinet and retrieved the instruments of her new confinements. He stepped up to the side of the bed and pushed aside her hair, exposing her neck. "Keep stroking yourself," he ordered her, as he closed a thick metal collar around her neck. It had rings in front and back. He took another band of steel and placed it around Leslie's left wrist. It made a loud, "Click!' when it closed.

Leslie was frantic. The band around her neck was cold and sinister. She suppressed a sob when she saw the ones that went around her wrists. When Faraq ordered her to give him her left wrist, she had thought momentarily of refusal, but the courage to challenge him fled right out of her as soon as it arose. When the bracelet clicked closed, she looked him in the face, searching for evidence of his intentions. He took hold of her right arm and closed another band around her right wrist. The wrist bands had rings on them too and she watched as Faraq attached a five inch long chain to one of them. He took hold of her other wrist, brought them both up to her neck, ran the chain through the ring on her collar and connected her steely bracelets.

Her arms were held up on her chest as if in an attitude of prayer. She felt him attach another chain to the back of her collar and, forcing her to move up towards the head of the bed, attached it to a ring in the wall.

Leslie looked up at him helplessly. He had a ferocious look in his eyes, as if he wanted to consume her. His cock was at full attention, ready to be wielded against her. She knew that he was going to fuck her and an involuntary thrill went through her body. When he knelt on the bed and began to maneuver himself between her thighs, a lump formed in her throat and her stomach quailed. Her loins burned at the thought of her upcoming use. She watched him carefully as he pushed her thighs apart with his hips, took hold of his rigid instrument and addressed it to her slippery slit. He glided its sleek head up and down it several times, tantalizing her. He then placed the head inside, moved up so that his hands were on the mattress on either side of her torso, and then slowly, slowly, slowly, eased himself the rest of the way in.

Leslie groaned with lust as she felt the cock expand her burning canal. He sunk himself to the hilt, pressing his flat, taut belly against hers. Her eyes were captured by his as if she had been hypnotized. Her thighs were trembling. When he began his motions, a wave of pleasure, tinted by her shame at her slatternly arousal, coursed through her.

He fucked her long and steady. His motions were slow, rhythmic. Leslie's heels dug deep into the bed and her hips started to rise and fall to meet his. When he leaned over, pressing his iron chest against her bound hands, and took her mouth, his hands on the side of her head, imprisoning it, a raging thrill went through her.

His pace was leisurely, but determined. Leslie's mind clouded with rapture. She came once, and then again, moaning into his mouth, her tongue writhing against his. Her legs circled around his back, pulling him in deeper, her hips thrust up seeking all of his fat, hard length.

When he came, he grunted loudly. His body tensed. His thrusts became hard and powerful. Leslie screamed and her pussy began another series of wild throbs and contractions.

He continued to stroke himself inside her well after he was spent. It was only when his prick was fully softened that he allowed himself to slide out. He said nothing to her as he dressed. He was going away again, she knew it. She would be alone once more, imprisoned deep within the bowels of the mansion, alone and in the dark. He tidied up a bit, folding the towels that he had used, closing the lid to the toilet, shutting the doors to the cabinet from whence her instruments of torment had come. As he did, he removed one more object. He brought it over to where Leslie lay and clipped it to the ring on her collar. It was a flogger with 6" long straps and a thick handle. The straps lay across her belly like evil snakes. Leslie shivered at the contact. She looked up at him miserably.

"That is for my next visit," he told her. "Think of it while you wait for me."

Leslie's face scrunched up into a mask of misery. She wanted to beg and plead not to be left alone again, but she knew somehow that any unbidden words from her mouth would trigger a ferocious response.

When the light went out and the door closed, Leslie uttered a forlorn moan. When she heard the outer door slam shut out in the hallway, she closed her eyes and brought her knees up, shrinking into a fetal position. She fought off her tears. Her pussy still simmered from the fucking Faraq had just given her and she yearned to stroke it, to take possession of it. She realized, though, that her current confinement was by way of a lesson. Her pussy did not belong to her anymore. It belonged to Mr. Moussa.

She thought of all the people who had used her in the past week, Jamilah, the cruel, heavy set Zarifa, the Queen and Captain Khalil, Mr. Moussa and now Faraq. She thought of how she had come for them all. What demon had gotten inside her, she wondered miserably, that made her succumb to their caresses, made her lusts rise rabidly as they used her. Even now, as she thought of her available, defenseless slit between her thighs, she ached to have someone, anyone touch it. Her confinements, her helplessness, her new status as a virtual sexual slave, made her pussy burn.

The knowledge that she was to be whipped again was a source of terror while at the same time, the fact that she was now a mere instrument for the pleasures of others, no matter how they obtained it, made her feel more alive than she had ever felt before. Before, her life had been sedate, planned out, serene. Now she was living on a plane of fiery intensity. Her life was out of her control, careening between one highly charged episode after another.

She castigated herself for her feelings. Although she had experienced thrills beyond her prior imaginings, she still yearned desperately to be freed. The prospect of being whipped again terrified her. Her body chilled when she thought of the agony she would have to endure. And then there was the prospect of being returned to the prison again, of a long, cruel sentence. She rebelled at the injustice of it all.

She had never thought of herself as a vulnerable person, but now she realized that she had been living under false assumptions: that somehow everything would work out, that the world was a vast, wonderful playground waiting to be explored, that her status and origins would protect her. Now she knew that none of those things were true. All along, she had been a victim waiting to happen, prey for the carnivores of the world. They had been just waiting their chance to devour her. And she had given it to them by strolling willingly into their den.

Eventually, she fell asleep. She did not dream. She was so exhausted from her travails that her mind sunk deep into oblivion. When she woke, she did not know how many hours later, it took her a few moments to understand why it was still so dark around her, why her hands were bound tight against her chest. When she remembered why, a pall of despair fell over her. There was nothing for her to do but wait.

CHAPTER SEVEN

When Leslie heard the door to her prison opening out in the hallway, her heart went into her throat. All she had been able to think of while she was lying in the darkness was that when Faraq came back, she would be whipped. The cruel instrument he had clipped to her collar had been a constant reminder to her. Its long, rough tassels brushed across her skin every time she moved. She could feel its thick, hard handle between her hands.

The door to her cell opened and the light went on. She blinked until she could adjust her eyes to it. It was Faraq again. He was carrying a tray. She watched him put it down on a small table in the corner. She began to whine when he came to her, leaned over and unclipped the whip from her collar. "Get on your knees," he said.

Suppressing a sob, Leslie obeyed. She kept her forehead down on the mattress, knowing that the cruel man wanted access to her tender posterior.

"I'm going to give you five strokes," he said, "to remind you of your duty to obey."

She wanted to tell him that she needed none, but knew that it would serve no purpose. She gritted her teeth and closed her eyes.

The hard, stiff tassels flashed across her rear. It was as if a sheet of fire had crossed them. He hit her again, and again, making her whine and cry. Twice more, the last seemingly with all his might. She sobbed and her body shook as she absorbed the blows. Her heart beat wildly and her body felt ill.

But it was over quickly. She had endured it. And even though there had been nothing suppressing her speech, she had overcome the temptation to whine and plead for mercy. In a way, she felt proud that she had endured it, as if she was recovering her strength and courage. She also knew, though, that the pain that had been administered was only a sample of what the cruel man was capable of and she resolved to be obedient in all things.

Faraq unclipped her collar from the wall and told her to get up. He put her breakfast down on the floor and snapped his fingers. Leslie fell to her knees, her arms behind her back and waited for permission to eat. He gave it to her with a nod.

It was a soft porridge mixed with raisins and flavored with cinnamon. It actually tasted good. Leslie slurped it up quickly, relishing every bit. It seemed natural today to be eating from the floor like a dog. When she was done, he wiped her face and released her hands. He left the chain dangling from one bracelet for future use.

"I will be back in half an hour," he told her. "You are to shower and wash your hair. There is some perfume in the cabinet behind the mirror over the sink. Use it under your ears, between your breasts, under your arms and on your belly above your sex. There is a razor there. Make sure that your pussy, legs and underarms are smooth. When you are done, you will kneel with your head down on the bed, your legs spread and your hands behind your back.

Faraq left without another word. Leslie scrambled to complete her tasks. She was going upstairs when he came back, she knew it, and she didn't want to do anything to miss the opportunity. She used the toilet, washed herself, shaved as instructed. It was somewhat difficult to shave her pussy. She had never done it before. It was strange to be handling it this way, pushing and pulling at the skin, tightening her labia so that she could scrape along its sides. Her confinements were always in her mind: the steel collar around her neck, the bracelets with the chain dangling from one.

It was strange, too to see her denuded lips, so child like, her slit so brazen. She knew that it would be used today, undoubtedly by Mr. Moussa and probably by Faraq too. She wondered who else. Hajib, Mr. Moussa's son? She blanched at the thought. Faraq and Mr. Moussa were one thing, but to be made available to the whims of a boy her own age seemed grotesque. And what about Jana, the daughter, or Mrs. Moussa? Surely Faraq hadn't meant them. Before she had gone to the prison, Leslie would have never thought of it. But now she knew that she had to. She dreaded being used by Mrs. Moussa who had been disdainful of her presence from day one. Now that Mr. Moussa was actually fucking her, she would be angry as a hornet. Leslie quailed at the prospect of being under her thumb.

She took the perfume, which smelled flowery and expensive, and adorned herself with it. She brushed her hair until it was smooth and shiny, cleaned everything up and put it back in its place, even putting back down the seat to the toilet. She didn't want to give Faraq any pretext to beat her. And then she climbed up on the bed, put her head down, spread her legs and put her hands behind her, crossing them at the wrist. And then, as instructed, she waited.

When Faraq came back, the first thing he did was clip the chain dangling from her right bracelet to the left, imprisoning her hands behind her back. Then he ordered her to get up and sit at the edge of the bed. He took some cream and placed it over the wounds to her breasts. They had faded somewhat but were still very evident. He ran his hands under her arms and down her legs, checking for smoothness. When he checked her pussy, he stopped at a spot just at the lower end of her right outer labia. She could feel him fingering a small amount of bristle there. Her heart began to pound and her mouth went dry.

"Lean back and spread your legs," he told her. He went to the cabinet over the sink and retrieved the razor. He applied it to the tiny area where he had found hair. He shaved it quickly. When he was done, he looked her in the eyes and told her, "There will be a punishment for that later."

Leslie suppressed a sob, but uttered no protest.

He went to the cabinet and removed a five foot long leash. He clipped it to her collar. "Come on," he said, tugging it. "Mrs. Moussa wants to see you."

Leslie had no choice but to follow where Faraq was leading her. She realized that he intended to drag her through the house naked and bound. The thought of everyone seeing her in her disgrace made her heart heavy with gloom. There were usually servants bustling all around the house during the day. They would see her shame. And then there was Hajib and Jana. And, she was to be presented to Mrs. Moussa naked! She remembered when she came into the house yesterday, when they brought her from the jail. Mrs. Moussa had called her "Whore!" If it had not been true then, it certainly was now.

Her heart raced and her belly churned as they traversed the passageway out of her prison. They passed through the outer door and then into the corridor that led to the surface levels. He marched her up the stairs. When they emerged on the ground floor, it was just as she had imagined it. One of the servants was sweeping the floor. He was an older man, tall and lean, with short, salt and pepper hair, wearing an off white colored caftan and leather sandals. He was wearing a traditional round, woven hat on his head. He stopped sweeping when he saw Leslie walking naked through the corridor and gaped at her. She could feel her heavy breasts swaying as she walked. She yearned to free her bound hands from behind her to try and cover herself up. The man's eyes went directly to her denuded loins, eying them hungrily.

From the light passing through the windows, Leslie could see that it was early in the day, well before 9 o'clock. It was the first inkling she had of what time it was since she had been sent to her underground prison.

They passed several of the maids. In the Moussa mansion, the maids wore staid white blouses that buttoned up to the neck and black skirts that went down to their calves. They were mostly young, but the house mistress was older, past middle age. She was usually dressed in a blue abaya that had a veil she pulled up whenever there were guests in the house. As Faraq pulled her into the wing in which Mrs. Moussa's salon was located, she was standing in the hallway giving instructions to a pretty maid with long, black hair, who looked all of 18 or 19 years old. They both stopped their conversation and peered at Leslie as if they had seen a ghost. Leslie clamped her trembling lips together tightly and tried to keep her eyes pointed to the floor. Tears of humiliation gathered in her eyes.

When they arrived at the door to Mrs. Moussa's salon, Faraq knocked. Leslie heard Mrs. Moussa's voice respond. Faraq opened the door and brought Leslie in.

Mrs. Moussa's salon was decorated in Arabic fashion. There were colorful tapestries and fabrics on the walls and a thick, Persian rug. The room was about 30' by 40', large enough to accommodate several guests but small enough to maintain an ambiance of intimacy.

There were no chairs in the European sense. Large pillows were distributed around the room for sitting or lying on. There was a 5' by 5' low, polished, gold inlaid table on one side. On the other was a low stool with a high backrest, well cushioned in hand woven, embroidered fabric. This is where Mrs. Moussa normally sat when she had guests, unless they were snacking at the table, and it was where she was sitting now. She was wearing a bright dress with a maroon top. The skirt was translucent with a gold backing and circled by narrow bands of muted, almost pastel, red, blue, yellow and green. It came down to her shins. The bodice had a curved neckline that showed the tops of her heavy breasts.

She was wearing stylish, bright red high heels and her face was elegantly made up, with turquoise shading on her eyelids, just enough blush to bring out the tawny color of her skin. She had long, curled lashes and her eyes were outlined in a light line of mascara. Her hair, long and black, was piled on her head in a bun at the back. It was pulled back at the sides and in the front, giving her an authoritative, business-like look. She had a long, elegant nose and almond shaped eyes. Her lips were full and covered with pinkish lipstick. Her hands were resting on the carved armrests of her stool. On her right hand was a large, gold ring with a diamond encrusted onyx crest. On her left was a large diamond wedding ring and next to that, a ring with a dark green emerald. She was wearing a bright white pearl necklace and had matching pearl earrings.

She had her legs crossed and gave Leslie a haughty, disdainful look as Faraq marched her across the room. There was a large woman dressed in a black abaya kneeling in front of Mrs. Moussa slightly to her right. She had raised her veil when Faraq had come in and she was holding it in place with a large, powerful looking hand. Her eyes were outlined in kohl. She looked over Leslie's naked body with a cold appraisal, as if she were judging her merits.

"Than you, Faraq," Mrs. Moussa said. "You may leave us now."

Being naked, bound and alone with Mrs. Moussa was just about the last thing on Leslie's list of things she wanted to do, but she knew that she had no choice. Faraq might have the authority of a master over her, but Mrs. Moussa controlled everything that went on in the house.

Faraq released the leash around Leslie's neck. Before he left, he handed Mrs. Moussa the key to Leslie's collar and bracelets. Then, without comment, he left.

There were a few moments of silence after the sound of the closing of the door while Mrs. Moussa perused Leslie's charms. Leslie was keeping her gaze down at Mrs. Moussa's feet, too embarrassed to look her in the eyes. She was conscious too, of the woman who knelt to her left and could feel her eyes crawling all over her.

After a short while, Mrs. Moussa spoke something in Arabic to the woman. She had let her veil drop and Leslie took a quick look at her face. It was soft and round and yet carried an aspect of coarseness to it. Her nose was long and broad. She had harsh looking eyes, cold and piercing. The woman said something back to Mrs. Moussa and Mrs. Moussa chuckled. The she spoke to Leslie.

"Get on your knees, whore," she said caustically.

Leslie hurried to obey. When she reached the floor, she rested her buttocks back on her calves.

"No, not like that, you lazy pig," Mrs. Moussa said. "Kneel up and spread your legs!"

Leslie rose up so that her back was straight and she spread her knees widely. There was something about Mrs. Moussa that terrified her and she suppressed a sob.

"I never want to see you standing in my presence without permission again, do you hear me, slut," Mrs. Moussa said. "In fact, from here on in, the only time I want to see you on your feet is when somebody is leading you on your leash, and then only if they tell you to get up, do you understand?"

"Y,yes, sayyadati," Leslie whined.

Mrs. Moussa laughed. "I see they taught you some manners in our prison," she said.

"Y,yes, sayyadati," Leslie replied meekly.

"I would like you to meet Sayyadati Latifah. Her name means the gentle one, but I can assure you there is nothing gentle about her. She is to be your caretaker while you are in this house. If I were you, I would obey her religiously in all things. She has considerable experience handling whores like you. She recently retired from a brothel in Tunis where the girls were, shall we say, under contract. Permanent contract. And under quite rigorous discipline. The same shall apply to you."

"Y,yes, sayyadati," Leslie moaned. She looked over at the woman. She had a sinister smile on her face.

Mrs. Moussa said something to Latifah and the older woman replied an assent. She rose from her knees, stepped over to where Leslie knelt and got back down. Leslie was kneeling about three feet away from Mrs. Moussa and Latifah was close enough that she was able to receive the key to Leslie's bonds by hand. She proceeded to unlock her collar and bracelets and toss them to the side. Leslie kept her hands behind her, not wanting to incur anyone's wrath by presumptuously moving them.

Latifah reached up and took a hold of Leslie's cheeks. She had a firm, authoritative grip. She looked deeply into Leslie's face, appraising her. She turned to Mrs. Moussa and pointed out several features around her eyes and mouth, commenting on them in Arabic. Mrs. Moussa nodded in reply.

The heavy set woman lowered her hands and captured Leslie's breasts. She massaged them and explored them, like she was assessing fruit. She put her lips to Leslie's nipples and suckled at them, bringing them into stiffness. When she was satisfied at their state of erection, she pinched them harshly, making Leslie squeal. A look of anger came across her face and she squeezed them harder, giving Leslie a harsh command. Leslie brought her lips together tightly, understanding the woman's order to keep quiet, and suppressed the moan of pain that wanted to come out.

After she released Leslie's teats, she ran her hands down her torso, drawing them across her belly. Leslie had lost a great deal of weight since her ordeal began and the woman seemed unhappy with the lack of roundness there. She said so to Mrs. Moussa who nodded again in agreement.

She felt Leslie's thighs, running her hands on the insides and measuring the smoothness of her skin. Her fleshy hand took hold of Leslie's hairless love lips, pinching them, running her palm over them, tracing her fat finger along the length of her divide. She turned and pointed something out to Mrs. Moussa who murmured a reply.

The former madam went behind Leslie, feeling her back and rear. She slid her fingers between the cheeks of Leslie's ass and inserted a finger about a quarter inch inside the dainty hole there. She pushed Leslie down until her forehead was on the rug and made her turn around so that her posterior was presented to the mistress of the house. She explained something to Mrs. Moussa while pushing her finger in and out of Leslie's anus, and she replied briefly in Arabic. She let her hand flow over her exposed love lips while saying something to Mrs. Moussa. She took hold of a portion of Leslie's lower right love lip, squeezing it tightly as if in explanation. Mrs. Moussa laughed, obviously liking the idea.

The woman forced Leslie back up and had her turn around again to face Mrs. Moussa.

During all of this examination and demonstration, Leslie had to strain mightily to suppress sobs of humiliation and shame. She was being displayed as if she was some kind of animal, a pet perhaps, and the woman was explaining how she could be trained and what her assets were. It brought home to her forcefully her new status. She trembled when she thought of what it would be like to be under the heavyset woman's tutelage. She was handling her so coarsely, so callously, like she was some kind of object. Her hands were strong and heavy and Leslie knew that in a test of physical strength, the woman would have it all over her. She could make her do whatever she wanted.

When Leslie was back up on her knees, her back straight, her hands crossed behind her, her knees separated as far apart as she could get them, the woman passed her hand between her thighs from behind, covering her pudendum, and asked Mrs. Moussa a question. Mrs. Moussa chuckled and gave an affirmation. At that, Leslie felt the woman's fingers begin a soft, sensitive dance across her mound. She nudged herself closer to Leslie and brought her other hand to Leslie's front and began to stroke and caress her belly.

Leslie felt an immediate rise in her lusts. When the woman drew a finger the length of her gash up and down, and then pressed lightly on her bud of pleasure, she realized what the woman was up to. She was going to make her perform for Mrs. Moussa's benefit, to display herself in passion, to make her come. She issued an unhappy whine.

The woman stopped what she was doing, came across Leslie's front and gave her a vicious slap across the face. Leslie cried out in pain and collapsed to the floor. The woman grabbed her by her hair and brought her rudely back to her knees, shouting something harsh at her in Arabic. Leslie, her eyes full of tears nodded desperately her readiness to obey, to endure whatever the woman wanted to impose on her silently. No sign that could be interpreted as resistance or protest would be tolerated.

As soon as she was satisfied at Leslie's compliance, she moved back to her position and recommenced her stoking of Leslie's fires. Her fingers nibbled at Leslie's cleft while her other hand gently and soothingly caressed her breasts, stroked her nipples, slid across her belly and up and down her thighs. Leslie closed her eyes and bit her lip. Her face still burned where it had been slapped. She didn't want to make any sound that would trigger another harsh blow.

It did not take long for the woman's expert manipulation of her puss, her caresses to her body, to begin to drive Leslie's lust. The fingers of her right hand probed and stroked and gently flitted over her sex. Leslie had had her cleft handled before, by boyfriends, and recently by Jamilah and the Queen and Zarifa too, but it had never felt like this. The woman's fingers were virtually magical, knowing just when to stroke, just when to glide over and agitate her bud of pleasure, just when to penetrate her and explore her interior, quickly finding the spots that made Leslie's lusts burn.

Her body was getting hot. Her thighs were trembling. The woman had her in a whirl of pleasure. She tried to suppress a moan, but failed. She readied herself for an immediate, violet retribution, but none came. The woman chuckled lightly and then cooed something soft and sweet in Leslie's ear, encouraging her passion. She switched hands, delving her left hand over Leslie's quim from the front, while her right hand began to caress her soft rear globes and slide gently in the valley between them.

Leslie moaned again. It was getting difficult to keep her back straight. Her torso wanted to bend over and absorb the waves of pleasure flowing through her. When she bent forward just a little, the woman's hand left her sex and pushed her back into place, and then resumed its wonderful torture. Leslie wanted to come more than anything in the world, but the woman seemed to know precisely how much she could take. She kept her tottering at the brink, her need growing higher and higher. When the woman leaned forward and began to suckle her breasts, Leslie moaned deep and loud. When the woman bit down on her teats, just enough to send tiny messages of pain to her, Leslie groaned.

Her hips were grinding at the hand that was teasing her quim. Her hands were clenched tightly into little fists. Her head was back and her mouth open. She was aware of Mrs. Moussa staring down at her, enjoying the spectacle she was making, but she didn't care. All she wanted was to come. She wanted to beg to come, to plead to come, but she knew that such things would be forbidden. Her mind burned. The woman slipped three fingers from her right hand deep into her crevasse and began a series of long, rhythmic strokes inside her. Two fat fingers from her left were slipping and sliding over her well lubricated nubbin. She started to sing some kind of musical chant, her voice low and soft. Leslie felt her orgasm growing larger and larger inside her. It was like some huge creature waiting to be born. She started a long, continuous anguished groan.

And then it came. Her body began to shiver and shake. Her pussy's walls contracted and throbbed. Her breasts were so tight, they felt like they were going to explode. She gave out a loud animalistic grunt each time her pussy's walls tightened. She arched her back, her hands gripped tight, her hips ground.

When her pussy's mighty convulsions started to fade, Latifah began a slow winding down of her ministrations. They were just enough to coax out of her a number of strong aftershocks. When her body began to sag and her breath began to return to normal, Latifah gave her head several gentle strokes, gave her breasts, loving squeezes and murmured sweet saying in her ear.

Mrs. Moussa released a gleeful peal of laughter and clapped her hands. She said something to Latifah that sounded appreciative and admiring. Latifah gave Mrs. Moussa a slight bow and beamed back at her, proud to have been able to show off her skills.

Leslie shivered in shame. Tears flowed down her cheeks. She had never been forced through anything so humiliating in her life. She had shown herself to be a slavish slattern. Her mind reeled at the thought of being under Latifah's powers, what she would turn her into. Her pussy glowed with energy still. Her skin seemed alive. She knew that the woman could do this to her any time she wanted.

"You certainly have found yourself at last," Mrs. Moussa said to Leslie. "I never saw such a blatant display of whorishness in my life. You are going to make everyone very happy. Especially me. And I think it's time you started. Come here!"

Leslie's body was still weak and sagging from her ordeal, but she knew that any delay in Mr. Moussa's order would be dealt with very severely by Latifah. She crawled over on her knees until she was at Mr. Moussa's legs.

"Reach under my dress and pull down my panties, whore," she told her. There was a passionate edge to her voice, whose genesis was no doubt triggered by Leslie's display of wanton lust. Leslie obediently lifted the edge of Mrs. Moussa's stylish skirt and crawled underneath it. She moved up between her thighs and felt her way along her smooth, graceful, mature, nylon covered thighs until she felt the soft sheen of her silk panties. She could smell her arousal. She gently slipped her fingers under the waistband and began to pull them down.

Mrs. Moussa raised her hips so that her undergarment could be slipped underneath her. Her fingers trembling, Leslie slid them down her thighs, backing up as she went. She slid them over her knees, down her shins to her ankles. She lifted Mrs. Moussa's pretty shoes, one by one and, and drew them over them. Her panties were bright white and made from a soft, delicate silk. They shimmered in the light. Leslie went to put them down on the floor beside her when Mrs. Moussa spoke to her.

"Kiss them, slut," she said. "Always kiss my panties when you take them off, do you understand?"

"Y,yes, sayyadati," Leslie whimpered back. She placed her lips on the soft material and kissed it and then gently placed it down on the rug beside her. She looked back up at her mistress.

"You know what to do, whore," the callous woman spat at her.

"Yes, sayyadati," Leslie returned, her voice low and obsequious. She pushed her head back under Mrs. Moussa's dress. She had spread her legs and raised her hips so that her cleft would be more readily available. Leslie moved up the darkened space, her hands caressing her mistress's thighs until she felt the wiry bush that shrouded her loins. Suppressing a whine, she leaned forward until her tongue found its target and then commenced a long leisurely lap at her crevasse.

Mrs. Moussa moaned and groaned while Leslie serviced her. Leslie tickled her clit with her tongue, slid it along the sweet divide, pressed it inwards as far as it could go, until her lips met the woman's slit. Mrs. Moussa gave her orders, her breath baited. "Suck my clit! Harder! Softer! Put your tongue in me! That's it! Yes! Yes! Caress my thighs! Lick my pussy lips!" Leslie obeyed her, administering her oral caresses as if she was paying worship to a powerful goddess.

She felt Latifah come up behind her. She slipped her hand over her quim and started to caress it. Leslie moaned as her lusts began anew. The pungent aroma and musky taste of Mrs. Moussa's loins, the hand that was manipulating her swollen purse, the thighs that pressed tightly against her cheeks, the sensation of being used, being a powerless tool of others' desires, all combined to overwhelm her. She licked and sucked the gushing, feminine organ as if she was being fed ambrosia. She felt Latifah's hands grab her arms and draw them back. She took hold of her wrists, pressing them firmly against her back with one hand, while her other resumed its agitation of her loins. She had only her mouth and tongue with which to worship Mrs. Moussa's slit. She buried her face hard against it, coating her face with her discharge, inhaling its lust bringing aroma and then took hold of her clit with her lips, pressing against it with her tongue.

Mrs. Moussa's hips began to grind against her face. She reached under her dress and took hold of Leslie's head, squeezing it tightly. She moaned and groaned. Her thighs began to quiver. She gave out a great shout and commenced a rabid series of groans while her pussy performed its magic on her. Her back arched. She clamped her thighs tightly around Leslie's head. She took hold of her hair with her hands and gripped it desperately. "Oh, yes! Suck me you whore! Suck my pussy! Suck it harder! Yes! Yes! Yes!" she exclaimed.

Her mistress's climax triggered one of her own, and Leslie groaned and moaned into her slit as the expert hand between her legs forced her pleasure.

Mrs. Moussa's body shuddered and she pushed Leslie's head away. Leslie drew back, emerging from underneath her skirt and looked up at her. Her chest was heaving and her face was flush. She had hold of one of her breasts and was gently squeezing it. It took her a while to recover. Latifah took possession of one of Leslie's breasts and was stroking it gently, as if satisfied with the performance of her pet.

When she had recovered, Mrs. Moussa sat up in her chair and smiled. "That was good, whore," she said. "We're going to have a lot of fun together." She said something to Latifah and the old, heavyset woman drew away, pulling Leslie behind her. She made sure that her ward was kneeling in the proper position and then she drew over a couple of large traveling bags. She asked Mrs. Moussa a question and Mrs. Moussa assented.

The first things she took out of her bag were several leather collars. They were brown and black, red, lavender and golden in color. Mrs. Moussa came down off of her stool and knelt down next to Leslie. She had Latifah put several of the collars around her neck to see what they would look like. They were wide and had golden rings attached to them. She took them and held them against her skin. She seemed to be torn between the lavender and the red. Latifah took a fold of Leslie's skin and pinched it hard, making her jump. She showed how well the red collar, more like a scarlet than an actual red, matched the color of the bruised skin. Mrs. Moussa admired and selected the red.

Latifah had Leslie kneel on her haunches while she applied the collar to her neck. She measured Leslie's neck and then with a very sharp knife on top of a square board she pulled out of the traveling case, she proceeded to cut it to the exact length. She applied it to Leslie's neck. While Mrs. Moussa held it in place, she took a long, leatherworking needle and sewed it closed. Leslie felt it drawing tight around her neck. It was not so tight that it would interfere with her breath, but tight enough so that she would always know it was there. It would also never slip or move, so that the rings in the front and back would always be in the right place.

When she was done sewing the collar closed, Latifah tied off the thick, leather thread and then applied a gooey substance over the seam. It hardened almost right away. No one would be able to remove the collar by merely cutting the thread. They would have to somehow cut through the thick leather of the collar itself.

Leslie suppressed her tears while matching leather bracelets were sewn around her wrists and ankles. Mrs. Moussa acted as Latifah's assistant, holding the leather in place while she sewed it closed. She gave Leslie little sardonic smiles as they proceeded. Leslie noted with fear her powerful, acerbic animosity. There was a steel hard edge to it and Leslie realized that she should expect no mercy of any kind from the elegant, refined woman.

The bracelets had rings on them too, and Latifah showed Mrs. Moussa how easily they could be clipped together. A golden chain hung from the bracelet on Leslie's right hand and Latifah drew it through the ring in the front of her collar and attached it to the other bracelet to show how Leslie's wrists could be confined. Then she did the same through the ring in the back, both bringing her wrists up over her shoulders, forcing her elbows out like little wings, and from behind her back, pulling her hands high up towards her neck. Leslie moaned in pain when her hands were brought up. Mrs. Moussa seemed to like this the best and played a little with Leslie's breasts while she watched her face and grim frown record her discomfort.

When the collar and bracelets were fully installed, Mrs. Moussa declared that it was time for a break. She went to a phone on a little table next to her small throne and barked out an order. While they were waiting, Latifah showed Mrs. Moussa how convenient it was to arrange Leslie in a hog tie. She made Leslie lie on her belly and she drew her arms behind her. She lifted her legs back, one at a time and threaded the chain dangling from her right wrist through the rings on her ankle bracelets. The chain then connected to the ring on her left wrist.

Leslie was in this position when a maid brought in a silver tray loaded with a brightly painted pot of tea, two small cups and a plate of gooey pastries. The maid, a pretty, tawny colored, young girl, looked at Leslie with undisguised horror as she laid the tray down on a little table in the middle of the room. She had long black hair tied in a ponytail and was wearing a white blouse buttoned up to her neck and a long, black skirt, the image of modesty. Leslie cringed when she saw her come in. But there was nowhere for her to hide. The maid put down the tray and scurried from the room.

Mrs. Moussa politely poured a cup of tea for Latifah and then one for herself. The two women carried on an animated conversation. It appeared to Leslie, from Latifah' gestures, that she was regaling Mrs. Moussa with stories of her days as a madam. Mrs. Moussa laughed heartily from time to time. She gave Leslie an occasional, malevolent look, but otherwise ignored her.

Leslie's shoulders started to ache. Her belly and breasts were pressed firmly against the rug underneath her. Her fingers were jammed up against the soles of her feet. Her knees were spread wide, baring her intimacies. She closed her eyes and lowered her head, disconsolate at the unfairness of it all. The light was shining brightly in through the large picture windows making Leslie think about the world outside where people were moving freely about in charge of their own destinies. How she yearned to be outside there with them, in a taxi maybe, headed for the airport in Tunis, going home, leaving her travails far behind.

Her muscles ached where she had been beaten with the cane by Faraq. She was conscious of the long streaks of angry red that covered her body. She couldn't help seeing in her mind's eye her body helplessly dangling from the chains in her basement prison, Faraq's cool, stern, callous face as he reared back with the whip. Would Mrs. Moussa beat her? She felt sure of it. The woman had a hardness underneath her elegant exterior which frightened her. She tried desperately to put the thought of it out of her mind.

Latifah was kneeling nearer to her than Mrs. Moussa and from time to time idly passed her strong hand over Leslie's buttocks and thighs. It was as if she had already taken custody of her and was reaffirming her proprietorship.

When they had finished their tea and eaten a few of the small pastries, Mrs. Moussa wiped her hands on a small napkin. Latifah presented her sticky fingers to Leslie's mouth. Mrs. Moussa watched, amused, while Leslie obediently licked them off.

The table was put aside and Leslie was released from her hog tie. Latifah made her come to her knees and cross her wrists behind her. She brought out another case. From within it she drew several bags of makeup and application tools. She explained her proposed design by drawing her fingers across Leslie's face, up around her eyes and around her mouth. Mrs. Moussa seemed satisfied with the proposal. They took out several colors, matching them against Leslie's skin and her scarlet confinements.

Mrs. Moussa liked the burnt orange color the best. Latifah had Leslie kneel stock still while she outlined her eyes with thick lines of mascara. She applied some to her lashes, brushing them until they were long and extended. She took the burnt orange eye shadow and covered her lids with it. She drew out two lines from each of her eyes with the mascara pencil, forming a small triangle like extension of them. Then she filled the interior with the burnt orange eye liner.

Mrs. Moussa selected a blood red lipstick that Latifah then painted on carefully. She outlined her lips with a thin line of black. The same color was applied to the tips of her breasts. They made her lie down on her back and spread her legs and applied it to the edges of her love lips, forming a bright, thick black edged, red border to her crevasse and tapering it towards the top, the point ending a few inches above the apex of her quim. The small area of flesh inside the lines above her clit was colored with the burnt orange eyeliner they had used. A similar color of red was painted on her toe and fingernails, a heavy lacquer being applied on top.

Mrs. Moussa made Leslie stand and walk up and down the room. She seemed delighted at what she saw. She made Leslie kneel down, facing away from her, her forehead to the floor, and spread her legs to see what her love lips would look like from behind. She laughed when she saw it.

The next case contained bright, golden jewelry. They tried several earrings up against her ears. Mrs. Moussa liked the ones that had little golden bells on their ends. Leslie's ears were pierced although she hadn't worn anything in them since coming to Tunisia, not wanting to be ostentatious. The holes were still open and the earrings went on without a problem. Mrs. Moussa ordered Leslie to walk and then crawl around the room to see how the bells would sound. They jingled and jangled lightly everywhere Leslie went to the merriment of the two older women.

Latifah pulled out of her bag a broad golden sheath, with crisscrossing narrow bands of gold. She showed how it could adorn Leslie. Gold colored straps went under her arms crossed her back and connected to the sheath over her shoulders so that when she leaned forward, it would stay close against her chest. Her skin showed through the gaps so that her aspect of nudity was not affected. It ended just above the swelling of her breasts, curving down from her shoulders in a wide arc. Mrs. Moussa liked it very much and it stayed on.

Next, Latifah showed Mrs. Moussa several golden chains that could go around Leslie's waist. Mrs. Moussa liked the one with tiny golden coins hanging from it. A large, gold medallion hung down in front, pulling the belt down and emphasizing the hollows of her hips and directing the eye down towards her loins. Again she had Leslie walk back and forth. She corrected her several times, telling her to sway her hips more so that the belt would accentuate her movements. Once Leslie got it down right, Mrs. Moussa was satisfied.

There was a full length mirror inside of a closet in the room and Mrs. Moussa brought Leslie over to it so that she could see herself in all her slave regalia. Leslie's gloom had grown deeper and deeper with each additional adornment. When she looked at herself in the mirror, she was aghast. She hardly recognized herself. Not that she wasn't alluring. Latifah had an expert's touch. Her makeup was just enough to emphasize her status as a whore, but not so much that she looked whorish. Her face was alive with color and she looked birdlike with her eyes accentuated. Her mouth looked succulent and inviting. Her breasts, so pale around the dark red discs of her painted areolas and teats, looked soft and malleable. The jewelry she had been adorned with glittered.

But it was her pussy that really shocked her. The servant who had seen her emerge from the basement had looked at her hairless loins as if seeing a strange creature for the first time. Now they would stand out even more, invite caresses, beg for penetration. The little tapering point made it seem like a temple where it would heaven to dwell. A darkness separated the two, daring red lines, promising passion, lust, ecstasy.

Despite its adornments, her body seemed more naked than naked. The places left undecorated stood out starkly. The unpainted portions of her labia seemed puffed out and prominent. Her breasts seemed larger, her belly, flatter and more delicate. Her thin, elegant thighs seemed smoother and longer. The bright gold jewelry made her pale skin seem even paler.

And if her other accouterments advertised her as a whore, her collar and bracelets advertised her as a slave.

Latifah had one more adornment. Miserable, deathly fearful of disobedience, Leslie followed her mistress on her hands and knees, her earrings jingling musically, as she stepped back over to where the large, powerful woman was kneeling next to one of her bags of tricks. When Leslie was kneeling tall next to her, thighs wide, back straight as she had been taught, Latifah showed Mrs. Moussa a four inch long, smooth tube. It was approximately five inches around. On one end it terminated in a rounded cone. On the other end was a bright, ornately decorated, golden colored disk about five inches in diameter, with a circle of red amethysts around it. It was designed to look like a large, blooming flower.

Mrs. Moussa didn't know what it was for, so Latifah had to explain it to her. Mrs. Moussa laughed when she finally understood. They made Leslie bend over. Mrs. Moussa spread her rear cheeks while Latifah, after applying a thin coating of lubrication, slid it into Leslie's rear portal. Leslie groaned as she felt it fill her. Latifah gave her a mighty swat on her left rear cheek that stung like the blazes. Tearful, Leslie quieted, but that did not allay her dismay at the presence of the new adornment to her body. Latifah, holding still a knob in the middle of the disk, turned the disk towards the right. Leslie gasped as she felt the tube expand inside of her. Latifah, for Mrs. Moussa's benefit as well as Leslie's, gave the device a couple of yanks. It did not come out.

Mrs. Moussa laughed and laughed. She rubbed her hands over Leslie's rear cheeks several times and then pulled at the device for her own amusement. She made Leslie crawl across the room. The disk stood out prominently from her rear. Then she made her walk back and forth, and it could still be seen clearly.

Leslie was in tears when she came back across the room. Latifah had to remind her with a loud clap of her hands and a stern, foreboding look to get back down on her knees.

"Well, you're all made up like the whore you are," Mrs. Moussa told her gaily when she was settled. "And if anyone wants to use your back side, and I can tell you that for some of Mr. Moussa's friends it is their preference, you will be all ready to receive them." She laughed and then patted Latifah on the knee, apparently profusely thanking her.

Leslie cringed at he woman's words. "Mr. Moussa's friends!" she thought frantically. "I'll have to fuck his friends! Oh, no, please don't let it be true!" Her body felt sickened.

Mrs. Moussa turned back to Latifah. They had a brief conversation. Mrs. Moussa's eyebrows raised and she asked her a short question. Latifah nodded affirmatively. Mrs. Moussa's face lit up and she smiled.

Leslie watched forlornly as Mrs. Moussa crossed the room. She picked up the telephone near her chair and punched in a number. When the phone was answered on the other end, she barked out an order and then hung it up. She gave Leslie a sinister smile and then came back and knelt down next to her, letting her beautiful, multicolored skirt flower around her.

"I heard that they gave you a new name at the prison," she said to Leslie. "Ghaniyah. It is a pretty name. That's what your name will be from now on here too. You are a pretty little whore so you should have a pretty little whore's name."

Mrs. Moussa let her pronouncement sink in. Leslie was deeply disturbed by the loss of her name again. She bit her lip and tried to fight back her tears.

Just then, the door to the salon opened. Leslie watched as the house mistress and two of the pretty, young maids came into the room. Leslie blanched at the idea of them seeing her as she was, naked and painted up like a whore. She watched as the house mistress handed something to Mrs. Moussa. It was a golden disk, oval in shape and about three inches long. There was some Arabic writing etched deeply into it.

"Latifah has brought you some very nice gifts, Ghaniyah, but I have something for you too," she said. "I was going to have it attached to your collar, but Latifah had a much better idea. I thought that she would have to do it some other time, but she tells me we can do it right now. Lie down on your back and spread your legs."

Trembling, Leslie complied. Cautiously, her suspicious eyes on her mistress, she spread her thighs.

Mrs. Moussa gave an order to the three women who had come in. The pretty, young maids, hesitated, but the house mistress repeated the order and clapped her hands for emphasis. They jumped to obey. They went to Leslie's sides, knelt down and took hold of her thighs. They pulled them until they were far back, raising Leslie's hips and displaying her painted love lips.

The house mistress knelt down by Leslie's head and took hold of her wrists, pinning them down to the floor above her.

Latifah had been busy at one of her bags. Leslie looked up and saw that she had adorned herself with clear, plastic surgical gloves and had a long, thick, silver needle in her hand. She watched as the woman washed it in a solution, drying it with a small, clean, white cloth. She gave Leslie a pleased look and then advanced until she was between her thighs. When Leslie saw her bend down towards her loins, a wave of fear passed through her. She started to struggle, but the three women held her down fast.

"Please don't! Please!" she begged. Latifah gave the other women an order and Leslie felt her hips raised and a thick cloth being slid under her. They let her back down. She looked up at Mrs. Moussa who was watching the unfolding event with a humored, disdainful look. "Please don't do this! Please!' Leslie whined.

"Shut up, whore, or I'll have you whipped to the bone," Mrs. Moussa said angrily. Leslie clamped her lips together and whined.

Latifah opened a small package and withdrew a square, white bandage. She wetted the bandage with the solution and then wiped it over the lower portion of her right, outer labia, covering it thoroughly. Leslie remembered Latifah pinching it and making a comment to Mrs. Moussa a short while before. Latifah tossed the bandage aside and picked up the needle. She bent over and took hold of Leslie's skin. Leslie felt the point of the needle press against her. She closed her eyes. A fierce pain shot through her as her labia was punctured. She screamed and her body shook. The women held her steady. The needle slid back and forth several times, making sure that the pathway was clear. Her wound burned and she broke into sobs.

Latifah put the needle aside and picked up a thick, golden ring, about two inches long. There was a gap in it about a ½ inch wide. She washed the ring in the solution and then brought it and a small pair of shiny, stainless steel pliers to her loins. She placed the ring through the hole she had made. Leslie squirmed and moaned as the ring abraded her wound. Latifah issued a small grunt as she strained to press the ring closed with the pliers.

She gave the ring a little tug. Leslie's body stiffened and she moaned disconsolately as more pain shot through her. Latifah smiled.

Mrs. Moussa handed her the disk. Latifah washed it with the solution and then brought it down to her loins. The disk had an unjoined ring through a small hole on one end. Latifah maneuvered that ring around the ring in Leslie's labia and closed it off with the pliers. She gave it a tug, making Leslie moan again, and then sat up and smiled once more.

Mrs. Moussa edged herself closer and leaned over. Latifah took hold of the disk so that Mrs. Moussa could see it. She laughed and clapped her hands.

"Oh, Ghaniyah, it looks so pretty. Do you want to know what it says? It says, 'Ghaniyah, Slave of the House of Moussa.' That's what you are now, a slave. Anyone who uses you will be able to see it and know what you are. You'll feel it every day when you walk or crawl, swinging below your pretty pussy, tapping against your thigh. And we can use the ring to chain you down when we want you to stay in one place. Or we can attach a leash to it and lead you around. It will be very useful."

Leslie moaned as she thought of what Mrs. Moussa was saying. Her eyes were full of tears. Her loins burned where the wound was. It was pulsing and throbbing. She could feel the disk laying against her thigh.

Mrs. Moussa gave the maids an order and they released Leslie's legs. They and the house mistress quickly left the room.

"Get on your knees, whore," Mrs. Moussa commanded. Despite the agonizing pain emanating from her piercing, Leslie struggled to her knees. She spread her legs and put her hands behind her back. She could feel the weight of the disk below her.

"We're almost done, Ghaniyah," Mrs. Moussa said pleasantly. "I have just one more thing for you. She got up and strode over to her chair. There was a small plastic bag on the floor to its left and Mrs. Moussa brought it over. She knelt down before Leslie, who had reassumed her position, and took something out of the bag.

It was a soft, round, bright blue rubber ball. There was some Arabic writing on it on one side. When it was turned around, the same word was spelled out in English. Leslie looked at it. In deep red letters, it said, "Whore."

"Open your mouth, Ghaniyah," Mrs. Moussa ordered. Disconsolate, Leslie obeyed. Mrs. Moussa pressed the ball in. It was just a little bigger than the opening of her mouth and it took a little pressure for it to pass over her lips. Once inside, it filled the whole cavity, making Leslie's cheeks bulge. It forced her lips apart and a crescent of blue could be seen between her teeth. Leslie pressed down hard, trying to bring her lips together, but while the soft ball would compress just a bit, it was not enough for her to close her mouth. She was about to whine her dismay when she saw Latifah looking at her sternly. Not wanting another slap, she suppressed it unhappily.

"You will keep this in your mouth at all times unless you are eating or giving someone pleasure," Mrs. Moussa informed her. "It will be a continuous reminder of what you are."

Mrs. Moussa rose to her feet and straightened her elegant, colorful skirt. She stood before Leslie, towering over her in all her awful beauty. Her face was hard and she looked down at Leslie with undiluted hatred. Her voice turned harsh and cruel. "You came to my house to flaunt you sluttish ways. I saw you eying my husband. You thought with your big breasts and big doe like eyes that you could seduce him away from me. Now you are just a thing to be used, an animal we will keep around the house for fucking. And if you fail to please anyone in any little way, you will suffer a terrible beating every time. I will make sure of it."

She took a deep breath. Her harsh words pierced Leslie's mind. She wanted to protest, to beg forgiveness, to promise she would go away and never return. But she knew that uttering a single syllable would result in immediate, harsh punishment. She knew too that any plea for mercy would be of no avail.

"Mr. Moussa will be back after lunch," Mrs. Moussa continued. "You will be presented to him then. I am sure he will enjoy making use of you. I want you to think of me when he has his cock in your mouth. It is I who put it there." Her voice grew harsher and her face arranged itself into a mask of rage. "I knew that you had gone out that day to show off your sluttish body to everyone," she shouted. "Who do you think it was who called the police? It was me! Who do you think told Captain Khalil to bring all those charges against you! It was me! You will be our little whore! And when we are through with you, you will be sent back to prison to serve a sentence of twenty years! My uncle is a judge and I will make sure that the case comes before him. That is what happens to slutty little whores who come here to steal our husbands! If I were you, I would be the best little whore I could be, because all that awaits you afterwards is a dark, dismal cell. So enjoy yourself as our guest while you can."

Leslie burst into tears. She had known that Mrs., Moussa didn't like her, but she had never guessed that it had burst into full blown hatred. To think that she was the one behind all of her troubles! And now she had to serve her, suck her pussy, crawl before her on her hands and knees! "…..eeeeeeeeeeease!" she tried to beg. "…….eeeeeeeeeeease! …on't …ooo is! …eeeeeeeeeeease!"

In an instant, she felt a resounding slap across her face. It was Latifah, enforcing her mistress's rules. She fell over, her face stinging and sobbed and sobbed and sobbed. She had been right! It was a nightmare! A living nightmare! She would never be free of it! "Why is this happening to me! Why!" she cried to herself.

She felt a harsh tug on her hair. Latifah pulled her back to her knees. She gathered her arms behind her, slipped the chain from her right wrist through the ring in the back of her collar and affixed her other wrist to it. Leslie moaned from the pain. Latifah moved in front of her. She took Leslie's right breast in the palm of her left hand and then came down on it ferociously with her right. It made a loud slapping noise and Leslie screamed. Then she did her left breast and Leslie screamed again. She grabbed her nipples and squeezed them harshly, making a face at her and uttering a long, insistent, "Shhhhhhhhhhhh!"

The pain was excruciating, but Leslie knew that it would not stop until she was silent. She used all of her concentration to bring her whines of pain to an end. She took a deep breath through her nose and held it, frantic to ease the torture to her breasts. Slowly, Latifah released them.

When Leslie looked up, Mrs. Moussa was gone.

CHAPTER EIGHT

Panic stormed through Leslie's brain. Mrs. Moussa had abandoned her to the custody of the other woman, the cruel former mistress of a harsh bordello. Any opportunity she might have had to plea for mercy had gone. She had never felt so alone in the world, so helpless. She fought back tears. She looked at the woman who would be her caretaker and saw a callous mistress who would mold her into a whore. She had already struck her cruelly many times. Her life was going to be a continuous hell.

Her shoulders ached from her wrists confinements. Her sex lip still burned from the cruel adornment they had installed there. She could feel the large, offensive instrument in her rear spreading wide her anal ring. The jewelry on her chest lay there heavily. Her earrings tingled at the slightest movement. Her mouth was clogged by the large ball they had put in it and the harsh word imprinted on it burned into her mind. She had come into the room as Leslie Harrington, a victim of cruel circumstance and would be leaving as Ghaniyah, Slave of the House of Moussa.

The heavyset woman moved towards Leslie and, putting her hand on the back of her head, pressed down until her forehead was touching the floor. She left her that way while she gathered the detritus of their playtime together. When she was done, she clapped her hands together twice. Leslie looked up and Latifah was making a sign that she should rise. Sorrowfully, she rose to her feet. Her minder had a golden leash with a fine, polished leather handle. In her other hand was a three foot long, supple stick. She clipped the leash to the ring in the front of Leslie's collar and pulled her forward. Leslie had no choice but to follow her.

They went out into the hallway, walked down the corridor to the hub of the mansion and then turned to go towards the dining areas. As they walked, Leslie's bells tingled musically. They passed a number of the servants who all gave Leslie long, astonished looks.

Instead of entering the dining room, Latifah brought her into the kitchen. It was a large room, big enough to cook for the huge banquets the Moussa's sometimes had. There were several cooks, all older women, dressed in dark shirtwaist dresses and wearing white aprons that covered their bodices and the front of their skirts and tied behind their necks. They all looked up at Leslie when she came in, towed behind Latifah. They formed a small circle around her. Leslie tried to shy away from them, but Latifah pulled her up with her leash.

The women oooouuud and ahhhhhed. They exchanged amused and incredulous statements between them. Latifah proudly showed her off. She made her spread her legs so that they could see her red lined purse and the golden decorations that dangled there and then turned her around so they could behold the golden flower that peaked out of her rear end. They admired her eyes when Latifah took hold of Leslie's chin and turned it this way and that. They fingered the jewelry on her chest and played with the bells on her ears. One of them reached out and squeezed a breast. Leslie issued a little squeaking sound that made them all laugh.

After a few minutes, the women all went back to work. Latifah spoke to one of them and the woman gave her a bowl of steamed couscous and lamb. Latifah guided Leslie over to the corner of the room, put the bowl on the floor and snapped her fingers, pointing down. She gave a command that Leslie came to learn meant, "On your knees." Leslie quickly lowered herself to the floor, a difficult task to perform gracefully with her hands still bound up high behind her. Latifah reached her fat fingers into her mouth and extracted the soft, rubber ball that resided there. Then she pointed to the bowl on the floor, giving a command that meant, "Eat."

Leslie hesitated for a second. She didn't want to have to eat like a dog in front of all these people. She got a harsh slap cross her face for her delay. She released a sob and bent her head down towards her food.

Latifah stood over her, making sure that she ate it all. When Leslie was done and licked the bowl clean, she got another one and made Leslie eat that one too. She was determined to fatten Leslie up right away.

When the second bowl was done, Latifah washed her face and gave her a long drink out of a water bottle, reinstalling her blue rubber ball afterwards. Then, grabbing a rag, she pulled Leslie to her feet and brought her out the rear door of the kitchen. The sun was bright and burning down harshly. Several of the servants were sitting at picnic tables eating their lunch. Latifah brought her past them to a little stretch of rough ground. She bent over and forced Leslie's legs apart. Then she pressed on her shoulders, forcing her down into a squat. She stood there waiting. At first, Leslie didn't know what she was waiting for. Then she understood. She had been ordered to pee on the ground.

A wave of misery went through her. The servants, two male ones and three pretty, little maids, were watching. One of them made a comment and they all laughed.

She couldn't do it! Not in front of all those people! She looked up at her oppressor beseechingly. Latifah just yanked at her chain and gave her a stern order. Leslie still couldn't do it. Latifah held out her hand, showing all five fingers. Then she closed her hand and counted them off slowly, one by one. When the fifth finger was out, she reared back and gave Leslie a mighty blow from her stick across her breasts. Leslie whined and cried out. She lost her balance and Latifah pulled her back into position with the chain. Then she held out her hand again, splaying her fingers. She closed her fist and started counting them out again, popping each finger out in turn. Leslie tried and tried, but couldn't get anything to come out. This time, Latifah struck her across her back. Leslie cried out in pain.

Latifah held her hand out a third time. Leslie was frantic to avoid another blow. She pressed down with all her might. She watched dolefully as the fingers began to pop out of Latifah's fist. Finally, when the fourth finger had emerged, she began a little trickle. It soon turned into a stream. It turned the light brown, water starved, sandy soil beneath her dark where it landed and permeated immediately into it. Tears were flowing down Leslie's face. Latifah didn't mind. It was what they all did in the beginning. She used waterproof makeup for just that reason. It was important that the sluts learned right away that their bodily functions were not their own and that for them, the concept of privacy didn't exist.

Once Leslie had released all of her water, Latifah wiped her quim with the rag, pulled her to her feet and brought her back into the kitchen. Leslie hadn't seen it when she came in, but there was a 4' by 3' cage against the wall near the door they had entered by. Leslie grimaced when they started walking over to it. Confirming her worst fears, Latifah opened it, removed Leslie's leash and motioned her to get in. Fearing a blow from the hot tempered matron, she went to her knees and shuffled her way in, bending her torso down so she could fit. When she was all scrunched in, Latifah closed the door and locked it. She hung the leash on a nail in the wall next to the cage.

Leslie watched forlornly as Latifah received her own bowl of food and walked outside to consume it. She disappeared from view.

The bottom of the cage was padded, but its area was small. Leslie had to shift herself around to get anywhere near comfortable. She found that if she pushed her back up against the bars, she could ease the strain that her uplifted arms were putting on her neck and shoulders. She sat with her knees up and her feet flat on the mat.

The bars to the cage were thin, reinforced wires, really, and they were about four inches apart. She had a relatively unobstructed view of the activities in the kitchen and knew that anyone looking would have a relatively unobstructed view of her. She dismally watched the women scurrying back and forth. Occasionally, they would glance at her and smile, humored by her predicament.

If it was near noon, it would be time for the family lunch. Before her days of woe had begun, Leslie had eaten with the family every day at every meal. The little dining room was just past a swinging door right in front of her. She knew that Mr. Moussa would not be back until after lunch, but she knew that

Mrs. Moussa, Hajib and his sister, Jana, were probably in there right now. It pained her to contrast the elegant lunch they would undoubtedly eat with her coarse repast. They would sit around the table, be waited on by servants and consume their meal while having a refined conversation. The thought of it, and the recollection of her own mostly pleasant meals there caused a wave of despair to flow through her.

Leslie's stomach soured as she thought about her upcoming meeting with Mr. Moussa. It would be her first formal use as a painted whore. She wondered what Mr. Moussa's reaction was going to be to all her decorations. She had been shamed when he fucked her yesterday, she would be shamed to be seen like this today. He would probably fuck her again, there was no doubt of that. A tear came to her eyes when she thought of it.

Her mouth closed down on the soft ball in her mouth, reminding her of its presence. And then she thought of the bright red writing on it: Whore. It sickened her to think of that word being in her mouth. It was like having a foul presence there. She had to admit that it was an insidious torment that Mrs. Moussa had devised. She was sure to think about the infamous word in her mouth many times a day. She pressed her tongue against the ball to see if she could urge it out, but she could not move it. She gave it up, disheartened.

At one point, Mrs. Moussa came into the kitchen. Her high heels made a distinctive, sharp clicking sound on the hard tile floor. She was still dressed in her elegant skirt and blouse. She had a piece of paper in her hand and she approached the head cook and showed it to her. There was a brief conversation and the cook nodded her head in understanding. While they were talking, Mrs. Moussa glanced at her. She gave Leslie a little smile and went back to her conversation. She left without looking at her again.

After about a half hour, Latifah returned to the kitchen. She handed her bowl over to a dishwasher, a skinny old man with mangy hair and a weather-beaten face. She came over to the cage, opened it and urged Leslie out. When she was standing outside, she hooked her leash to her collar and gave it a tug.

They returned to the central hub of the mansion and approached Mr. Moussa's office. Leslie looked down forlornly at the desk where she used to sit. Latifah opened the door and brought Leslie in. She saw that some work had been done in the room since yesterday. There was a large ring in the floor about three feet away from Mr. Moussa's desk. There was a six foot long chain attached to it. Latifah hooked the end of the chain to the ring on Leslie's right ankle bracelet and then she ordered her to her knees, facing away from Mr. Moussa's desk. She unhooked the leash from her collar. She gave her an order, that Leslie understood by the hand motions that accompanied it, meant for her to place her forehead on the floor, raise her hips and spread her legs. She complied immediately. She heard Latifah's soft footfalls on the thick carpet as she left. The door closed behind her.

Leslie realized that she was locked into position as firmly as if she had been bound in place. She didn't dare lift her head. She couldn't imagine the consequences if Latifah came back in and saw that she had moved.

While she waited, her mind kept drifting back to the plug that filled her rectum and the bright golden disk that abutted its end. It would be the first thing Mr. Moussa would notice when he came into the room. His friends would fuck her there. Mrs. Moussa had said so. She couldn't stand the thought of it. Strange men would use her. They would laugh and joke about her whorishness and then use her callously.

Maybe it would be better to be in prison, she thought. And then she recalled the brutal guards, Sergeant Malikeh and Captain Khalil, being used by Jamilah every night, her rapes by Zarifa. She thought of the hard, cruel inmates, the long days and nights of boredom, the merciless stone walls. And once she went inside again, there would be little, if any, chance of escape. The same might be said for her current condition, but at least she was not in a prison. There were windows and doors and sometimes people forgot to lock them. Somehow, she pledged, she would find a way to get away, to be free again. It was the only thing she could cling to.

When the door opened, she gave a little jump. She heard Mr. Moussa's feet on the carpet. She sensed him going by her. He stopped for a couple of seconds, looking at her, and then sat down in his chair. He picked up the telephone and punched in a number.

She envisioned with dismay his eyes flitting over her proffered, decorated rear, her painted love lips that peeked out under her, the dangling medallion that hung so heavily from her love lip. She heard him go through about four or five conversations while she knelt unhappily on the floor fretfully awaiting the moment he would take notice of her again and order her to get up.

It happened about twenty minutes later. She heard Mr. Moussa put the telephone back in its receptacle. His chair turned. There was silence. She knew he was looking at her. She began to tremble. Then she heard his voice.

"Get up, whore," he said to her sternly. Leslie slowly struggled to her feet. The bells on her ears chimed daintily.

"Come here," he said.

She edged her way to him. When she was standing a foot away from his knees, he began to examine her. He reached out his hand and jiggled the gold belt around her waist. He reached up and took hold of a breast, pinching it lightly between his thumb and forefinger. He made her turn around. He tugged playfully at the glittery flower in her rear and laughed. She felt him turning the dial, causing the intruder to narrow and then he glided it in and out of her a few times. When he pushed it in the final time, he turned the dial in the other direction, returning it to its uncomfortable fullness.

Placing his hands on her hips, he made her turn around again. He played with her breasts, then ran his hands down over her hips and down her thighs. His hands were hot and strong. Leslie felt herself watering as he touched her. The thought of him using her, without her consent, being powerless to stop him, made her heart beat heavy and her breath short.

"Spread your legs," he told her. When she did, he ran his hands up the insides of her thighs. He halted at her painted pussy. Looking down at his hand, he ran a thick finger along the gap between her red lined lips. Leslie moaned as a thrill passed through her. He slipped the finger inside her tunnel, gliding in easily and sawed it back and forth a few times. Leslie felt her knees go weak. He took hold of the medallion that hung from her loins. Leslie hissed with pain as it tugged at the still raw hole. He looked at the inscription, gave a satisfied smile and then lowered it gently.

When he pointed to the floor, Leslie sank to her knees. He took hold of her heavy breasts with his hands, weighing and assessing them, running his thumbs over her stiffened nipples. He took hold of her chin and turned her head this way and that, getting a good look at Latifah's artistry. He saw the ball lodged in her mouth and, curious, he thrust his fingers in and pulled it out. He read the writing on it and it humored him. He put it down on the desk, spread his legs and lowered his fly. His prick emerged like a snake slinking out of a hole. Leslie took a deep breath, leaned over, opened her mouth and took it in.

He kept her pace nice and slow. His one hand rested on her head, the other on her shoulder. Leslie could hear her little bells chiming lightly as she bobbed her head up and down. She washed his pole with her tongue, suckled on it gently, kept her lips formed tightly around it. Apparently dissatisfied with the depth of his penetration, his hand forced her head down, thrusting the tip of his cock into her throat, making her cough and choke. He held it there for a second or two and then let her resume her motion. Leslie learned from her lesson and sank her head down each time until his cock rubbed up against the back of her mouth before rising again.

The telephone rang. He picked it up with his right hand while his left took hold of her head and stopped her motion. She heard him talking and a tinny voice in Arabic on the other end of the line. The conversation took a couple minutes. She knelt there, motionless, his stiff wand filling her mouth. She remembered Mrs. Moussa's words. She was the one who put his cock in her mouth. She gave a little sob. Mr. Moussa, mistaking it for impatience, gave her head a hard swat. She silenced herself. When the phone call was over and he replaced the handset onto the receiver, she began her motions again.

He was leaning back in his chair, enjoying the workings of her mouth. Once in a while, he released a soft sigh, but that was the only sign of the pleasure she was giving him. That and his rigid cock.

When he finally groaned, Leslie took it as a sign that he wanted her to increase her pace, but she was wrong. He pushed her head off of his loins, took hold of the ring in her collar and pulled her to her feet. He pushed her torso over the desk. Leslie spread her legs and arched her back in anticipation of his use of her steaming canal. She needed him to fill her. Her lusts were so high that she felt ready to burst. She whined in disappointment when she felt him turning the dial on the device in her rectum. He slipped it out and put it down on a piece of tissue on his desk. Then he aimed his cock at the dainty, expanded hole, pressed against the still small entrance and plunged within.

Leslie gave a moan of pain when her delicate ring expanded. When his motions began, thrusting her torso back and forth across his desk, she felt a tingling there. It traveled through her gut right to her pussy. It was like someone was passing a low voltage charge of electricity through her loins. She began to moan. He took hold of her wrists, dangling on their chain and brought them together until they were crossed, straining the muscles of her shoulders even more. Holding them with one hand, he pressed them down on her upper back, while his other hand held onto her hip.

The incessant motion of his thick, rigid instrument was driving Leslie wild. Her moan got deeper and louder. His hand left her hip, took hold of the blue rubber ball, and shoved it back between her lips, silencing her.

He began to fuck her with earnest. His hips banged against her rear cheeks. He pressed her down onto his desk harder. He took hold of the hair on the back of her head and pulled it until she lifted her chin from the desk and brought her head back. Her throat stretched and it became hard to breath. He was grunting now, giving her mighty thrusts, sinking deep within her.

Suddenly, he groaned, his body stiffened and his cock began to throb and spurt. Leslie came too, her pussy shuddering and convulsing. She bit down on the ball in her mouth and, as her paroxysms of pleasure made her body shake, she remembered what was written on it. Whore. She was a whore. It was official.

He stood leaning over her while he caught his breath. He released her wrists and slipped from her. She heard him open a drawer and pull out some wipes. He cleaned off his cock and tossed the wipe into the trash. He took the plug and reinserted it into her expanded anal ring. He turned the dial a couple of turns more than before. She would have to get looser back there if she was to accommodate him without problem.

Leslie was still laying on his desk when the door opened. Small feet made their way to the desk. Leslie looked up. It was one of the maids. She had Mr. Moussa's mail. She gave Leslie a disdainful look as she handed it to him. Then she turned and left.

Moussa ordered Leslie back to the floor, where she had been kneeling before. When she was settled, he sat down and began opening his mail. "I used to do that," she thought miserably. "That was my job." He would get someone new, probably a local girl. It would have to be someone who wouldn't blanch when they saw Leslie naked and bound kneeling on the floor, or draped over the desk, or on her knees servicing his cock with her mouth.

Mr. Moussa didn't use her again that afternoon. She knelt there, motionless, for about an hour and a half until he got up from his desk, without a word, and exited his office. A few moments after he left, Latifah came in and collected her.

And that was how her life as the household whore began. Latifah brought her to a bathroom where there was a bidet. She let her pee and then felt around in her pussy to se if Mr. Moussa had left any of his spunk in there. Finding none, she withdrew the intruder from her rear and tested that hole. When she discovered Mr. Moussa's slime, she took a nozzle from the bidet and rinsed it out. She washed the aperture with soap, replaced the plug and brought her back to the kitchen.

Before placing her in her cage, Latifah, the merciful, finally released her arms from her back. She had to extend them slowly to guard against muscle strain. She brought Leslie's wrists before her, circled the chain on her right wrist through the ring in the front of her collar and attached it to the other bracelet. She then ordered her into the cage.

Leslie stayed there while Latifah had tea with one of the cooks. After a little while, a telephone rang. It was for Latifah. She said something affirmative into the phone and hung it up. She swallowed the rest of her tea, released Leslie from her cage and guided her out of the kitchen.

This time it was Hajib. He was waiting the hallway. He took the leash and rushed Leslie upstairs to his room. He used her callously, laughing and joking, mocking her, relishing his right to violate her. He let her go after an hour or more. Latifah was sitting on a chair outside his room. She collected her charge, washed her in the bathroom and brought her back to the kitchen. She was fed a coarse meal from a bowl on the floor and then returned to her cage.

After dinner, she was brought to Mr. Moussa's den where she sucked him off and then to Mrs. Moussa's sitting room outside her bedroom where she serviced her pussy once again. Each time, Latifah waited patiently outside of the room until her abuser was through with her, washed her, and brought her back to her cage.

About ten o'clock, Faraq appeared. He pulled her from her cage and, after reminding her of her promised punishment from this morning, gave her seven harsh lashes across her rear. Her screams echoed off the kitchen walls. After, he had her suck his cock right there in front of the kitchen staff. Then he put her back. A little after twelve, when it was clear no one would call for her again, Latifah brought her down to her cell in the basement.

She used a cream to remove all of the makeup. She brushed her hair. She let her move her bowels and pee. The she brought her to the bed. She ordered her to lie down and then chained her wrists to the ring at the head of the bed. There was a small nightstand next to the bed. Latifah went to it, turned on a small table lamp and then went to the door and turned off the over head. The room was suffused with a soft light. To Leslie's surprise, she started to remove her clothing. When she was naked, she got up on the bed and laid down next to her. She was heavyset and slightly chunky, but not obese. Her breasts were

large and fluffy. She stroked Leslie's hair and murmured
something sweet sounding to her. She leaned over, merged their
lips and slipped her tongue into Leslie's mouth.

They fucked for the better part of an hour. She teased
Leslie's pussy until she screamed. She suckled and massaged her
breasts. She made her come three times, twice with her hand and
once with her mouth. She released her hands from the ring,
fastening them to the front of her collar, and made Leslie kiss
and mouth her large breasts and lick her pussy. When she came,
she squeezed Leslie's head with her hands like she was trying to
burst it.

When she was done with her, she connected the back of
Leslie's collar by chain to the wall, pulled a light covering over
them and went to sleep.

Leslie lay there a long time awake. She had had sex with five
people that day: Faraq, Mr. Moussa, Mrs. Moussa, Hajib and, of
course, Latifah. Some of them more than once. What was
amazing to her was that she was just as responsive at the end of
the day as she had been in the beginning. Even now, her
unreachable pussy hummed between her thighs. She squeezed
her thighs together in an attempt to relieve herself from the
feeling.

It was clear that her fate from now on, until Mrs. Moussa
tired of her, was to be a totally controlled human being. She
would even be subject to regulation at night when she slept. She
could hear Latifah's soft snores behind her as she lay on her side
with her back to her, her legs all scrunched up. At any moment
that the heavy set woman desired, she could reach over and make
use of her. There was no way for Leslie to stop it.

Moreover, while anyone in the household could do anything
they wanted to her, feel her breasts, stroke her loins, use her rear
portal, her body was essentially off bounds to her. Her hands had
been bound in one way or another virtually the whole day. They
were bound even now. Her wrists lay upon her breasts, but her
hands could not touch them. Her pussy was way out of reach.
Although she was technically still a human being, she had lost all
her human rights.

Eating on the floor like a dog in front of the staff had been an act of extreme humiliation for her. The kitchen workers had smiled and joked about it while they watched her. She realized that as long as she was Mrs. Moussa's prisoner, she could expect the harshest, most demeaning treatment. She remembered her wan smile at her when in the kitchen. There had been a frightening coldness to it. The fact that she could go back to the dining room and calmly consume her midday meal knowing that less than 30' away Leslie was suffering dismal, soul wrenching humiliation proved that she had a heart of stone.

She was thankful, at least, that her mouth was free. For now, at least, she didn't have that terrible word in her mouth. She knew that it would be returned there tomorrow. But tomorrow was tomorrow and now was now. She realized that she would have to learn to think that way and find peace and freedom from domination wherever and whenever she could.

She had been overwhelmed when Latifah kissed her mouth. She could still feel the sensation of her large tongue twirling around her oral cavity, stoking her lusts. The woman was a demon. She was casting a spell over her, eroding her sense of individual personhood a step at a time. She would be her ever hovering shadow, the enforcer of Mrs. Moussa's dictates. She hadn't permitted Leslie the slightest deviation from her orders, permitted even a sound of rebellion or unhappiness. When Leslie had broken down into tears while in Mrs. Moussa's salon, she had slapped her viciously, had belabored her breasts and nipples until she stopped.

And she had total control of her body. Latifah determined when and how she ate, where and when she pissed and shat, how she was bound, when she would reside in her cage, when she would go to bed and how she would sleep once there. Even throughout the night she would be a constant, over bearing presence, her large body lodged next to her. She was in charge of decorating her like a whore. Tomorrow morning, she would probably wash and clean her too. There would be nothing volitional left about her life at all.

And yet, despite her rigid, overpowering control of her, there was an element of sweetness to her too, murmuring little encouragements to her, petting her, stroking her. After dinner tonight, she had given her a piece of chocolate. It was a small piece, but it had been an island of pleasure after a hard, hard day. And when she made love to her, she was tender and considerate. Her touch was gentle and soft. Her kisses had been powerful, permitting no resistance to them, but they had been sensual and, in a way, comforting too. She might be a fuck animal for everyone else, but she was still human, in some small way to Latifah.

After a while, Leslie was able to fall asleep. She had been right about Latifah's control over her though. During the night, she felt the woman's hand caress her thigh. She pulled Leslie to her back, pressed her thighs apart and made her come while stroking her head and cooing to her. When she was done, she kissed Leslie on the lips and moved her back to her side. Leslie slept the rest of the night with the large woman's arm draped across her body, snuggled up against her.

Leslie slept deeply. She did not awaken when Latifah rose. Only the sound of the shower brought her to consciousness. She watched as the large woman washed herself. When she saw that Leslie was awake, she gave her a big smile. Once she had dried herself off, still naked, she unlocked Leslie's chain from the wall, let her pee and then brought her to the shower. She released Leslie's hands and washed every inch of her body. When she was done, she locked Leslie's wrists back up to her collar. She shampooed her hair. After she had dried it and brushed it out, she shaved Leslie's legs, arm pits and loins.

This last she had done with Leslie lying on her back on the bed, her knees up and spread and a pillow under her hips. She applied lotion to her pudendum, rubbing it in gently. She slid her thumb over Leslie's bud of pleasure and caressed it until Leslie moaned and her slice had moistened. Then she had Leslie lie up further on the bed and turn on her belly while she gave her body a thorough, comforting massage. Her hands were expert at loosening Leslie's taut muscles. Her ministrations put Leslie in a daze. Latifah hummed a little song while she worked on her, letting out pleasant sounding endearments from time to time. Once she had spread a sweet smelling lotion all over her skin, she rolled her to her back, and did the same for her for her front, massaging the fronts of her thighs, her breasts, her arms and shoulders, even her hands and feet.

As she was applying the lotion to her front, running her hands lightly over Leslie's breasts, belly and thighs, Leslie began to get aroused. She felt Latifah kiss the tips of her breasts. She ran her lips over her belly as she stroked her sides. She placed her strong hands on the insides of her thighs and spread her legs. When she put her mouth to Leslie's sex, the young girl moaned. She kept her on fire for a long time and then finally gave her release, as Leslie screamed her pleasure.

She had just finished doing her makeup, lining her lower lips, decorating her eyes and the tips of her breasts and all the rest and was about to put on her jewelry when they both heard the sound of the outer door opening and closing. Latifah leapt up and quickly donned her black abaya, pulling the veil over her face. The door to the cell opened. It was Faraq. He made a motion for Latifah to leave the room. She had just finished decorating Leslie's breasts and the young girl's hands were temporarily free. She was sitting on the edge of the bed at its foot.

Leslie's heart grew cold when she saw the icy demeanor of Mr. Moussa's factotum. A knot formed in her stomach as she worried that he had come to beat her. But he had not.

He ordered her up on the bed. Leslie scrambled to obey. She remembered his order of the day before and as soon as she laid down on her back, she raised and spread her knees and started to pet and caress her coosh. She watched the man undress. By the time he crawled up on the bed between her widespread thighs, she was wet and ready for him. His cock was already hard. He moved up, probed at her opening and slid right in.

There was something special about when Faraq fucked her that wasn't present for the others. While he possessed her, dwelt inside her, she felt totally and irrevocably controlled by him. Her mind grew fevered and her body rejoiced. He took her to a singular zone where she felt that pleasing him, satisfying his carnal appetites was her life's charge. She moaned and thrust her hips up to meet his. She circled her arms around him, enclosed the back of his legs with hers, drawing him in. When she came, she gripped him tightly, reveling in the feel of him, the heat of his body. And when he came inside her, she was overwhelmed with joy at having served him.

Afterwards, when he withdrew, she was filled with shame at her sluttishness and her fear of the implacable man returned.

When Faraq was finished with her he left. He had not said a word to her, having told her to get on the bed with a wave of his hand. Leslie felt debased, used and discarded. She knew that she was nothing but a depository for him. To her, he was her true master, the dark, foreboding ruler of her soul.

When he left, Latifah returned, patted her on her head and urged her from the bed. After she washed her loins, she finished adorning and perfuming her, locked up her hands to the front of her collar, attached her leash and led her upstairs.

And this was how her day began, first for days and days, then for weeks and weeks and then for months and months. While Latifah mouthed her to completion every morning, Faraq's morning visits were intermittent. Sometimes, in the middle of the day, or in the early evening, when no one had called for her, her would bring her down to her cell and fuck her long and hard. When he spilled himself into her mouth, her womb or her rear, his cock throbbing, his muscles tensed, his mouth emitting a deep, almost angry groan, she felt like he had given her a great gift. During their couplings, Leslie would feel like she was on fire as he used one or another of her entrances. When he was done, Latifah, who always waited outside, would come in and reclaim her, wash her and then bring her back upstairs.

Some days, he would not use her at all, although she would see him as she was led through the hallways or while she was in her cage in the kitchen. Sometimes, he would pull her out of her cage and make her suck him. He rarely said any words to her. On occasion, he beat her or left her grotesquely bound in her cell, hooded and gagged for several hours just to impress on her that he still retained power over her. Sometimes, when Mr. Moussa was away, he would fill her crevasse with the soul stealing, body wrenching dildo he had used on her the first day, bind her as he did then, and leave her there to suffer for several hours. These sessions always resulted in a redoubling of Leslie's commitment to obedience, which was the whole point.

Mrs. Moussa used her often, sometimes several times a day. Usually, she had Leslie mouth her pussy to completion while on her knees before her, but often she actually took her to her bed. She would drive Leslie to shattering orgasms. She would lay atop her, press her mons down hard against hers and fuck her, abrading their sex lips together. She would take possession of Leslie's mouth, not like the strong but yet comforting efforts from Latifah, but with a forcefulness and aggression that left no doubt who was the slave and who was the mistress. Leslie hated the feeling of her tongue in her mouth. It was like the ultimate invasion of her being. When Mrs. Moussa took possession of her quim with her mouth, she would ravage it like a demon.

Mrs. Moussa was particularly cruel and often had her beaten, and sometimes beat her herself, for the slightest perceived infraction or just on a whim. When Mr. Moussa was away, which was often, Latifah would deliver Leslie to Mrs. Moussa's salon. She had had a little cage installed there and Leslie would be placed in it. It was even smaller than the one in the kitchen and she would be all scrunched up, her flesh pressed through the bars. Mrs. Moussa would let her languish there for hours while she talked on the phone, read a magazine, had her tea, awaited her guests. She would cast an occasional glance at her, just often enough to let Leslie know that she was aware of her presence.

At night, when she was delivered to Mrs. Moussa's room, she often had her wait upon her soft, luxurious bed, her forehead pressed down, her hips up, her legs spread, her wrists locked behind her back, while she tended to her personal needs. Leslie would hear the slither of her silk coverings as she disrobed, listen as she bathed herself in her large, brilliantly decorated tub in the adjoining bathroom, hear her brushing her long, silky black hair. It was as if she were purposely flaunting her freedoms and luxuries so that Leslie could contrast them with her own lack of these things. When she finally came to bed, she would take her time, exploring each facet of Leslie's body with her hands and her lips, demonstrating her ownership, before commencing her main assault.

Because she was the one who had essentially enslaved her, Leslie's resentment against Mrs. Moussa burned more fiercely than against anyone else. She would look at her elegant exterior and contrast her gracious, lush life with her own miserable one. She would hear her fashionable heels click clacking in the tiled hallways as she approached and a raw anger would rise up inside her. Latifah, leading her now with the leash attached to the ring in her loins, would make her fall to her knees and put her forehead to the floor as she went by. The cold, indifferent looks that Mrs. Moussa gave her chilled her to the bone.

And she had the power to return her to that hellish prison. So Leslie kissed her back passionately, serviced her with anxious vigor, accommodated her every use of her, obeyed her every command with slavish devotion, and paid obeisance to her as if her life depended on it.

From time to time, Mrs. Moussa would have female guests. They would gather in her salon where Mrs. Moussa often used her. Mrs. Moussa would order Latifah to demonstrate for her friends her skills at the manipulation of female flesh and, kneeling before them, her legs spread, her hands bound cruelly up her back behind her, Leslie would moan and groan, tremble and shudder before them until Latifah finally took mercy on her.

Afterwards, the women would admire her markings and decorations, giggle and laugh when they saw the golden flower in her rear, comment admiringly on the medal fused onto her loins. Mrs. Moussa would have her kneel in presentation position while she and the other women ate their lunch and drank their tea or coffee. Afterwards, they would undress and make love to her, each in their turn, or merely lift their stylish skirts and have her mouth their pussies until they came.

From time to time, Mrs. Moussa called in their chauffer, a tall, muscular, dark skinned Bedouin, and had him fuck Leslie for their amusement. He would pierce her mouth, making her suck him long and hard before spilling himself on her face. He would then plow her lower apertures while she was on her hands and knees, her cum covered, enraptured face held up for Mrs. Moussa's guests to see, until she groaned and shook with pleasure. He had incredible stamina and was capable of quick recovery and would not finish with her until he had filled her with his spunk at least three times.

The women often returned all by themselves and Mrs. Moussa would let them use Leslie in one of the guest rooms.

Mr. Moussa's use of her was always remote and cool. While Mrs. Moussa often verbally tormented her, reminding her of her delicate status, calling her a whore and a slut, Mr. Moussa rarely spoke to her at all except to give her orders. When he was home, she would spend a couple hours each morning and afternoon in his office with him. He would take a break and have him suck his prick or have her bend over the desk and fuck either one of her lower holes. Sometimes he took her to his large, overstuffed couch and, lying her on her back and raising her thighs, plowed her furrow relentlessly until she moaned with pleasure and then released his spume into her.

If Mrs. Moussa came in, as she did often, and he was using her, she would wait patiently until he was done, sitting in a chair smoking a cigarette or reading a magazine, before speaking to him. Those times when Leslie was kneeling, her ready, twin portals in presentation position, her head to the floor, she would listen with dismal rancor as they chatted happily together, discussing this or that. When Mrs. Moussa left, her distinctive, musky perfumed scent would linger in the room, reminding Leslie of her former presence.

Mr. Moussa would have her come to him and he would tumble her over his lap and then absent mindedly stroke and caress her sex while talking on the telephone. He would bury his fingers deep inside her, making her flush with passion and then, just as nonchalantly, push her aside and go on to other business, leaving her to burn.

He did get another secretary. It was a young French girl. She was appalled at first when she saw Leslie, all made up like a whore, bound and naked in her employer's office, but she soon got used to it. Sometimes, when Mr. Moussa got bored with her, he would have the young girl come in and lead her from the room with her leash and turn her over to Latifah who always waited outside.

And, as Mrs. Moussa had foretold, Leslie had to fuck his friends. When a business acquaintance came by the office, Mr. Moussa would order Leslie to service him with her mouth. If they were inclined for other pleasures, he had one of the servants show the man to a guest room, Leslie in tow, and he would fuck her there.

At night, he sometimes had guests in his den. There was a large, 3' by 3', leather covered hassock there where Leslie could be placed on her back and used. Or she would be ordered to kneel on it, present her rear haunches and, as Mrs. Moussa had predicted, suffer the use of her rear aperture. Mr. Moussa never used her when other men were present, but would wait until the end of the night when they had all left. He never took her to his bed, never undressed, and used her only in his office or at night in his den.

After a few weeks, Hajib went back to Paris. Leslie was grateful that he had because he was the most callous user of her body. He would slap her around, whip her, make him lick his toes, crawl around the room and fuck her hard. He never lasted long and Leslie rarely experienced an orgasm with him.

The best, or the least worse, depending on how you looked at it because she was still being used as a whore, was Jana, the Moussa's 24 year old daughter. She missed sorely the marriage bed. She had some suitors, but none of them could compete with the memory of her dead husband. She would treat Leslie with loving affection whenever she used her. She never bound her or beat her. Her kisses were like delicious fruit and her touch soft and caring. Leslie responded in kind and they spent hours in bed together, sometimes drifting off to sleep after their bouts of lust. Jana missed the use of a cock most of all. She had a dildo that she made Leslie wear around her waist and use to fuck her.

Mrs. Moussa caught them lolling about in bed together one evening. She had told Latifah to bring Leslie to her bedroom suite when Jana was done with her and had gotten impatient with waiting. She burst through Jana's door and saw them lying together exchanging sweet kisses. She gave Jana an intensive dressing down in Arabic and then brought Leslie to her room where she beat her brutally. Leslie did not couple with Jana for a few weeks after that and when they finally resumed their lovemaking, their sessions were brief.

All during this time, Latifah was a constant presence. She would wait outside the room while Laura was being used and then wash her up when they were finished with her. She fed her her every meal, always on the floor, her hands bound behind her. She washed and decorated her every day, slept with her every night. She would place her in her cage in the kitchen, letting her languish there for hours until someone called for her. Leslie often saw Mrs., Moussa in the kitchen, always elegantly dressed and made up, wearing her imported high heel shoes, but she hardly ever acknowledged her presence, and if she did, it would be with a slight, ironic smile.

There was a lounge off the kitchen for the female staff and sometimes, when Latifah was certain that no one would call for her, she would take Leslie back there so that she could drink tea and gossip with the other girls. She would have Leslie kneel by her side with her legs spread and her forehead on the floor while she sat cross legged next to her and petted and stroked her while she talked to the other women. She would keep Leslie on a slow burn for the longest time, letting her orgasm every once in a while, to the amusement of the other women, and then begin her casual ministrations all over again.

Every night, when everyone was through with her, she would make love to Leslie for an hour or more down in her cell and then go to sleep next to her, sometimes waking her up later for another session.

She was not overly cruel, but remorseless when she felt that Leslie had erred. She always carried her three foot long, flexible stick and she would give Leslie an immediate, fierce stroke with it when she was hesitant to obey, failed to walk properly through the hallways, her hips swaying enticingly, made a mess at her bowl, whined at any discomfort, stepped out of line in any way. There was a chain dangling from the ceiling in the kitchen and if Leslie's sin was particularly egregious, she would give her ten or twenty harsh strokes right there.

She gave Leslie lessons too. She had many years of experience with whores. She had a model of a prick and sometimes at night, before they made love, she would give Leslie tips on how to improve her techniques. She showed her how to pleasure a pussy too, showed her where to luck and suck and, more importantly when. It became Leslie's only source of revenge to have Mrs. Moussa tottering on the edge of release, in near agony, moaning and yearning for completion. She taught Leslie how to use her pussy's muscles too, how to clamp them around a cock and they engaged in exercises every night until Leslie got it right.

Generally, she saw Leslie as a slightly subhuman creature with all the attributes of a wonderful pet. She would sing to her, caress her tenderly, feed her little scrumptious tidbits from time to time. She loved making her up and varied the colors of her makeup and the jewelry that she wore around her neck and waist. Leslie always wore the belled earrings and the golden flower in her rear. Some nights, she would hold Leslie in her arms after they had finished making love and croon to her, letting Leslie cry and sob from her unhappiness.

Leslie was expressly forbidden to talk. Even the words, "Yes, sayyadati, no, sayyadati," were eventually forbidden to her. There were only two occasions when she was permitted speech.

Once a month, on a Friday, under Faraq's direct supervision, and Latifah hovering nearby, she was allowed to call home. This was to prevent her parents from becoming too upset and complaining to the American Embassy. They had been informed of Leslie's charges and that Mr. Moussa had kindly gone her bail. Leslie's father was a retired Air Force officer and he was always asking Leslie whether he should do something to help her. Leslie, under the keen eye of Faraq, who listened on an extension, always demurred, saying that she preferred to let justice take its course. She always reassured him and her mother that Mr. Moussa was treating her well although she had to obey the court's rules as far as phone calls and letters were concerned.

It was so incongruous to be kneeling on the floor in Mr. Moussa's office, naked and decorated like a whore and talking to her parents, while Latifah idly caressed her coosh. She did her best to sound normal, but some of her bitter disquiet about her treatment inevitably came out and her parents would ask her repeatedly if she was all right.

When she hung up there were always tears in her eyes. Faraq always made her suck his cock while Latifah stroked her to completion before she was returned to her other duties. Each night after a phone call, after Latifah went to sleep, she would cry and cry and cry. If Latifah heard her, she would draw herself up behind her, circle her with her large, strong arms and comfort her.

The only other occasion she was allowed to speak was the day the man came from the American Embassy to talk to her about her charges. It was about a month after her slavery had commenced. Leslie had not known about it in advance. All she knew was that when she woke up, Latifah did not put on her decorations. Faraq came down, and after stringing her up in the chain that dangled from the ceiling, gave her ten vicious swats with a cane. When her miserable sobbing relented, he opened the armoire in the room. It hadn't been opened since her imprisonment began. He took out one of Leslie's business dresses. It was cream colored with little brown buttons that went up the bodice. The skirt was knee length and had small pleats. It was one of her favorites.

Leslie was shocked to see all her things in there. She had wondered what they had done with them and now she knew. Afterwards, in the mornings, when Latifah was decorating her, she often stared at the closet dismally, pining for different days.

Faraq had her put on the dress. He installed the blue ball in her mouth, locked her bracelets behind her back and then brought her upstairs. She was led to Mr. Moussa's office where he was already sitting at his desk. She was made to kneel, her head to the floor, her hips raised while they waited for something. Mrs. Moussa came in to join them. Leslie got a glimpse of her shiny high heels and smelled her musky perfume. When she passed Leslie, she flipped up the back of her skirt so that her portals would be fully displayed. The three sat in casual conversation for a while. A maid brought in a tray of iced tea. Mrs. Moussa and Faraq smoked cigarettes. When the intercom buzzed, Mr. Moussa picked up the phone and received some news. He nodded to Faraq who ordered Leslie to get up and sit in a chair. He released her bracelets from behind her.

The dress had long sleeves that covered her bracelets and buttoned all the way up to the top, hiding her neck. Faraq had dressed her in her Nikes and pulled white socks up over her ankle confinements. So when the man from the embassy came in, there was nothing special to see except a rather prim and proper young lady.

He said his hellos to Mr. and Mrs. Moussa and Faraq and then to Leslie. He said that his name was Tom Martin. He wanted to know how she was being treated. Leslie cast quick glances at Mrs. Moussa and Faraq. They had all moved to Mr. Moussa's couch and easy chairs on the other side of the room. A mat had been placed over the ring in the floor. Mr. and Mrs. Moussa were sitting on the couch, the same couch on which Mr. Moussa occasionally fucked her.

Mrs. Moussa was, as always, dressed elegantly. Her top was a dark gold color, made of silk. It had large deep green, fabric covered buttons. The vee neck opened to the middle of her considerable cleavage and there were wide lapels. On her ears were small, thick, golden loops. She was wearing one of her trademark, flowing skirts. It was olive green and had abstract designs on it of yellow, blue and red. Her high heels were a very light green as was her eye shadow. Her lips were a soft red. She was wearing her regular rings and had a thick, woven gold chain around her neck that rested near the tops of her breasts.

She was a beautiful woman, refined looking, pleasant in her demeanor, gracious in her speech. How different she was from the Mrs. Moussa that Leslie knew and whose pussy she sucked. Leslie saw that she had picked up the ball from her mouth that had been left on Mr. Moussa's desk and was holding it in her right hand, squeezing it tightly. It was not a good sign.

Mr. Moussa was, as usual, stiff and correct and wearing a well tailored, pinstriped business suit. Faraq, dressed in khaki pants and a black tee shirt, was standing behind them, his eyes smoldering, his jaw set. Leslie's throat went dry when she saw him looking at her. Her body ached from her beating, her bruises pulsing. Now she knew why she had gotten it. It was to remind her that whatever happened here today, whatever she said, she would not be leaving with Mr. Tom Martin today or any other day. If she told him that the respectable Mr. and Mrs. Moussa had turned her into a sexual slave, she doubted that he would believe her, but even if he did, there would be nothing he could do but protest to the government. If things got bad, the Moussa's would simply ship her back to prison.

Leslie sat in one of the armchairs and Mr. Martin sat in one opposite her. They were facing the couch and Martin had to turn a little to his left to talk to her. It was strange to be seated in an actual chair after so many weeks. It was strange not to be on her knees in front of her oppressors. She had to fight the urge to fall to the floor and beg forgiveness.

She looked at the American. He was dressed in a cheap, grey business suit. He was wearing a white shirt and a wide, paisley tie. He was young, about 27 or so. He was clean shaven and fresh faced: an America abroad. Mrs. Moussa offered him tea but he declined.

"Ms. Harrington," he stated formally, "my name is Tom Martin, as I said. I am an undersecretary at the American Embassy in Tunis. Part of my duties is to obtain access to Americans accused of crimes in Tunisia and make sure that they are being afforded their rights and treated well. Are you familiar with the charges against you?"

Leslie looked quickly around the room, then down at the floor and then at Mr. Martin. The thought of speaking in Mr. & Mrs. Moussa's presence seemed sacrilegious, never mind Faraq. She had to jump start herself. Mrs. Moussa noted her distress. She put the ball in the pocket of her skirt, took hold of the pitcher of iced tea and poured a glass. "She's very nervous, Mr. Martin," she said gracefully. She had a deep, melodious voice that flowed like heavy cream. She got up from the couch carrying the glass.

"Here, take a long drink, Leslie," she said. "It'll make you feel better."

Leslie's hand was shaking as she took the glass. She had not been permitted to feed herself or drink anything but the water from a bottle that Latifah gave her for a long time. She brought the glass to her lips and took a small sip. It tasted so good! She drank a little bit more and then a little bit more. Then she looked up at Mrs. Moussa standing next to her and, seeing her patience starting to slip, put the glass down on a small table next to her chair.

She looked at Martin. "What was the question again," she asked. Her voice sounded funny to her, unfamiliar.

"The charges, Ms. Harrington. Do you know what they are? Has anyone told you?"

"Y,yes," she replied softly.

"Do you have an attorney?"

Mrs. Moussa interrupted. She was standing behind Leslie and had put her hand on the back of the chair. Leslie felt her dangerous presence behind her.

"We've hired the best attorney in Dar Al Jamah," she said. "He's very expensive, but cost is no object. We've become quite fond of Leslie since she's been with us. She's like another daughter to me." Mrs. Moussa stroked Leslie's hair. It made Leslie shiver.

"Well, I'm glad of that," Martin said writing something down on a little pad he had produced from his jacket pocket. He returned to Leslie.

"Are you being treated well?"

A thousand responses rushed into Leslie's mind. But they only caused a second's delay. She knew the right answer. "Y,yes," she said.

"That's good. It must be nice to have Mr. and Mrs. Moussa helping you. Otherwise you'd be rotting in that awful jail. I've heard some very nasty things about it. You're lucky. Bail on a criminal charge is very unusual in Tunisia."

Leslie didn't know whether this called for a response, but she eked out a "Y,yes," just in case.

"Is there anything that you need, anything that I can help you with?" he asked her.

His voice was so earnest, so desirous of being helpful that Leslie felt like she was going to cry. Then she felt a tear falling down from her right eye. She wiped it away with her hand. "What's going to happen to me?" she asked timidly.

"Well, these are some very serious charges. It's hard for me to conceive a nice person like you of having committed them. I've checked out your background and you come from a very nice family and have a good education. Maybe you'll be found innocent." He looked away from her as he spoke. Leslie knew that he knew that there was little chance of that. Sergeant Malikah had told her in the jail that the courts in Tunisia had a 95% conviction rate, and Mrs. Moussa's uncle was going to be the judge.

Leslie started to cry. She couldn't help it. She was overwhelmed. Here, a mere three feet away from her was a fellow American. He was from the American government. It was like having the agent of her liberation right in front of her and him being helpless to assist her.

Mrs. Moussa leaned over and put her arm around her shoulder. "There, there, now Leslie, don't cry. It will work out all right, I promise you." She turned to Mr. Martin. "See, you've upset her."

"Oh, I'm terribly sorry. I didn't mean to. It's just my job, that's all," the American replied. "I guess I'll be on my way."

"Won't you stay and have some lunch?" Mrs. Moussa asked graciously.

"No thank you. I've got to get back to Tunis by dark. It was nice having met you all." He rose from his chair and extended his hand to Mr. Moussa. They shook and Mrs. Moussa extended hers to his. They shook as well. Martin gave a polite nod to Faraq.

He turned to Leslie who had remained seated. No one had told her to get up.

"It was nice to have met you, Ms. Harrington. If there ever anything I can do for you, please give me a call." He reached into his jacket pocket and pulled out a businesses card. He handed it to Leslie.

"Call anytime. I wish you well and good luck."

Leslie took it and looked at it. Her tears were gone, but her heart was filled with despair. In a few moments, this little interlude in her new life would be over and she would revert to being the Moussa's private whore. Her lips began to tremble.

She knew that the likelihood of her ever seeing America again, or even another American for that matter, for a long, long time was very small. She looked up at Mr. Martin. She saw sympathy and helplessness in his eyes. "Thank you," she said meekly.

Faraq escorted Mr. Martin from the office. A wave of panic shot through Leslie. Her only hope of being freed was leaving! What should she do? What could she do? And then he was out the door and it closed behind him. Mr. Moussa went to his desk and lit a cigarette. Mrs. Moussa poured herself a glass of iced tea and took a long drink. She said something in Arabic to Mr. Moussa and he just waved her off. He picked up the phone to make a call.

Leslie was shaking. Nobody had told her to move. She didn't know what to do. She knew she should be on her knees, but she hadn't the power to move a muscle. Mrs. Moussa looked at her like she had forgotten that she was there. "What are you waiting for you stupid whore," she said coldly. "Take off that silly dress and get on your knees."

Leslie suppressed a sob and started to move. She still had Mr. Martin's card in her hand and Mrs. Moussa snatched it away. Leslie had just begun to get off her seat.

"Wait!" Mrs. Moussa commanded. She took the blue ball out of her pocket. "Open your mouth slut," she said caustically. Leslie complied and Mrs. Moussa shoved the ball home. "There, whore," she said. "Now get naked."

Normally, that is in her prior life, Leslie would have gotten to her feet to take off a dress. But she was too afraid to stand. She sank immediately to her knees and started unbuttoning the dress. Her hands were wet with perspiration and the buttons kept slipping out of her fingers. Mrs. Moussa got impatient and she grabbed the two sides of the bodice and tore them apart, causing the buttons to fly off. "Head to the floor!" she ordered. Leslie obeyed instantly and put her arms behind her back. She heard Mrs. Moussa ask Mr. Moussa a question, an affirmative response from him and then the opening of a drawer. Mrs. Moussa stepped closer to Leslie. She felt the hem of her dress being lifted and then heard the sound of a scissors at work.

Mrs. Moussa cut all the way up the back of Leslie's dress. She took one arm and cut the dress all the way to her shoulder and then did the other arm. Leslie was crying the whole time. This was her favorite dress. She knew that the likelihood of her ever wearing it again was close to nil, but to see it being wantonly destroyed by the cruel Mrs. Moussa was too much to take. And all this on top of having to watch Mr. Martin walk out the door. She started blubbering and sobbing. Mrs. Moussa tore the rest of the dress from her body. She crouched down and pulled her Reeboks from her feet and tore off her socks. Before she got up, she connected the chain from the bracelet on Leslie's right hand to the one on her left.

Just then, Faraq returned to the room. "Take this pig down to her cell and give her a thorough beating," Mrs. Moussa said in English so that Leslie could understand her. "She needs to put all the foolishness that took place here today out of her mind. And when you're done, have Latifah bring her to my salon. I'll be waiting for her there."

Faraq snapped his fingers and Leslie jumped to her feet. She was still sobbing. Faraq connected her leash to the ring in her loins and pulled her from the room. She sobbed all the way down the hall, down the stairs and along the corridor. She was till sobbing when Faraq mounted her once more in her cell, her hands pulled far up above her, her ankles anchored to the floor. He took a long, thin whip out of the closet and, without delay, laid into her with a powerful stroke.

When Latifah brought her up to Mrs. Moussa's salon an hour later, she had been decorated as usual and was wearing all of her accouterments. Her body was covered with a dozen angry, red stripes.

CHAPTER NINE

As the months went by, Leslie felt herself slipping deeper and deeper into her role as a sexual slave. She got so used to being referred to as Ghaniyah that, at times, she forgot that she once had been called Leslie. All she thought about was sex and, occasionally, her freedom. During the long, boring hours she often spent in her cage in the kitchen, she would begin to yearn to have somebody ring for her. Her pussy would become wet when she saw Faraq or Mrs. Moussa moving through the kitchen. With Mrs. Moussa, it was always tinged with a feeling of revulsion. Faraq took all of his meals there and she would burn as she watched him, hoping that when he was done he would take her downstairs and fuck her or, at least, release her from her cage for a short while so that she could suck his prick.

It was in December, some nine months after her enslavement, that events coalesced that would change her status.

Hajib was home. Mr. and Mrs. Moussa were away in Rome, along with Jana. Faraq had left for a few days to see to some business for Mr. Moussa. To Leslie's dismay, Hajib had virtual sole use of her, except for Latifah of course. For three days running, he kept her in his room for hours, abusing her, fucking her, whipping her. He brought two of his friends home with him one day and the three of them used her repeatedly in turn, or in pairs, while drinking themselves into a stupor. It was early in the morning that Latifah was able to rescue her.

On the fourth day, Latifah received a telegram from her sister in Tunis that their mother was ill. She was beside herself. Via telephone from Rome, Mrs. Moussa gave her permission to go and see her. It was arranged that the house mistress would take care of Leslie.

She, of course, had little experience with how to handle the house slave, but she did her best. By the second day after her departure, Leslie was pining for Latifah's return.

It was that night that it happened. The house mistress had dropped Leslie off in Hajib's room. Normally, Latifah would have parked herself outside of his door and waited until he was done with her. The housemistress had other duties, however, and she left, intending to return in an hour or so.

Hajib was a typical rich man's son. He was juvenile in the extreme, irresponsible and wild. When he discovered that the housemistress wasn't there, he telephoned a few of his friends. When he got off the phone, he left Leslie chained to his bed while he went out to get something. He returned with a long, black ayala. He bound her hands to her front collar and made Leslie put it on. He brought her down the stairs to the outside and put her in the passenger seat of his car. He drove her to one of the first class hotels in town and brought her upstairs to the penthouse.

The party had already started. There was loud rock and roll music, laughing, dancing young men and women, and a table full of booze. It was one of the hotel's largest suites and there were as many as twenty five people there. When Hajib brought Leslie into the room, he made an announcement. The music stopped and everyone crowded around. He lifted Leslie's abaya up from the hem, whisking it from her body.

Leslie had been frightened when Hajib took her from the house. She was deathly afraid of him. He had no limits as far as she was concerned and he had beaten her very badly a few times, so much that she had to stay in bed the next day to recover. Although he was scolded by Mrs. Moussa, he was not punished.

When she saw all the fashionable young people gathered in the room, Leslie's stomach fell. She knew that Hajib would make her available to them. There were so many and most of them appeared to be drunk. When Hajib took off her covering, she whined in misery.

They made good use of her. The crowd watched her first few blow jobs, issuing catcalls and witty comments that made everyone laugh. After that, the party resumed again and she was dragged to the bedroom where the real fucking started. Boys and girls had their fun with her. It didn't take long before she was covered with cum and women's slick discharge. Her tongue and pussy and rear started to become sore.

The party went on and on. People came and went. Hajib was nowhere to be found. Leslie saw people doing lines of coke and smoking hash. They made her smoke some and she welcomed the dizziness and dullness it brought. They filled her full of booze too. Eventually, someone brought her to the bathroom, gave her a shower and then brought her back to the bed for more fun.

At some point, Leslie passed out. When she awoke, she was on the bed. There was absolute silence in the suite. Bodies of boys and girls, in various states of undress were strewn about the room. It took Leslie a few moments to realize that she wasn't chained to anything. It was the first time in almost a year. She understood immediately that her chance for escape at come at last.

She went to the bathroom and threw up. After she washed her face, removing her makeup with soap and water, she felt a lot better. She tiptoed out into the bedroom and gathered some women's clothes that she thought would fit. She selected a nice pink blouse and a black miniskirt together with a pair of black high heels. There were a dozen abayas strewn about the room and she picked one up. Then she looked around for women's purses. In the third one, she found a passport. The girl didn't look much like her, but she would have to do. She went through the pockets of some of the pants and found wads of cash. She found Hajib lying in a pool of his own vomit. His pants were around his ankles. Resisting the temptation to piss on his face, she reached in them carefully and found his car keys. A moment later, she was out the door.

She took the stairs rather than the elevator in case she might meet someone coming up who would stop her. When she got to the parking lot, she found Hajib's car right away. It was a Mercedes sports model, a two seater, brand new. She hopped into the driver's seat, started it up and roared away.

She didn't know where she was going at first, but she knew that she needed to get away from the hotel in case Hajib came looking for her. She drove about five miles outside of the city and stopped by the side of the road. Her adrenaline was pumping high. She realized, too late, that she hadn't anything to eat or drink. She didn't dare stop anywhere because, even after all these months, she only had a smattering of Arabic and that had mostly to do with spreading her legs, kneeling down or opening her mouth.

She tried to gather herself and tried to envision a map of Tunisia. She knew that to the east was Libya. She certainly didn't want to go there. To the west was Algeria. That sounded a little better. But which road should she take? How far was it and did she have enough gas? If she was able to sneak into Algeria, she could find the American Embassy and get a ticket home. They just had to help her. She was still an American, wasn't she?

She opened the glove compartment and found a map. When she unfolded it, she saw immediately that her options were very limited. Algeria was many, many miles away. And once she reached the border, it was many, many more miles to the coast and the capital city where the embassy would be. Libya was only about 75 miles. She couldn't remember if there was an American Embassy in Libya anymore, but there had to be something. Tripoli was a huge city and was very close to the border. She had some money. She could call home and her dad would find some way to help her.

So Libya it would be.

She took the car out on the roadway. Fifteen minutes later, she was on the coast highway traveling at 75 kilometers per hour.

She felt so happy she began to laugh. She drew back the hood to her ayala and let the wind from the window blow through her hair. It was about 7 a.m. and chilly. There were a few cars passing the other way, but not many. She turned on the radio and tuned it to an Italian station where she could hear good old rock and roll music. Hajib had left a pack of cigarettes in the console and she took one out and smoked it, even though she had never smoked before. She coughed at first, but then got it down. It made her head feel light and dizzy, but that felt good too.

When she thought that all of her travails were behind her, she started to cry. No more whippings, no more chains, no more

Latifah. She could sleep in a bed alone. She could go out for walks. She could sleep all day, stay up all night and watch TV. Go to movies, find a boyfriend, see her family, use the telephone. All of these things were going to happen. No more 20 year prison term looming over her horizon.

After a while, she held back her tears. She would have a good cry and a mental breakdown when she was home and free for sure. Now there was still danger out there. She remembered that she had to cross the border and that she had somebody else's passport. But she had a huge wad of cash too and, from what she understood, in these Middle East countries, cash talked and bullshit walked.

A little over an hour later, she came up to the border crossing. There was a high gate and customs offices on both sides. She started to get nervous. "This has to work! This has to work!" she thought. She remembered the collar around her neck. She worried whether seeing it might set off alarm bells. But if she kept the ayala up high, covering her neck, she might be all right.

There were three cars ahead of her when she pulled up to the border crossing. Two sleepy guards were manning the actual gate and a thin man in a poorly fitting uniform was checking passports. He had a military style cap on his head and red epaulettes on his shoulders. She remembered the last time she had seen red epaulettes and she shivered.

It only took a minute or so for her car to be next. The man leaned over into her window and said something in Arabic to her. She just smiled and handed him the passport. She had put two 100 Dinar notes in it, about $150.00. His eyes bugged out a little when he saw them and he looked around. Then he looked at Leslie and then back at the passport. He lifted the cash from it and looked at the picture. There was a pause that, for Leslie, lasted a lifetime.

He closed the passport, put the money in his pocket and pointed to his left, saying something in Arabic. Leslie didn't understand him, but his tone didn't sound too good. She reached down into the little purse she had stolen and pulled out another wad of cash. It was about 400 Dinar. He took that too, put it in his pocket and repeated his motion for her to pull out of the line. Leslie started to panic. She grabbed all the cash that she had and she proffered it to him. "Please! Please let me through! Please!" she said. The she repeated it in French. The man said something angry to her. The men at the gate were taking notice.

Overwhelmed with fear, Leslie considered gunning the motor and running the gate. But then there were the guards on the other side, the Libyans. She would have to run that gate too and then she would be a fugitive in Libya. She realized that she didn't have much choice. Maybe the man just wanted her to wait until a better time. Maybe he wanted sex or something. Maybe he'd let her go if she could talk to him in private.

She gave the car some gas and pulled over to where the officer had indicated. She pulled the veil over her face and got out of the car. He took her by the elbow and escorted her into the low, brick building. There was a small reception area with a number of dirty, worn, yellow plastic chairs and a window behind which sat another officer. The man who had brought her in said something to the man at the window. He pressed a buzzer and the door to the right of the window popped open. The officer led Leslie through the door, down a long hall paneled in faux oak, and to another door. He opened the door, pushed Leslie in and then closed it.

The room was about 10' by 20' with an 8' high ceiling. It had a scuffed up wooden floor and a bench that ran along one wall. Ominously, there were chains bolted into the benches with hand cuffs at their ends. The room had a series of small windows about a foot wide along the top of the wall covered with chicken wire. Its walls too were covered with cheap, fake oak paneling. Leslie realized that she had been detained. She sat down on the bench and cried.

She knew that if she was returned to the Moussa's she would be in a world of trouble. She couldn't imagine the punishments she would receive. And then there was the distinct possibility that she would be taken directly to the prison where she could commence her 20 year sentence capped off by whatever they would give her for trying to flee the country. A wave of despair flowed through her so intense that she began to vomit. A thin line of bile and other foul smelling liquids emerged from her mouth and spilled onto the floor. She looked around the room to see if there was anything there she could kill herself with. There was nothing, of course, unless she could break a window and cut her wrists with some glass. But she had nothing to break it with. And she had the chicken wire to contend with too. She bent over and curled up on the bench and sobbed.

She had been cried out for about an hour when the door opened and another officer came in. He was dressed like the first, but without a cap. He looked at the floor where Leslie had puked and made a disgusted face. Leslie looked back at him. "I'm sorry," she said. "I couldn't help it."

The man waved for her to come with him. When she reached the door, he took hold of her elbow and marched her deeper into the building. He had a tight grip on her arm. She was led to another door. He knocked and she heard a man's deep voice answer. He opened the door, guided her through and closed the door behind her.

This room was elegantly appointed. The walls were painted a deep green and there was a plush rug on the floor. On the walls were mounted beautiful watercolors of desert scenes. There were a few official looking plaques. On the far wall was a picture of the country's ancient dictator and in the corner hung the national flag.

Immediately in front of her was a large, dark oak desk. It was neat, with a small pile of papers to the right and a telephone to the left. It had a large, green desk pad on it. Behind it, sat a broad shouldered man with a full, black moustache and black, wavy hair, neatly barbered. He had red epaulettes on his shoulders too, but also had what looked like golden eagles on his lapel. Leslie's passport and the wad of cash she had given the border guard were sitting on his desk. He had a scowl on his face. He didn't look evil, but he didn't look friendly either. Leslie guessed that he was about 50 years old.

"Please sit down," he told her.

Nervously, Leslie made her way to a wooden chair in front of his desk and took a seat.

"Now I know that this isn't your passport. You're not even Tunisian. So you might as well tell me who you are and why you are trying to sneak into Libya."

Leslie's throat constricted and she started to cry. "Please let me go! Please!" she said miserably. "You can have all my money. You can even have the car. I just want to go home!"

"My name is Colonel Abib," he announced. "I am the commander of this border crossing. When a foreigner hands one of my men a Tunisian passport and some cash, the subject is arrested and brought in here to me. Your only chance of crossing this border today is to convince me that you have a good reason to flee Tunisia. So I want the truth. Now. You are an American, no?"

Leslie nodded. She began her tale of woe. She told him everything from her arrest by the police in Dar Al Jamah to her stealing of the car. She showed him her collar and bracelets. Her face was awash with tears and the colonel twice had to give her tissues to wipe it.

"That is a very sad story, Miss Harrington," he said finally. "Alas it is not too uncommon in our country. There is much corruption. Let me tell you this, the last thing I want is you serving 20 years in a Tunisian prison."

Leslie's face brightened. "You mean you'll help me."

"Of course," he said.

Leslie burst into tears again. "Oh, thank you!" she said over and over. "Thank you!"

"For official reasons, I cannot let you cross the border until tonight when I get off duty. This way I will not be committing an official act of misconduct. You will have to wait until then. I assume that this is acceptable."

"Oh, yes! Yes!" Leslie blurted out. "Anything you say! I can't thank you enough!"

"It is all right. I will have my reward," he replied.

He pressed a buzzer on his phone and the office who had escorted her to his office returned. The colonel gave him some instructions and he snapped to attention.

"My man will take you to a waiting room. I assume you haven't eaten. He will bring you some food and something to drink. The room is air conditioned so that you will be comfortable."

"Thank you," Leslie replied.

The man led her even deeper into the building and into a room much like the first one except that this had a table and some chairs and no windows. As soon as she was alone, Leslie removed her ayala and sat in a chair. About a half hour later, the man returned with a plate of mixed beef and vegetables and a Coke. Leslie wolfed them down.

She sat in the room for hours. Twice, Colonel Abib came back to assure her that all was well. When he saw Leslie's long, bare legs, he brought himself up quickly and returned his gaze to her face. In the middle of the afternoon, an officer came back with more food and another Coke. He let her use the bathroom down the hall and then brought her back.

Leslie didn't know how late it was when the colonel finally came to get her. He had his officer's cap on and was wearing a heavy jacket. She saw, to her dismay, that he was carrying a pair of handcuffs.

"These are just a formality, Miss Harrington," he said to her apologetically. "I can't have my officers seeing me take you out without them. Please turn around and let me put them on you, and then we will leave."

Reluctantly, Leslie got to her feet, turned around and put her arms behind her. The colonel had trouble putting the cuffs on her because of her scarlet leather bracelets, but he managed.

Down about thirty feet from the room in which she had spent most of the day was a door to the outside. Leslie was able to glance out of a window and she saw that it was dark. Colonel Abib unlocked the door with a key on a chain that led to his belt and they stepped outside.

It was a little chilly, maybe 50 degrees Fahrenheit. Leslie shivered as they walked along a macadam path and then into a parking lot. Colonel Abib had a loose hold on her right arm. They were walking quickly.

"There, ahead is my car," the colonel said, pointing out a shiny, black, late model BMW sedan. When they approached it, by its rear, they came to a halt. "Excuse me while I get my keys," the man said. He reached into his jacket pocket.

Swiftly, he stepped behind Leslie. In a second, he looped over her head a long cloth with a 6' by 3' pad in the middle. He pulled the pad over her mouth and quickly tied the cloth off behind her head. Leslie barely had time to protest. He used his key chain to pop open the trunk. He pushed the shocked Leslie towards and then into it. She screamed, but only a muffled sound came out. He swiftly had a rope around her ankles and tied them together. While Leslie struggled and screamed, he flipped her to her belly and connected the rope around her ankles to the handcuffs, hogtieing her. Leslie had just turned her head back to issue a plaintive whine when the trunk lid closed.

The car drove for about 45 minutes. All kinds of things were going through Leslie's fevered mind. Was he taking her back to Dar Al Jamah? If he was, was it to the Moussa's or to the prison? Or had he kidnapped her on his own behalf? If he intended her to go back to prison, all he would have had to do was put her in the back seat of his car with the handcuffs on and take her there. The same went for the Moussa's house. Therefore, she concluded, he had taken her for his own purposes, whatever they were, although Leslie knew that they wouldn't be good.

She then realized that there would be no record of her at the border crossing. As far as the authorities were concerned, and they must be looking for her by now, she would have just disappeared into thin air. But then there was the car. Hajib's car was at the border crossing. Someone would report it and her trail might be tracked from there. But what good would that do her? She would be returned to the Moussa's or prison. It was no choice at all.

But what did Colonel Abib intend to do with her? If he intended to rape her, she could handle that as long as it was the price of freedom. She remembered how he had looked at her legs. Maybe that was it. She hoped that was it, because anything else was too dreadful to bear.

She felt torn apart. She had been so close to freedom she could taste it. What he had told her in his office had lifted her spirits so high that many times during her wait in the small room, she had had to resist the urge to get up and dance. Now she had no idea what her future would bring. Had she gone from the frying pan into the fire?

When the car stopped, Leslie's heart went into her mouth. She dreaded the opening of the trunk and what it would reveal about the man's intentions. She heard the car door open and close and then, for a few moments, nothing.

When the trunk lid opened, Abib leaned over and freed Leslie's ankles. He took hold of her arm and began to lift her out. "Come on, sweetie pie," he said merrily. "We're home."

It was dark out, but from the lights on neighboring properties, Leslie saw that they were in what seemed to be a middle class neighborhood. She didn't have much time to look around because Abib quickly dragged her towards his house. The building was one storey and had a car port with an older model Toyota Celica was parked in it. There was a grass lawn in front of the house and a walkway to the street covered in small white stones. A side door off the carport led into the house. Abib took her through it.

They were inside a regular, American style kitchen. It was small and unkempt with dishes in the sink and packages of food, some of them open, strewn around the counters. Leslie heard a woman's voice and a moment later, an older, somewhat plump woman with long, loose, salt and pepper hair came around the corner. She was dressed in thin, purple cotton pants and a yellow pullover blouse. When she saw Leslie, her face fell. She looked at Abib and she started to yell excitedly in Arabic.

Abib started yelling back. It was clear that the subject of the argument was her. The argument went on for a few minutes. Then Abib, dragging Leslie along, pushed the woman aside and went into the next room. It was a living room and there was an old brown couch and a dark blue reclining easy chair along with a long coffee table. They passed through that room and went down a short hallway. Leslie tried to fight the man, but he was immensely strong and just yanked her every time she tried to dig in her feet and stop. Abib opened a door and they entered a small bedroom. He snapped on the light. It was painted in blue, with a made up twin bed, an old oak dresser and a nightstand with an old brass table lamp on it. There was a closet with sliding doors. One of the doors was off track.

The woman had followed them and was still shouting excitedly in Arabic. Abib ignored her. He threw Leslie down on the bed. She tried to scramble off of it, but he was on her quickly. He pressed her belly down on the mattress. The rope he had used on her ankles was still tied to the handcuffs and he captured Leslie's ankles one by one and tied them off with it, returning her to her hog tie. Her short, black skirt had risen up over her hindquarters, and before he got up, Abib rubbed his rough hand over them appreciatively. The Arab woman's screeches got louder and she went up to Abib and started hitting him with her fists. Abib relented his assault on Leslie's ass and got up off the bed. He took the still arguing Arab woman, presumably his wife, by her arm and pulled her from the room. The light went out and the door slammed shut.

The arguing went on for a full ten minutes. Leslie struggled to free herself from her bonds, but could not. She tried to scream, maybe one of the neighbors would hear her, but all that came out was a barely audible screech. She gave up her struggles and waited for whatever would happen next.

Eventually, the voices calmed down. They faded away as if they had gone into the kitchen. She heard more shouting and what sounded like pots and pans and dishes flying. Abib was undoubtedly complaining about the state of the kitchen. After a while, those sounds calmed down too.

For a long while there was relative silence in the house. She heard the TV go on and the voice of an Arabic announcer. Shortly afterwards some kind of drama show came on with police sirens and gunshots and a lot of talking.

It was about two hours later that the door opened again and the light came on. It was the woman and she was holding a tray with some food and a glass of juice on it. She came over to Leslie and sat down on the bed, putting the tray on the nightstand. She spoke to Leslie.

"I give you food and some drink. I take off cloth on mouth and feed you, you make noise, no eat, cloth go back on. Okay?"

Leslie was famished. She didn't want to go the night without something to eat. She was thirsty too. Leslie nodded.

The woman leaned over and released one of Leslie's ankles. She looked at the scarlet bracelets around them curiously. The she helped Leslie sit up with one leg under her. She untied the gag. When she released it, Leslie whispered urgently, "You've got to help me! He's kidnapped me! I'm an American citizen! You've got to help me get away!"

The woman put her finger to her mouth and said, "Shhhhhhhhhhhhh! If husband hear he beat me. He beat you too. No talking. He said."

Tears went to Leslie's eyes. The woman looked kindly. She obviously had sympathy for Leslie's plight. But Leslie clearly saw that she would not help her. This was not America where women had rights. If Abib wanted to beat his wife, there was no law stopping him. This woman obviously, despite her vitriolic temper, lived under his thumb. If she let her escape, Abib might kill her.

And so, Leslie disconsolately silenced herself. The woman took the plate from the tray and started spooning out food to her. It was a salty stew which seemed to have some bits of lamb in it. The woman ladled it into Leslie's mouth gently. Leslie chewed it slowly. She figured the longer she took to eat, the longer she would not have the gag around her mouth. And maybe, just maybe, the woman might be convinced to help her. Maybe not now, but maybe later, depending on how long Abib expected to hold her as his prisoner.

Every once in a while, the woman let Leslie have something to drink. The drink was a carbonated lemon juice with what seemed like a ton of sugar in it. While a prisoner at the Moussa's, Leslie usually had only water to drink so she actually delighted in having something to taste. When the stew was gone, the woman took up a pita, tore some off and scraped up the rest of the sauce. Leslie ate every bit.

When the meal was finished, the woman put down the bowl and spoon and said to Leslie, "You turn over now. I tie foot."

"Please," Leslie sad, "I have to use the bathroom."

The woman hesitated. This was not within her instructions. She thought about it for a moment. Then she pointed to her loins. "You make?" she asked.

Leslie got her meaning. "Yes," she said.

"You move," the woman told her. Leslie realized that the woman wanted to take off her underwear. Unfortunately, when she had escaped from the hotel, she hadn't thought to grab any. She moved anyway, shifting herself so that her loins were raised off the bed. The woman leaned forward to raise her short miniskirt. When she brought it up Leslie's thighs, she gasped. Not only did she not have any underwear on, but her pussy was shaved bare, outlined in red and there was a golden medallion hanging from her loins. She leaned over and took hold of it, reading it carefully. The she looked up at Leslie, horror in her eyes.

Leslie grimaced both in embarrassment and sorrow. "You see, I need help," she said.

"You name Ghaniyah," she said quietly. "You belong to Moussa."

"I'm trying to escape, please help me," Leslie asked again. The woman shook her head. She took the bowl from the tray and placed it under Leslie's loins. Leslie concentrated for a few seconds and her flow began. She filled up the whole bowl.

The woman carefully brought the bowl back to the tray and put it down. "You lie down now," she told Leslie after wiping her. Her voice had grown a little sterner. Leslie bit her lip and, seeing no choice, obeyed. The woman tied off her free ankle to her hands. Then she took the cloth gag, centered it over Leslie's mouth and tied it off tightly. She picked up the tray, turned out the light and closed the door. A few moments later, Leslie heard the toilet flush. A few moments after that, the argument outside her room began all over again.

The house eventually quieted down. The TV went off. Leslie heard someone in the bathroom brushing their teeth. She heard the unmistakable sound of liquid going into the toilet from a high distance and she concluded that it was Abib taking a piss. Soon, there was another person brushing their teeth. There was quiet and then the toilet flushed. A door down the hallway closed. And then there was silence.

For about an hour, Leslie tried to free her hands from the handcuffs. She could not get them past the heel of her hands. She moaned in frustration and gave up. Soon, she fell asleep.

She woke up to someone untying her ankles. It was dark in the room. For a moment she thought hopefully that it was the woman. But when she felt a rough hand on her thigh, she knew that it was Abib. When her ankles were free, her quickly flipped her to her back. She knew that he was intending to rape her and so she kicked out with her feet, landing one blow to his belly. He swiftly captured her feet and flung himself on top of her. His hand went around her throat. He squeezed it until Leslie started to choke. "If you give me any more trouble," he told her, snarling, "I'll choke you to death and bury you in the back yard!"

A chill went through Leslie. She gave up her struggle. For all she knew he would do just as he said. No one would miss her. No one knew she was here.

Abib was naked. He insinuated himself between her thighs and then raised them with his arms. He took hold of his cock and pressed it against her opening. Despite all her nonconsensual fucking while the Moussa's sex slave, nothing about Abib turned her on. She was as dry as the desert when he went to enter her. She moaned with pain as he advanced. He placed his heavy thumb over her clit and pressed it down, but that did nothing for her. She whined desperately under her gag. This slowed him down a bit. He pressed and he pressed and he pressed, slowly but surely until her cavern lubricated in self defense. When he was fully inside her, he began an energetic rogering. Leslie did not assist him, but lay still and lifeless, absorbing his thrusts. It did not take him long. He groaned and stiffened, thrust into her four more times and then collapsed.

He lay there for a few moments, panting. Then he arose, slipping his softened cock from her slit. He flipped her to her back once more and retied her ankles to the handcuffs. Then he tiptoed from the room and closed he door.

CHAPTER TEN

Leslie did not get back to sleep for a long time. She cried for a while. And then she stopped. She just lay there, miserably recounting all the terrible things that had happened to her since she had come to Tunisia. She thought of home, tried to visualize the faces of her family, but had a hard time doing it. She thought of her friends and how excited they had been for her when they found out about the great job she had gotten. She would certainly trade places with any of them now. She thought of how close she had gotten to getting away and then realized that it had not been close at all. She would have been better off going to Tunis and trying to find someone who would smuggle her out of the country. Maybe she could have stowed away on a cruise ship or something. Why hadn't she thought of that before? Trying to cross the border without her own passport had been a foolish decision.

She eventually did fall asleep and awoke when she heard noise around the house. It was early morning. She heard Abib using the bathroom again and taking a shower. A little while after, he came into her room.

"Let's see if we can get you tied down a little better," he told her as he released her ankles from her wrists and then pulled her to a sitting position. He tied her ankles together again and then released her hands from the handcuffs. He pulled her arms in front of her and examined her scarlet leather cuffs. He saw the chain dangling from her right bracelet and drew the right conclusion. He passed it through the ring in her collar and then hooked it to her left wrist. For good measure, he slipped the rings on her wrists together too. He untied her ankles and lifted her from the bed. He took her to the bathroom and sat her on the pot. "If there's anything you have to do, you better do it now," he told her.

Leslie emptied herself. She had done it so many times in front of Latifah, it didn't bother her one bit. He raised her from the seat and wiped her and then brought her back to the bed. He made her lie down on her back and then clipped the rings on her ankles together. He tied them to the bed frame at the end of the bed. Then he did the same at the head of the bed with the ring in the back of her collar. "Now that's much better, isn't it," he said happily. "My wife will be in later. She has strict instructions not to loosen your bindings except to feed you and let you pee. She knows that if you somehow get away, I'll slit her throat and chop her up into little pieces."

He went to leave and then turned. "In case you're wondering, the car you were driving was taken over the border yesterday into Libya. It's probably already been sold. It will bring a nice price, but not as much as you will." He laughed and left.

An hour later, the woman came in and released the tie to the back of her collar. After helping Leslie to sit up, she fed her some oatmeal for breakfast. It had raisins and honey in it. She let Leslie drink another glass of carbonated juice and then regagged her and tied her back down. They hadn't exchanged two words.

Leslie had a lot of time to think. The idea that Abib was going to sell her to someone had already occurred to her, but now she knew that her speculation had been true. She worried fretfully as to who it could be. She realized that her escape had actually landed her in a much worse position. While she was at the Moussa's, everybody at least knew where she was. She had a paper trail. It was actually possible, although unlikely, that someone would intervene on her behalf. Now, God alone knew where she would end up.

She had heard about harems in Saudi Arabia and such places and had always wondered if they were true. A harem had to be a better place than the Moussa's or prison, she thought. She would probably have to fuck only one guy and that only once in a while. They would treat her nice and she would have a nice bed and good food. Maybe she would get pregnant and the Emir, or whoever her captor was, would marry her and make her a queen. She did not have to worry about pregnancy at the Moussa's.

They fed her a regular diet of birth control pills. Mrs. Moussa was happy when she observed that they made her breasts bigger.

Nothing much happened in the house during the day. She heard the woman moving around a little bit. She vacuumed the living room at one point. There were a few phone calls. Someone came to visit. Leslie heard the door bell ring. But the woman chased whoever it was away. She watched TV for a long time. One of the programs was in English, a soap opera. Leslie thought it might be General Hospital.

When the woman came in to feed her lunch, Leslie indicated that she had to pee again. Rather than freeing her ankles, she untied them from the end of the bed, raised her legs and put the bowl under her quim. Leslie felt herself dribbling into it. The woman wiped her off and retied her ankles to the bed frame. Then she loosened the tie that went to her collar, helped her to sit up and fed her some soup. When done, she tied her back down again.

It was dark when Abib came back to the house. This time there was little shouting. He fed Leslie, playing with her breasts at the same time. He brought her to the bathroom again and actually brushed her teeth.

Later that night, he came to her again. It was the same story, only tonight, Leslie still had the abrasions from the night before. She moaned and whined while he entered her. He had just gotten buried to the hilt when Leslie heard his wife begin an awful racket. She was hitting him with a stick. Abib leapt from the bed. He started yelling back, but his wife's position was morally superior and she soon had him defeated. He slunk back to his bedroom. The woman tied Leslie's legs back up and left.

In the morning, Abib didn't stop in to see her. Leslie heard the woman and him have an argument which she apparently won. Then he left.

The woman came in with her breakfast a little while later. She helped her pee. After she fed her, she put down the bowl and restored her gag. She tied her collar off to the head of the bed and then looked at Leslie thoughtfully. She looked at her loins and then pointed to her own. "You hurt?" she asked. Leslie nodded her head.

She got up from the bed and returned with a tube of ointment. She freed her ankles. She made a motion for Leslie to raise her knees and lift her hips. Pushing up the hem of Leslie's black miniskirt, she put a little dab of the ointment on her finger and pressed it against her hairless love lips. "Men bastards," she said as she dipped her finger into Leslie's slit. She slowly reached her finger in as far as it would go and applied the ointment to the walls of her crevasse.

The gentle handling of her quim soon had Leslie lubricated. She didn't want to, she couldn't help it. She had been handled so many times with lustful intent that her reaction was automatic. While at the Moussa's, if she did not lubricate quickly, she would be beaten.

After a few moments, the woman noticed that Leslie was getting aroused. At first, she pulled back. Then she tentatively brought her finger back and slid it along the rim of her crevasse. She brought it up and touched her stiffened love bud lightly. Leslie gave a little jump. She looked Leslie in the eyes. She put down the tube of ointment and edged closer. Placing her hands on Leslie's thighs, she pushed them further apart. She brought her hand back to Leslie's pussy and, placing her fingers gently above it, started stroking her moist divide with her thumb. When she ran her thumb over her love bud, Leslie moaned. She slipped it inside her, stroked up and down her gash and returned, circling her clit slowly, running over it back and forth, tickling it softly. Leslie moaned again and her hips started to thrust gently back and forth.

The woman drew her hand from Leslie's puss for a moment. Her eyes were soft and moistened. Her chest was heaving. She was wearing a cheap, flowered, cotton skirt that went down to her ankles. She reached under her skirt and slid her panties down her thighs, over her knees and over her feet, dropping them on the floor. Her left hand returned to its task and her right snuck under her skirt.

She pleasured Leslie slowly and lovingly. Leslie could see her hand moving under her skirt. Her legs were spread wide. Her face was getting flushed as was her chest over her breasts. After a while, her hands, as if synchronized, began to pick up speed. Her breathing came heavier and heavier. Leslie felt her lusts growing higher and higher. Her thighs started to quiver. When the woman began to groan and shake, her torso doubled over, her left hand frigging Leslie's clit excitedly, Leslie's dam burst and her pussy began a series of intense, familiar contractions. The room was filled with both women's voluptuous groans.

After their passions had crested, the woman kept a gentle stroking of Leslie's quim until her pussy came to rest. She paused for a moment. Then she gave Leslie a shamed look. She picked up the tube of ointment and, after putting on the cap, shoved it into the pocket of her skirt. She pulled Leslie's legs down, hooking them together, and then tied them off to the foot of the bed. She pulled down her miniskirt to cover her. All the time, she kept her gaze averted from Leslie's face. She picked up the breakfast tray and retreated from the room, closing the door behind her. A few moments later, she returned. Her face was red with embarrassment as she picked up her white cotton panties from the floor. Her eyes downcast, she fled the room.

Leslie luxuriated in the afterglow of her orgasm for a long time. It had certainly been unexpected. The fact that the woman had taken pleasure with her, in Leslie's eyes, would increase the chances that she would eventually help her. Seeing her as another human being with feelings and desires could only be a good thing.

The day went on as yesterday. There were a few telephone calls. The doorbell rang twice, but the woman sent the people away whoever they were. And for a while, the TV blared. Early in the afternoon the woman came back into the room with Leslie's lunch. When she removed Leslie's gag, Leslie tried to engage her in conversation. "Please help me," she said. "My name is Leslie Harrington and I'm from Buckstown, Pennsylvania. My father's telephone number is 717-555-1717. Please call him and tell him I need help."

"No talking," the woman said angrily. "No talking or no soup!"

Discouraged and afraid of not getting to eat, Leslie remained silent.

When the soup was done and Leslie's collar tie restored, the woman released Leslie's legs again and let her pee. When she had removed the bowl of urine and wiped her down, she took the ointment from her pocket again and proffered it to Leslie. "I do?" she asked tentatively. Leslie nodded yes.

It was the same as earlier. Her ministrations to Leslie's wounds soon turned into a delicate, gentle manipulation of her sex. She quickly had her underwear on the floor. When they were both greatly aroused, she looked Leslie in the eyes, hesitated, and then removed her hand from Leslie's puss. Leslie watched as a wave of lust passed through her. She leaned forward, pushing Leslie's right thigh wide with her left hand and lowered her lips to Leslie's quim. She started slowly at first, licking her gash along its length, lightly touching her stiff clit with her tongue. After a short while, though, she began addressing Leslie's lusts with alacrity. She moaned and sighed as she washed Leslie's gash with her tongue. She suckled on her nubbin of pleasure, flicked it with her tongue and drove her tongue deep within her.

Leslie was driven beyond distraction. Her hips ground back at the mouth that was pleasuring her. She moaned and arched her back. She spread her legs wide, raised her knees, curled her feet.

The woman went on and on. Leslie came, groaning and shaking on the bed, and yet the woman continued. Suddenly, she groaned loudly. Her own hand had brought her over the top. Her tongue licked Leslie's quim excitedly. She gave her clit a long, hard suckle. She flattened her tongue and drew it up and down, delving into Leslie's fevered tunnel and then lathering her clit. Leslie howled with pleasure. She thrust her hips madly towards the mouth that was pleasuring her.

The woman continued to lick her while Leslie's climax wore down. She was moaning softly. Finally, she sat up and gave Leslie an embarrassed look. She wiped Leslie's goo from her face with the sleeve of her blouse and then quickly restored Leslie's legs to bondage. She took up the bowl and tray, this time remembering her underwear, and left the room, closing the door.

Leslie lay there, her body suffused with warmth. Her pussy glowed. After a while she passed off to sleep.

She awoke somewhat later. The TV was on. She spent an hour or so listening to the voices. It was some kind of game show and there was much audience laughter. The commercials came loud and brash. Everything was in Arabic except once she heard a Coke commercial.

The light was just starting to fade in her window when the door opened again. It moved slowly, tentatively. The woman's face peered around it, as if checking to see if Leslie was still there. When she came in the room, she closed the door. She hesitated for a moment and then began to strip off her clothes. Her breasts were full and although a little low on her chest, still firm. She had released her long, salt and pepper hair from its bindings and it flowed down over her shoulders and shrouded her breasts.

When she had cast away her panties, she sat on the edge of the bed and began to stroke Leslie's thigh. She pushed up her black miniskirt and flitted her hand over Leslie's pudendum. Then she slowly released her ankles. When Leslie's legs were free, she edged her way between them and slid her body forward. Leslie spread her legs widely to accept her. When their bellies matched, the woman pressed down her hips, bringing their sexes into contact. She gave a great sigh and began to abrade them together.

Slowly, surely, the women's lust rose. She pulled Leslie's blouse free of her skirt and ran her hands up over her belly and took hold of her breasts. She massaged them gently, plucking nimbly at her teats.

Leslie raised her hips the better to facilitate the friction between their loins. Her hands were crushed to her chest by the woman's weight. She was staring intently into Leslie's eyes. Leslie was moaning behind her gag. She knew that what the woman was doing was a form of rape. She had no power to deny her, but she was so gentle, so passionate that Leslie gratefully accepted her assault. Only with Jana, the Moussa's daughter, and, at times, with Jamilah, her cellmate, had making love been so soothing and comforting.

The woman reached her hands behind Leslie's head and released her gag. She mashed her breasts against Leslie's bound hands and took her lips. Their tongues merged and danced together. Their pelvises ground. Their breathing, matched, became heavy. They moaned and sighed. Leslie came first, a soft, glowing orgasm that drifted out from her quim and spread throughout her body. The woman quickly followed suit, issuing high pitched squeals as her pussy sent her wave after wave of delight.

When they had crested, the woman laid on Leslie for a long while. She kissed her softly, murmuring her name again and again. "Ghaniyah. Ghaniyah. Ghaniyah."

Leslie tried to speak, but the woman placed her fingers on her lips. Carefully, as if making sure that she caused her no discomfort, she lay the padded gag across her mouth again and tied it behind her head. Slowly, as if in a daze, she tucked Leslie's blouse back into her skirt and then rebound her ankles. She pulled the miniskirt back down to cover Leslie's froth covered mound. Then, after giving Leslie a sorrowful look, gathered her clothes and left.

Abib returned just after dark. He took Leslie to the bathroom to use the toilet and then fed her. He turned out the light when he left.

The house was unusually quiet. At one point, voices raised for a little while and then calmed back down. Leslie had the sense that something was going to happen.

She had fallen asleep. When she felt her ankles being untied, she awoke. It was still dark out. Abib was dressed in civilian clothes. He released her collar from the bed frame and pulled her to her feet. He undid the clasp to her miniskirt and pulled it down over her hips to the floor, making her step out of it. He unbuttoned her blouse. Before releasing her hands, he reclipped her ankles together. When he had the blouse removed, he refastened her hands to the front of her collar, released her ankles and, after removing her gag, brought her to the bathroom.

The woman was standing there naked. She refused to look Leslie in the eye. The shower was on and the woman helped

Leslie step into it. She took a sponge from a ledge, soaped it up and began to wash Leslie's body.

Leslie started to cry. She knew why they were washing her. Today she was going to be sold. Abib wanted her nice and clean for when the buyer inspected her. She stood there docilely while the woman cleaned her. The sponge ran over her breasts, her belly, her legs. She washed her pussy carefully. The shower head was on a hose and she took it out of the holder and ran it through her hair. She applied shampoo, washed it and then used a sweet smelling cream rinse.

When she turned the shower off, she dried Leslie with a big, fluffy, cotton towel. She helped Leslie step from the shower stall and brought her to sit on the toilet lid. Leslie saw, as the woman gently brushed out her hair, that she was crying.

The man had been watching the whole time. When the woman had finished with Leslie's hair, he barked out an order to her. The woman nodded, went to the medicine cabinet and removed a pink lady's razor. She made Leslie spread her legs and she shaved the few days' growth off of her loins. When she was done, she covered the area with lotion and rubbed it in.

Abib stepped up and took Leslie by the arm. He dragged her into the bedroom and pushed her onto the bed. He had two pairs of pliers in his hands. He made Leslie spread her legs. He grabbed the ring that held her medallion to the ring in her labia with the teeth of the two pairs of pliers, one on each side of the ends and, with some difficulty, pulled them apart. He removed the medallion denoting her as "Ghaniyah, Slave of the House of Moussa," and tossed it aside. The woman came in with a glass of lemon soda. She had dressed. She proffered it to Leslie, but Leslie refused to drink it. She knew that she might need the liquid in her system later, but she didn't care. She didn't want the woman's conscience to be assuaged by this last act of kindness. She was letting her husband sell her into slavery of some kind and Leslie wanted her to have all the guilt of that in her mind. The woman started to cry again and left the room.

Her captor removed her gag and made her stand up against the wall. He took out an ancient, Polaroid camera and took a few shots of her. He locked her hands behind her back so that he could get a good shot of her breasts and then made her bend over, with her head on the bed and her legs spread so that he could get a shot of her nether holes. He put the pictures in his pocket and then joined her ankles together.

A wave of fear passed through her. "Please don't do this, please," she murmured. Abib paid her no mind. He applied the gag to her mouth and tied it off behind her head. He pulled her towards him and lifted her up over his shoulder. He carried her from the room, through the house and out onto the carport. It was still dark out. Apparently even Colonel Abib couldn't keep a naked woman prisoner and he had to hide what he was doing from his neighbors. He popped the trunk and placed Leslie into it. She whined and cried. He pushed her to her belly, connected her ankles to her hands and closed the trunk.

The car didn't start for a long time. Leslie speculated that Abib was having some breakfast or was waiting until daylight so that he could arrive at the buyer's at the right time. An hour later, she heard the car door opening and closing. The engine started. The car backed out of the driveway and they were off.

They drove for a long time. The smooth macadam eventually gave way to a bumpy road. Leslie let the rhythm of the road lull her. There was nothing she could do. Why cry after all she had been through? One form of slavery was much the same as the rest. She would never be free again. She just had to accept that. This was her life now, to be owned and used, sold and resold, until she reached some more final end.

It was starting to get very hot in the trunk. Leslie began to rue her rejection of the drink proffered to her by Abib's wife. Her mouth was dry and she was sweating heavily.

When the vehicle finally came to a halt, there was about a twenty minute delay. She figured that Abib was showing the buyer her pictures and doing some preliminary negotiating. When the lid finally popped open, Leslie had to squint before she was able to see outside of it. She could just see the outline of her assailant and a woman with long hair standing next to him. She was shorter than Abib, maybe 5'5" or so. She seemed young.

The woman's voice said something excitedly in Arabic. There was a piercing quality to her voice. Abib leaned over and released Leslie's ankles and then pulled her out. He set her on her feet.

They were in the middle of a large oasis. There were long strands of brownish green grass, tall palm trees that curved this way and that and a number of large, black tents. In the background, she could hear people talking and she heard the bleating of a goat.

The woman was scanning her admiringly. She had brown skin and a sparkly diamond lodged in the side of her right nostril. Her hair was chestnut colored and very long. She was wearing a rust red halter top that came down to just below her belly button and a pair of colorful, clinging pants that hugged her hips. Several long strings of beads hung around her neck, settling around her small breasts and she had red and orange ribbons in her hair. She had a long but narrow nose. Her face was attractive, but in a manly way. Her eyes were a bright blue, standing out starkly on her dark brown face. Her lips were thin and her jaw sharp. On her wrists were a number of shiny, thin, gold and silver bracelets. Large, concentric, golden rings of various sizes ran through her earlobes.

She had a bright smile on her face. "Welcome to El Hamma, Ghaniyah," she said brightly. "Maybe you come stay with us a while, eh?"

"My name's not Ghaniyah," Leslie thought to herself. She tried to put on a brave stare, but she was shivering inside.

The woman was small, a little smaller than her, actually, but she carried herself in an aggressive, masculine way that bespoke toughness and perhaps cruelty. There was a man with jet black skin standing to her right a little behind her and she said something to him in Arabic. When she turned to walk towards one of the tents, the man stepped forward, took Leslie by the arm and hauled her along.

Inside the tent it was cooler than outside. The floor of the tent was covered by several layers of soft Persian rugs. It was, perhaps, 200 feet or so around. A tall, heavy pole stood in its middle and a number of other, thinner poles were strewn about holding up the black canvas above them. Pillows lay about, large, bright colorful ones with hand woven covers. An 8' long polished mahogany table sat off to one side. It was about 2' off the floor. Abib and the woman knelt down beside it while the black man took Leslie over to a pole run horizontally between two of the tent supports. He released Leslie's hands from behind her back only to tie them off to the horizontal pole about five feet apart. When he was done, he picked up another pole from the floor, about 8' long, and tied off her ankles as far apart as they could go. Leslie was effectively spread-eagled, ready for inspection by her buyer.

Abib and the woman drank tea and talked for a while. There was a large gold rimmed plate filled with figs, small slices of oranges and almonds on the table. Abib and the woman picked at it as they talked. The woman had a ready, free laugh. The black man, who was wearing a dark green, sleeveless t-shirt and loose, black, cotton pants, knelt down with them. He had a broad gold band around his left arm, up past his elbow and a large, gold earring in his right ear. The woman poured him a cup of tea.

In back of the tent, Leslie saw a group of older women, dressed in colorful, flowing robes that covered their heads, kneeling in a little circle. They seemed to be shelling peas or something. Several wild looking children came running in and out chasing a small, very thin, brown dog. They gave Leslie's naked body only a cursory glance.

Finally, the moment of truth came. The black man shoed the children from the tent and lowered the flap. The very top of the tent was open and bright sunlight shown through it. The woman approached Leslie confidently. She gave her a not unfriendly smile and began her examination. She ran her hands all over Leslie's flesh, testing her skin for smoothness. She held her breasts in the palms of her hands, weighing them, letting them bounce up and down lightly, admiring the shimming flesh, and then squeezed them gently. She picked at Leslie's teats until they hardened.

The black man removed her gag and she took hold of her chin and turned it back and forth, admiring the lines of her face. She looked at her teeth. Her fingers toyed with her scarlet, leather collar and the dangling ring in front. She ran her hands through her hair, down over her hips and over her belly. She tested the inside of her thighs. Crouching, she inspected Leslie's slit, delicately pulling her love lips apart, playing with the ring lodged in her labia.

When she went around the back, she caressed her back and her rear cheeks, and slid her hands down the backs of her thighs. Leslie felt her parting her rear mounds. Her hand traced over her little brown star and a finger pressed in and twirled around as if she was testing the flexibility of the pursed tissue.

The black man stood in front of Leslie, watching her carefully. Leslie tried to avoid his eyes, but she kept going back to them. He had a noble nose and thick lips. His cheeks were scarred. His eyebrows and hair, which was captured in a long ponytail behind him, were jet black. His chin was firm and strong. His hands, which he kept on his wide hips, were large and strong looking. He stood about 6'4" tall. His arms and thighs were thick and muscular. His eyes were piercing and he had a determined, stern look on his face.

The woman came back around Leslie's front. She caressed her face several times, her aspect soft and almost enticing. Then she stepped closer. She leaned her thin body up against Leslie's and began kissing her face lightly. Her mouth hovered over Leslie's lips. Leslie could smell her sweet, hot breath. She flitted her tongue over Leslie's lips while her hands ran down her head and over her shoulders.

Leslie could feel the heat from the woman's body. She felt her lust begin to rise. She wanted to beg the woman to stop, but she was too afraid to speak.

Slowly, her hands descended Leslie's torso. She lowered her head and subsumed her nipples in her mouth, suckling on them gently, washing them delicately with her tongue. Her hands caressed her hips and then pressed on to caress the insides of her thighs. When one found her mons, a finger slipped in between her love lips. It was then that Leslie moaned. She closed her eyes and cursed herself. The woman had no reaction, but her finger began to slip up and down Leslie's divide, probing deeper and deeper each time. Her hand caressed her mound, her fingers trickling over it softly. Then she stood back, placed the tip of her finger on Leslie's love button and began a slow, gentle rotation on it.

Leslie felt her blood rising. She pressed her lips together and closed her eyes. She knew what the woman wanted and she was trying with all her might to deny it to her. But the finger was incessant. It rolled and rolled over her clit, pausing only, from time to time, to gather some of her moisture and spread it over it. Before long, Leslie's hips started to match the finger's motions. She caught herself and tried to stop, but each time, the mesmerizing, tantalizing motion of the finger brought her back. She shook her hips to try and dislodge it. She moaned again. She clasped her hands open and shut again and again in frustration. Part of her wanted the finger to leave her, but another wanted the woman to seize her mons fully, to begin a steady, sure, all out assault.

And then she could feel it coming. She opened her eyes and looked into the startling, blue eyes of her assailant. There was something captivating about them, mysterious and distant. Mrs. Moussa often played with her quim, tantalizing her, bringing her to the brink of completion again and again, but her purposes had always been to demonstrate her mastery over her, to demean her. With this woman it was different. Her gaze bespoke no intent to humiliate Leslie, not even really to test her. Instead she seemed to be entering into a conspiracy with her, inviting her to take a journey of rapture. It was as if she could look inside of her, transmit her will into her.

The finger stopped its rotation, but did not break contact. It commenced a rhythmic stroke, so soft that Leslie had to concentrate to make certain that it was touching her and that it was not just her imagination. Her lust kept rising and rising. Her thighs began to shake and then her hips and then her whole body. She closed her eyes again and felt herself being carried rapidly down a swiftly flowing stream of desire. The entire universe came down to the minute point of contact between her clit and the phantom finger.

When her orgasm came, she moaned loudly. Her body quivered. Her pussy exploded into a series of hard, jolting contractions. She screamed, "Oh! Oh! Oh! Oh! Oh!" Her hands strained at her bindings, frantic to remove the source of the ecstatic stimulation from her loins. Her orgasm went on and on until she found it hard to breath. When she gave out a deep, animalistic groan that emanated from the depths of her throat, the woman finally granted her mercy.

She watched Leslie carefully as her pussy's throbs wound down. Leslie's chest was heaving and her heart was racing wildly inside her. Her body was covered with a shiny, sheen of sweat. She sagged in her bindings.

The woman smiled at her, not a smile of irony and disdain, but one of welcome. She patted Leslie on her cheek and she returned to the table with Abib and the black man.

There was some bargaining and bickering back and forth. Abib was not really in the driver's seat because there weren't too many places you could sell a woman way out here in the desert. He might take her up to Tunis to sell her to a brothel there, but there weren't too many of them who would take the chance on a stolen American.

On the other hand, Leslie had proven her immense value. And the woman seemed to like her. She kept on glancing at her and smiling. The black man seemed to have a deep interest in her as well. But his glances were more fear inspiring. If Mrs. Moussa was a devil, her soul evil and black, this man seemed more like a demon, a djinn, a spirit of the desert. Leslie had done some reading on Arabic myths and stories before she came to Tunisia, and she remembered djinns has having been described as being made up of smokeless flame or 'the fire of a scorching wind'. They could be evil or good, had their own souls and possessed magical powers that they often used for their own ends.

As the talking went on, Leslie became more and more apprehensive about being left here. She had thought one form of slavery to be more or less the same as the other, but she sensed that being owned by the slender, powerful woman and her djinn would cost her her soul. She wanted to shout out, to beg Abib not to leave her here. She was afraid, though, that if she did, her new owners would extract a fiendish punishment for it. Aside from that, she knew that once Abib got his price, she was doomed.

Abib and the woman seemed to come to an agreement. They slapped their hands and gripped the edges of their fingers together in a ritualistic hand shake. The woman called out to one of the older women in the back of the tent. She got up and hustled out while another round of tea was poured. She came back a few minutes later with a heavy, steel strongbox and put it on the table in front of the woman. The woman had a small key hanging around her neck in the midst of all of her colorful beads and she opened the strongbox with it. She counted out a large pile of bills. Abib took it and counted it again. He nodded at the woman, they shook hands again in their ritualistic way and he downed the rest of his tea.

When he stood up, Leslie knew that her fate was sealed. All restraint left her.

"Please don't leave me here! Please!" she begged. "I'll do anything for you! I'll fuck you every night! My parents have money! I can get you some! Lots of money! They'll pay anything to get me back! Please don't leave me here! Please!"

Her body was wracked by panic. She started to yank and pull at her bonds. "Pleeeeeeeeeease!" she screamed. "Pleeeeeeeease!"

Abib just smiled at her as he passed by. He was stuffing the bills in his pockets. The woman and the man walked out with him, leaving the flap down as they exited. A few moments later, Leslie heard the engine to the BMW come to life. It revved and then she heard it beginning to fade away.

She was trembling with fright when the man and the woman returned. Her face was twisted into a piteous mask. She started to sob.

The woman came over to her, and began to stroke her head, her body pressed up close next to her. "Poor Ghaniyah," she said. "You cry. It good for you. You like Jaida, you see. You stay with us now for a while. You like it, you see."

The black man had a sharp knife and he began cutting away her ankle and wrist bracelets. Leslie had hated wearing them, but now was sorrowful that they were being removed. Being the prisoner and sex slave of the Moussa's seemed eminently preferable to whatever was going to be her fate here. They had possession of her body, but she feared that this wiry sprite of a woman and her companion were going to steal her mind.

Jaida kept giving her tender kisses while the black man kept at his work. When he had all the scarlet, leather bands removed from her extremities, Jaida stepped back and let him remove her collar. Leslie's body shook as he sawed away at the leather. When he removed it, Jaida stroked and caressed the pale flesh which had been underneath. "Poor little Ghaniyah," she said. "We take good care of you."

"M,my name's Leslie," Leslie managed to croak out.

Jaida laughed. "No, you see. You name Ghaniyah." Her laugh wasn't mocking, but rather, pleasant, almost sisterly.

"No it's not!" Leslie asserted with more confidence. Jaida just petted her cheek and smiled.

"This be Khuzaymah Najib Mu'awiyah Juzam," the woman said, stepping back and pointing to the black man. "He my servant. You call him Najib. You get to know him very well." As she said this, she slipped her hand into the front of his pants and took hold of his cock. "You learn to treasure him."

She opened her mouth and gave Najib a deep kiss. Najib circled her torso with his powerful arm and kissed her back. When the couple broke, Leslie could see his stiffened cock bulging behind his pants. It was longer and thicker than any one she had ever seen.

"For now, we busy. We deal with you later." She turned to Najib and said something to him in Arabic.

"Naän, sayyadati," he replied. His voice was low and musical.

Jaida left the tent. Najib turned to the old women sitting in a circle and spoke to them. His voice was stern, commanding. Two of the women leapt up to obey him, their eyes darkened. One brought over a brown, ceramic lidded pot, about three feet around. Bowing, she opened it for Najib. Leslie could see into it. There were a number of round balls of what looked like dense sponges floating in a milky substance. He reached in and took hold of one and approached Leslie. "Open mouth," he said sternly.

Leslie considered disobeying him. Clearly, he was going to put the dripping object in her mouth. But she looked at the size of the man, his flexing muscles, remembered the look on the older woman's face when he gave her his order, and decided against it. Meekly, a tear running down her face, she spread her lips. Najib popped the ball inside.

It had a sweet taste, almost like coconut. The ball filled her mouth, spreading her lips apart. Her tongue started to tingle right away. Some of the liquid slid down her throat.

The other woman had brought over a large wicker basket. She put it down at Najib's feet and bowed, as had the other woman. Najib waved her away. He opened the basket and took out a black, leather harness. He approached Leslie and put it over her head. It had a cup that went under her chin and extended up over her mouth, smothering her lips. Najib pulled the two thick straps that extended from it behind her head and connected them, pulling them so tight that Leslie's jaw was pulled closed over the ball in her mouth.

Two straps went up on either side of her nose. There were pads on them, oval shaped, and Najib slid them into position so that they would cover her eyes. A horizontal strap ran along the back of the pads. He brought its ends to the back of her head and pulled them tight as well. Leslie's eyelids were forced down and she was closed into darkness. Another strap went over her head and connected behind her, sealing the harness in place.

Leslie started to wail and moan as soon as she was closed into darkness. She tried to beg for release, but no sound would come out. Then she felt the man daub a thick, gooey substance along the line of her crevasse, delving his finger in until her pussy's walls were coated with it. When he was done, he applied some to her pleasure bud. A moment later, she felt him applying the substance to her little rear opening. And then, two dabs went over her nipples.

Leslie was terrified that the man had put some kind of substance in her that would burn and torture her. She yelled and screamed and protested, but no one seemed to pay her any attention. She strained her wrists, trying to get free, but she was tied too tightly and surely. She started to cry.

But when no fiery plinth erupted in her crevasse or her rear, she began to get a hold of herself. There was warmth there, but not a fiery one. It was soothing and almost comforting. Her mind started to wander too. It was like a cloud was descending over it. It was a little like getting dizzy, but not quite, more like a film had encircled her brain and was gently squeezing it. Her body began to relax. A pleasurable sensation came over it as if a thousand warm, gentle hands had started to caress it. Her pussy began to glow. It seemed to radiate and her consciousness started to surround it. The circle of tissue surrounding her rear entrance began to trill. Her nipples felt like someone's warm mouth was gently suckling them

After a while, Leslie just forgot where she was. Her fear and anxiety had disappeared. She felt so good that she started to hum to herself, letting the sound buzz inside her head. She knew that the sensations were coming from the substance leaking from the ball in her mouth and she tried to squeeze it to get more. Her body was stretched out to its extremes. It felt more open and free than it had ever felt before. She began to believe that if she could just get a little push she could soar into the sky and fly.

Once or twice, she felt gentle, woman's hands touch her skin. They lightly flew over her breasts, her belly and up and down her sides, over her mons and her hips, her rear. She heard Jaida's voice, soothing and mesmerizing, saying, "Pretty little Ghaniyah. Happy little Ghaniyah," over and over again. While her body rejoiced at the touch, her mind rejected the appellation. "I'm Leslie," she thought. "I'm Leslie."

Some time later, she didn't have any idea of how long, she felt Najib's strong hands loosening the leather straps confining her ankles. When he released her wrists, she fell to her knees. The effects of the drugs she had been given had passed. Her body felt like she had endured a marathon. Her pussy and rear felt tired and dull. A loop went around her neck and was pulled tight. It urged her to her feet.

She found that she could barely stand. Her arms were drawn behind her and her palms joined together. She felt something slide over them and in between and then a thong wrapped around them, securing them in place. Her shoulders were pulled back and she attempted a wan struggle to free her hands. She didn't have time to concentrate on that. She felt a tug on her leash and she was moved forward. She was brought out of the tent. The sun was rabidly hot. Her feet burned on the sandy soil as she was marched along. They traveled about a hundred yards and she was brought into another tent. This one seemed much smaller than the first. Najib's large hands forced her to kneel.

He spread her ankles about a foot apart and tied them to stakes in the floor of the tent. He spread her knees and tied them off too. A strap was tied to her joined hands and pulled back and tied off to a stake. She felt a block of wood close around her neck. It had ropes attached to the ends and it was pulled just high enough so that she could rest on her haunches and yet her back was pulled straight, her neck extended.

A few moments later, Jaida came into the tent. Leslie recognized her scent, spicy, like burnt cinnamon.

"Hello, Ghaniyah," she said sweetly. She gave her breasts gentle caresses and then ran her hands lightly over her thighs and belly.

She loosened the harness from behind her head and pulled it off, removing the ball that had been in her mouth. The light in the tent was dim. A battery powered lantern was behind her suffusing a gentle light throughout the small tent. Jaida had a tray with her holding a bowl filled with stew and two earthenware carafes filled with some kind of liquid.

Leslie had come out of the stupor she had been in. She shivered at the recollection of how lost she had gotten under its effects. She knew that her initial impression had been right. Jaida was going to capture her mind. "I won't let it happen!" she thought desperately. "I won't!"

"Ghaniyah need to eat," Jaida said. "Good food. You like."

"P,please…." Leslie started to say.

Jaida put her hand over Leslie's mouth. "Ghaniyah no talk. Ghaniyah never talk. Ghaniyah silent always."

A tear floated down Leslie's face. She wanted desperately to beg and plead for her freedom. She also knew that she was entirely at Jaida's mercy. Her and the ominous Najib. She knew what pain was, and no matter how many times Mrs. Moussa or Faraq or Latifah had whipped her, it was always agonizing. She never got used to it. Najib looked like he would be merciless with a whip. So did Jaida, despite her outer sweetness.

Jaida fed her spoonfuls of the stew. It had an earthy flavor, slightly spicy. It tasted like yogurt or goat's cheese had been mixed in with it. There were some spices that Leslie couldn't place. The carafe held a sweet juice, thick and creamy, like apricots. There was a second carafe full of water, and Jaida made Leslie drink that too. She put the empty bowl underneath her pussy and told her, "Ghaniyah pee."

Leslie did as directed, happy to release her water. Jaida patted her quim with a soft cloth. Then she knelt back and smiled. She caressed Leslie's face and then leaned over and kissed her lips. It was a soft kiss, their lips just touching. She pressed her lips down a little harder and slipped her tongue between Leslie's, just enough for a shiver to go through Leslie's body. Her hand drifted down her side, over her belly and atop her quim. When the fingers started to dance lightly upon it, Leslie issued a moan of despair. At the same time, her tongue intertwined hungrily with Jaida's, eager to accelerate her lust.

Her orgasm came quickly. It shook her body. Her pussy throbbed and convulsed. The cream that Najib had placed in and around her crevasse seemed to have brought the tissues to life. It made Jaida's fingers feel like they were full of electricity. At the end, she was panting like before.

While she was recovering, Jaida placed all the things she had brought with her back on the tray. There was a little bowl with a top on it. Jaida opened it and Leslie saw another one of the sponge like things that Najib had placed in her mouth earlier.

"Please don't," she whined. "Please."

Jaida put her fingers over Leslie's lips. "Ghaniyah no talk," she said, repeating her earlier mantra. "Ghaniyah never talk. Ghaniyah always silent."

Leslie quieted, but she refused to open her mouth to allow the infernal object in. She shook her head this way and that, her lips compressed, little whines escaping them.

Jaida knelt back. There was a sorrowful look on her face. "Ghaniyah bad," she said. "Make Jaida sad."

She took hold of Leslie's harness and began to apply it to her head. Leslie tried to turn her head to avoid it, but Jaida quickly had it in place, her jaw locked closed, her eyes blinded.

"Jaida back quick," she said.

About two minutes later, she returned. She knelt in front of Leslie and applied two six inch long rods against her labia, one on each side. Leslie desperately tried to move her legs to avoid it, but there was nothing she could do. She had the sensation that Jaida was twisting something and the bars started to move closer and closer together. Very quickly, a fierce pain erupted in her labia. She moaned and whined and twisted her head. Jaida stopped tightening it when the pain became exquisite.

She stroked Leslie's head. "Poor Ghaniyah," she said sadly. "I be back not too long. You see. Ghaniyah bad. Ghaniyah get pain. Poor Ghaniyah." She stroked her head one more time and left the tent.

The pain from her labia was agonizing. The device was crushing her flesh. She swished her hips back and forth, desperate to dislodge it. She cried and whined. In her darkness, the pain became a huge beast that had gripped its jaws on her sex and wouldn't let go. She howled. Her body shook. She cursed her life, cursed the world, cursed Jaida, Abib, Mrs. Moussa, everybody. She prayed for relief, tried to listen for Jaida's footsteps on the soft sand outside her tent. Longed for the sound of the tent flap opening.

When it happened, her mind leapt for joy. She trembled as Jaida's fingers freed her sex. When the blood returned, her pussy ached and she groaned. Jaida removed the harness from her head. Tears streamed down Leslie's face. Tears of joy and sorrow. Jaida caressed her head. "Poor Ghaniyah," she said. "Jaida make pain go away. Ghaniyah must thank Jaida."

"Th,thank you," Leslie murmured. Jaida placed her fingers on her lips again and repeated her formula. "Ghaniyah no talk. Ghaniyah never talk. Ghaniyah always silent," she said. "Ghaniyah thank Jaida this way," she proffered. She lifted her rust red halter top, exposing her coffee cup size breasts. "Kiss Jaida," she instructed.

She leaned forward so that Leslie could place her lips on her teats. Leslie suckled them gratefully. When Jaida thought she had sufficed on one, she tendered her the other. She leaned back when Leslie had thanked her enough.

Jaida opened the bowl again. Leslie whined. But she opened her mouth, her lips atremble, while Jaida slipped it in. "Good Ghaniyah," she said happily.

It only took her a few moments to restore her halter, forcing her jaws closed, blinding her eyes. Leslie heard her opening a jar and she felt her swipe the goo over and inside her crevasse. As had Najib, she applied some to her teats and her rear entrance as well. She ran her hand over Leslie's quim and up her belly and then stroked her breasts. She left without a word.

Leslie tried to fight it, but before long she was asea again. For the life of her, she could not recall why she had put up such a fight. Her body felt wonderful. Her sex purred and her breasts tingled as did her rear. All that was missing was a warm hand to caress her, something to fill her. She tried to imagine her pussy, wet and dilated, her golden ring sparkling. In her mind, she tried to kiss it, imagining her tongue taking a long trip up her divide ending at its crux, lathing the little button atop.

She was startled when the tent flap opened. She knew that it wasn't Jaida, the size of the body was too big. It smelled of man's sweat, deep and pungent. It was Najib, she knew it. When she heard him undressing, she imagined his strong, black body, his long, thick cock. A moment later, she felt his hot hands on her flesh and she trembled. It felt so good. He caressed her breasts, plucked and pinched her vibrating teats. He ran his finger along her divide. The sensation was so thrilling, it made her jump. As if he had tested her readiness and found her ripe, he began to untie her from her bonds. When she was free, he released her from her blinding harness. He gently parted her lips with his fingers and withdrew the sponge from her mouth.

Leslie was floating in space as he guided her to the back of the tent, away from the stakes that had imprisoned her. Before he laid her down, he tied her wrists together in front of her and drew a soft, black cloth over her eyes. When she was on her back, eager and moaning, he slipped between her knees. A moment later, his rigid member pushed aside her outer lips and entered her.

What began was a long, intense session of delirium. Leslie moaned and groaned as she fucked her. When his mouth took her breasts, she writhed and squirmed. His strokes were long and sure. Slow and steady. When she came, she felt like her spirit had been touched. He poured himself deep within her, deeper than anyone had penetrated her before. She came again. He rolled her over and pulled her to her knees and entered her bowels. Leslie shook and shuddered. The rasping of his prick along her energized ring sent electrical charges through her. She felt him come and her lust exploded. He remained hard, made her come again and followed suit.

All the while he was fucking her, he kept murmuring, "Good Ghaniyah. Beautiful Ghaniyah. Sweet Ghaniyah." There was a hypnotizing quality to his voice and Leslie soon joined the mantra, repeating in her mind, "Sweet Ghaniyah. Good Ghaniyah. Beautiful Ghaniyah."

When he finished with her rear, he washed himself off and then pulled her mouth to his cock. Leslie subsumed it with joy. She suckled it hungrily. Najib's strong hand guided her along it, slowly, incessantly, probing it into her throat. Jaida joined them. Leslie reveled in her cinnamon smell. She washed Leslie's pussy with her tongue, making her body vibrate. Leslie still had Najib's cock in her mouth and she clamped her lips down firmly on it when Jaida made her explode with passion. When Najib's cock began to spasm and jerk, she pushed her head down hard so that it would pour directly into her belly.

When they were done with her, they laid her down, retied her hands behind her back, bound her ankles and tied them to a stake. They restored her head halter. Leslie was asleep even before they left.

She awoke much later. Her head was woozy and her body sagged. She tested her bonds languidly. It took her a while to remember what had happened. When she recalled it, she moaned in misery. It was like she had become another person. Leslie had flown away, replaced by Ghaniyah, a creature enthralled with lust. They were doing that to her. They were stealing her. She had to get away somehow before she was all gone.

Jaida came in a while later and after she mounted her again on her stakes, she fed her. This time, after she ate, she did not install one of the fiendish sponges, but instead had her drink a thimble full of the watery, white liquid that the sponges had been soaking in. Leslie did not dare refuse.

She left her there, blinded and silenced. A short while later, Leslie, her mind numbed by the drug, heard the sound of car engines. A little while after that, she heard music. There were drums, flutes, some kind of stringed instrument. More cars pulled up and some left. She heard a man's and a woman's laughter outside her tent. It went on for hours. Jaida came by and gave her something to drink, let her pee, made her come and left. One of the old women came in and fed her. Later, after the music stopped, Najib came by and fucked her again, spilling himself in her pussy and in her mouth.

Day after day went by. She never left her tent. Three or four times a day, she would be forced to accept one of the sponges in her mouth. Jaida would come in, tantalize her with her hands and whisper sayings in Arabic in her ear, always following them up with reminders that, "Ghaniyah love Jaida. Jaida love Ghaniyah. Ghaniyah belong to Jaida. Ghaniyah do anything for Jaida." Then she would make her come.

One of the older women would come by and bathe her. They all seemed to be in milk, and they would feed Leslie from their breasts. There was a strange, spicy taste to it, reminiscent of the milky liquid that the sponges were soaked with. Each time, afterwards, dizziness would come over Leslie and her loins would burn.

She spent long times affixed to her stakes, her halter affixed to her head, awaiting someone to come to her. There would be long, fevered sessions of sex. Sometimes it was with Najib, other times Jaida. Sometimes both. As Jaida had promised, she came to treasure Najib's prick. Even when she was not under the influence of the drug, her pussy clenched when he discharged himself in her mouth.

She never had to be punished again. The thought of making Jaida sad was too much to bear. Jaida loved her. She kept telling her. She caressed her, kissed her. Sometimes she just lay with her, for an hour or more, kissing her, stroking her, caressing her, telling her how beautiful, sweet and good Ghaniyah was.

Najib was an overpowering force. When she smelled his flesh enter her tent, a shudder would go through her. He never harmed her, never beat her, never hurt her, but her fear of him was rabid. He emanated a power that pierced her inner self. Her memory of her sessions with him were always sketchy. She would remember his long, thick cock filling her canal, stroking languidly along it. It seemed alive inside her. When he presented it to her lips, she felt compelled to worship it. He had an otherworldly stamina as if he drew his powers from an unearthly source. When he left her bound in her tent after filling her with his seed, she could feel it seeping into her cells, claiming her, marking her as his.

But it was Jaida that she came to love. Her fingers were so deft, her kisses so sweet, she melted every time that she saw her. When she lapped at Jaida's pussy, making her writhe and moan with pleasure, she felt like she had been given a great gift. When Jaida licked hers, Leslie's mind and body spun away into space. When they were conjoined, mouths pressed to sexes, one atop the other, and Jaida was always on top, it felt like their bodies had become one, that Jaida had crawled inside her.

The sessions that were hardest to remember were when either Jaida or Najib would light some incense and bring Leslie's face to it, forcing her to breath in the fumes deeply. She would pass off into a fog and recall only their murmuring words, soft, mesmerizing, enchanting, rhythmic and strange. The words were not Arabic, not any Arabic that she had ever heard and she had been around it a lot since she had been enslaved by Mrs. Moussa. They sounded close to it, but rougher, more guttural. Later, she could not remember a single one. They would use her afterwards, Najib's cock buried in her body, her face buried in Jaida's loins, but she would never remember anything once they had begun. The next thing she would know is when she woke up, mounted on her stakes, her halter affixed firmly around her head.

She lost the urge to speak. When the idea entered her head to beg or plead for freedom or forbearance from the potion, or to be able to spend even one day, a few hours, without the steady diet of lips, fingers, cocks and cunts assaulting her, Jaida's mantra would enter her head: "Ghaniyah no talk. Ghaniyah never talk. Ghaniyah always silent."

Eventually, they did not have to resort to the sponges. Jaida or Najib would proffer her a cup of the milky white liquid and Leslie would drink it willingly. She lost her fear of losing herself. Or rather, she forgot it. Jaida would ask her every day, "What you name?" It was the only time Leslie was given permission to speak. When she answered that it was Leslie, Jaida would laugh sweetly and contradict her. "No, you Ghaniyah. Beautiful, sweet Ghaniyah. Jaida love Ghaniyah. Ghaniyah belong to Jaida. Ghaniyah do anything for Jaida."

Finally, one day, when she was mounted on her stakes, Jaida came in and freed her from her halter. There had been a long, intense session the night before with both her and Najib. She had been fed several large cups of the potion. They had used the incense on her several times. When she awoke, mounted to her stakes, it was morning. She could hear the morning birds outside. When her mouth was free, Jaida asked her again, "What you name?" Leslie went to answer and she couldn't remember. She scoured her brain. She started to cry. She had a name! She knew she had a name! What was it? Jaida saw her tear filled eyes and began to stroke her head lovingly. "You know," she said comfortingly. "I tell you many times. You remember."

Then it came to her. "Ghaniyah?" she asked uncertainly. It was wrong somehow, but she knew it was the right answer.

Jaida broke into a broad smile. She gave her a loving kiss. "Yes, you name Ghaniyah. Jaida love Ghaniyah, beautiful, sweet Ghaniyah. Now I think you ready to learn to dance."

And learn she did. That day, Jaida introduced her to the other girls. There was Falak. She was a tall, buxom Spanish girl who had been sold by her boyfriend for four pounds of hashish. Bahira was a petit French girl originally named Nicole, scooped up off the streets of Marseille. Lama and Rasha were Germans. They were kidnapped right off a cruise liner in Tunis one night.

They were sisters, Lama with fiery red hair and Rasha a blond. Azizah, formerly Veronica, was Italian with jet black hair and olive skin. She was the most voluptuous of the clan, with big breasts, wide hips and plump, pursed lips. They all loved Jaida and Jaida loved them. They greeted Ghaniyah with open arms, kissing and petting her, making sweet sounds in her ears. Jaida's girls never talked. Jaida's girls were always silent.

Every day, for hours and hours, Ghaniyah was taught how to move her hips, to shake her bare breasts gently so they shimmered, to move seductively with the music. She was adorned with jewels, given colorful diaphanous, revealing clothes to wear and taught how to shed them delectably.

Her sessions with Najib and Jaida continued, although they started spending less and less time with her. There were the other girls to take care of after all. From time to time, Ghaniyah's mind would falter. She would remember that she had forgotten something. She would cry and sob in Jaida's arms. But those occasions became fewer and fewer as the weeks progressed.

Soon after her dancing lessons began, at night, after the music had started, Ghaniyah would be given a large draft of potion and bound hand and foot in her tent. The men would come and untie her and use her, several every night. She would fuck them with fury, although, at first, the next morning she would be sad and ashamed. Jaida would comfort her though and would remind her, "Beautiful, sweet Ghaniyah. Jaida love Ghaniyah. Ghaniyah belong to Jaida. Ghaniyah do anything for Jaida."

When her dancing skills came up to par, she would entertain in the main tent. Her price went up then, of course. She would lead the men she had enticed gaily into her tent and bring them a world of delight.

The girls were all fast friends. Jaida let them make love to each other from time to time. She paired Ghaniyah off with Bahira, the little, black haired French girl, and, for a special price, the men could watch them make love. Ghaniyah loved Bahira's pretty little breasts, her doll like body. But it was Falak, the Spaniard, who she really lusted for. She and Falak would approach Jaida after a practice dancing session, holding hands, and supplicate her with their eyes. If she allowed it, it would be in her own luxurious tent while either she or Najib watched.

Najib was the constant, ominous presence. All of the girls were afraid of him. When he took one of them to his tent, she often stayed there for several days. He would perform his ceremonies; drive the girl to intolerable passion. She would return ever so much more devoted to her duties.

The girls were always supervised, and if they were not practicing their dancing, or lounging around the main tent with Jaida or Najib in attendance, they spent their times alone and bound in their tents. Every day, they fed from the breasts of the older women who seemed to be somehow embonded to Jaida, as docile and compliant as a herd of cows, with Najib as their harsh taskmaster. Daily, Najib would mix special herbs and spices for them and mix them in their food. They dutifully and morosely consumed it while he watched, casting dark, fearful looks at him.

Over the months, the camp was moved several times. The older women, with the help of the men of the camp, would pack up Jaida's tents. They moved by truck, not by camel, with the men of the camp as drivers. They also served as the musicians and had their families with them. This helped provide cover for Jaida, making their encampment seem pedestrian. It was clear that she had some kind of power over them and they would obey her orders with slavish deference. Their women and daughters served refreshments to Jaida's guests at night, dressed in colorful Arab garb, although it was always clear that they were not available for other, carnal duties. Jaida's girls traveled in little cages, gagged and bound, in a locked truck driven by Najib. They would cross over to Algeria from time to time and into Libya. With Najib at the head of the column, for some reason, they never had any trouble at the borders. Business would always pick up when they moved near a new city.

The spring came. In May, Falak was sold to a wealthy shipping magnate from Oman. Before she was allowed to leave, she spent a week in Najib's tent. The night after she left, the remaining girls were all brought into a circle in Jaida's tent. Once they had all breathed deeply of Najib's incense, they joined hands while Jaida and Najib made love on top of a large, silk cloth decorated with strange pentagrams and obscure writings. Within a few days, her replacement appeared, a tall, languorous Dutch girl who fell afoul of some drug dealers in Marrakech. She was given the name Anisah.

Little Bahira, the French girl, was sold in August, after a week in Najib's tent, to a man who owned a rich mining concession in Morocco. She was replaced two days after the subsequent ceremony by another American girl, Barbara, who they named Fatima. She was an athletic brunette with a fine, compact body who had disappeared from a bazaar in Cairo while on vacation.

Business was brisk, so much so, that the girls strained to accommodate it. As a result, in October, another ceremony was conducted and within a week, a sultry, black haired, dark eyed Irish girl was added. She had been with a UN team in Darfur when the village they were stationed at was overrun by raiders. The other team members had been released after some tense negotiations, but Cassie, later given the name Yaminah, was never found. Ghaniyah and Yaminah quickly became good friends.

In December, they were encamped by a small town called Daghagra in southeastern Tunis, about 60 miles from the Libyan border. It was Ghaniyah's one year anniversary, but she didn't know that. She didn't think about those things. She had spent the last few days in Najib's tent just to make sure that her commitment to her new life was reinforced. All of a sudden, business dropped off to a mere trickle. Najib went into town and came back with the news that there had been riots in Daghagra. All the girls were brought to the main tent and locked into their cages. Jaida and Najib debated what to do. They considered moving back to Algeria, but had been told that border security had been heightened on the Algerian side due to the disturbances. The same was true on the Libyan side. They decided they would sit it out.

The girls were scheduled for refreshers. They practiced their dances. Business started to trickle in again. After two weeks, they decided to move nearer to a big city. They relocated outside the coastal city of Zuara. Business picked up. One night, in January, the 14th, news came in that the government had fallen. The next day, the 15th, some of the wealthy merchants from Zuara, who had been members of the opposition, sent word out that they wanted to reserve the next night, the 16th for a great celebration. Tantalized by premium rates, Jaida agreed.

The party started a little after sundown and carried on all night. By 11 o'clock, Ghaniyah had made five trips back to her tent. Liquor was flowing, the band was playing, the girls were dancing up a storm. Ghaniyah had developed, under Jaida's tutelage, a special routine. She was wearing a golden circlet around her head on which dangled small, golden coins. Around her waist was a golden chain. A few months ago, Jaida had given her a bright diamond to wear in her nose, she had cried with happiness when she received it, and it sparkled in the bright lights that shined down over the dancing ring. She was in the middle of her performance, had discarded all of her diaphanous coverings, when suddenly three Humvees pulled into the circle of tents. Men dressed in desert camouflage uniforms jumped out and started firing their weapons in the air. They were in the main tent within moments. The girls started to scream, men ran for the exits. Jaida and Najib sprung to their feet. Ghaniyah had been so entranced by her dance that when the music stopped it took her a few moments to realize it.

A boyish looking man, dressed in a jacket and tie approached her. He grabbed her by the arms and started shaking her. "Miss Harrington! Miss Harrington! It's me, Tom Martin! From the American Embassy! Don't you recognize me?"

Ghaniyah was in a daze. "Why is this man shaking me?" she thought. "What is Harrington? What does it mean?"

"Leslie!" the man shouted. He shook her some more. "Leslie! Wake up! Wake up! Your father sent us. These men are Air Force commandos. We've been looking for you for a year! The woman, Colonel Abib's wife, called your father a year ago. Told him everything. We got Abib to talk, but we hadn't been able to find your caravan. You're going home!"

"Home?" she thought. "Leslie?" And then, from deep in her mind's recesses, the name came floating back to her. "Leslie! That's my name, Leslie! I'm Leslie Harrington! Oh my god!"

She turned and looked around the tent. Najib was staring at her with his demon's eyes. Jaida looked as if she were on fire. Martin pulled at Leslie's arm.

"Come on, we've got to get going. All hell's broken loose in Tunisia and the border is wide open. We can be there in an hour! You're going home!"

Leslie realized that she was stark naked. Martin pulled on her arm again and she started to go with him. They ran out of the tent. He dragged her into a Humvee. It fired up and sped away.

Martin had a blanket and he covered her with it. Leslie started to cry. It was all over! She was going home!"

An hour later, the Humvees pulled through the unmanned Tunisian border and into Libya. Special arrangements had been made with the Libyan government and they were waived right through.

Martin was holding Leslie tightly in his arms. She was dazed, half awake. Her hand was between her legs. She thought of the gold ring in her pussy, which she had never been allowed to touch. Her fingers found it now. It was smooth and hard. She recalled its sparkling color whenever she had been given permission to see it. She thought of all she had been through, all the men and women who had used her, her life as a slave, owned and controlled by others, her life of fevered sexual abandonment. Strong, confining arms were holding her, controlling her. Her fingers rolled over the ring and then drifted north, into her lubricating divide. "Ohhhhhhhhhhhhh," she moaned, and began a slow, languorous manipulation of her sex.

POSTSCRIPT

Three months after she returned home, Leslie received in the mail an envelope postmarked from a town in western Tunisia called Talah. It contained a single colorful piece of paper coated with an aromatic dust. There were strange, Arabic words on it drawn atop a pentagram. Her fingers tingled as she held it. After scrutinizing it carefully, she threw it away and forgot all about it. For reasons she was not quite sure of, a week later, without telling her family, she boarded a plane to Madrid and then caught a connecting flight to Algiers. She stayed at a hotel on the outskirts of the city. The next morning, she resumed her journey, taking a train to the small Algerian town of Biskra. She was met at the station by a tall, dark skinned man who seemed to know her. She got into a taxi with him, leaving her small travel bag on the platform, and they drove to an encampment a few miles outside of town where Jaida was waiting.

The end.